HEATHER MANNING

Swept to Sea

PUBLISHING

To the best English teacher ever, Mrs. Fosburgh, who ignited my love of writing. Thank you for being so awesome and reading my short stories—no matter how LONG they were. Thank you also to my family, especially to my mom and dad, who let me go to my first writer's conference this spring, and to my sister, Cortney, who listens to all my ramblings about my stories. Finally, thank you most of all to God.

Foreword

Hello and thank you for joining me on this journey. *Swept to Sea* was originally published in 2013, while I was 16 years old. Since then my publisher has closed, and I decided it was time for my *Ladies of the Carribean* series to be out and accessible for those who wanted to read it. I like to call this *Swept to Sea* (Heather's Version) as a fan of Taylor Swift. Thank you for your support, and I can't wait to share many books to come with you. Please keep in touch with me via my website, www.heathermanningofficial.com or my social medias.

Chapter 1

L ondon, England
   1696

Lady Eden Trenton dashed into her bedchamber and slammed the oak door. The bang sent an echo through the chilled room. A loud crash sounded behind her but she ignored it. At one time she would have felt guilty if something broke as a result of her temper, but now she truly did not care. She threw herself onto her four-poster bed and curled into a ball.

She hated Lord Rutger. Hated him and what he had tried to do.

How could he? How could she have let him turn her into this crying, weak little woman who she hardly even recognized?

Eden shoved those thoughts from her head even as she pushed herself up onto her elbows.

I will not be his victim. Not now, and not ever again.

She couldn't just lie here in self-pity. That would get her

nowhere. Instead of lying there, she had to do something or she feared she would not make it through the night without going insane.

Her tear-clouded gaze drifted to the wooden writing desk in the corner. Where a glass vase had once proudly sat, harboring a bouquet of fragrant red roses, a pile of shattered glass now lay. The once-vibrant roses now lay withered, mingled with the glass. Their demise must have been the crash she had heard when the door slammed. Good. When Eden saw it was Lord Rutger's vase she had destroyed, a thrill of rebellious excitement coursed through her. He had given her the flowers, along with a sapphire necklace, when their engagement had been announced publicly. 'Twas a shame such a beautiful piece of jewelry was so tainted.

Eden gathered up the shriveling flowers in one hand. She bit her lip when a shard of glass pricked her finger but did not care it hurt her. It was worth the pain to see Rutger's gift in such a tortured state. Her sole regret was that it marked the flowers' demise and not that of the cruel man himself.

Eden hurried toward the other end of the room and tossed the petals out her open window, willing them to fly away. Fly away and escape this cage they were in—just as she longed to do herself. Bright lightning forked across the night sky. A deafening crack of thunder caused her to jump. The storm seemed to mirror the myriad of emotions churning deep inside her.

Feeling every bit a madwoman, she began to take up a pace around her bedchamber. She had no idea how she could escape this wretched, heartless man, this man to whom her own father had promised her hand in marriage. Her chances of survival were slim if she *did* marry him.

Oh, what will become of me?

She sank back onto her bed with a grimace. Her ribs ached from Rutger's latest assault.

I need to get out of here. I need to leave this town, this country. But where could she go? She had no family but her father here in London and her brother Adam, wherever he had run off to.

An idea burst into Eden's mind as she thought of Adam. Against their father's wishes, her brother had visited the colonies in the Caribbean on a sailing trip a few years ago. He had come back regaling them all with fantastic stories of clear turquoise waters, white sandy beaches, and lush, green palm trees. Since then, she had always dreamed of visiting the colonies for herself.

What Eden needed was to talk to her dear friends Aimee and Ivy and ask for their advice, but the evening had grown far too late for a social call. She would have to wait until morning, which seemed ages away. Plopping back onto her pillow, she tried to sleep. A few dragging hours passed before she finally fell into a fitful slumber.

* * *

When the first rays of daybreak streamed through her window, Eden rose to seek out her friends. She dressed, grabbed her reticule, and tiptoed down the grand staircase, tugging on her gloves as she went.

She winced as a floorboard creaked under her weight.

Although many of the servants had been released of their services because of the Trenton's dwindling estate, Eden did not doubt the remaining few would notify her father of her activity. No one made social calls this early in the day.

One more step brought her to the parlor. Eden took a deep breath and glided past.

She collided with a tall, hard form.

Fear coiled through Eden as she realized a man towered above her. Her pulse accelerated. Had she been caught?

It took only a moment for her to recognize Gregory, one of her father's footmen.

"Gregory, you gave me a scare. I thought you were ... I thought..." Eden inhaled shakily. How would she get to Aimee and Ivy now that a servant knew her whereabouts?

"I apologize, Lady Trenton. May I ask, where are you planning to go so early in the morning? You are hardly ever awake at this time of the day." He clasped his long hands together behind his back.

"I ... I ..." Eden worried her bottom lip with her teeth. If her father heard she was making mysterious trips out of the manor, he would suspect something. But if she didn't leave the house herself ...

"Could you stay here for just a moment, please, Gregory? I will be right back."

"Of course, Lady Trenton."

Eden dashed off to her father's study and grabbed a few pieces of paper from his desk. She dipped a quill in ink and jotted down the same message on both papers: "Meet me in my parlor as soon as you can—it is an emergency."

She signed the notes and folded them in half. If she couldn't summon her friends personally, she would have one of the footmen do so.

Eden tucked the notes under her arm, picked up her skirts, and sped back to the entryway. Gregory was waiting as she had asked.

"Yes, Lady Trenton, what may I do for you?"

Eden hesitated, but decided to trust him. It was just Gregory. Nothing to worry about. He had been one of Adam's best friends when they were youths. Surely he would not tell her father what she was doing if only she asked.

"Please, take these missives to Lady Aimee Dawson and Lady Ivy Shaw. Do not tell anyone you did this for me." She handed him the notes.

He bowed. "Of course, milady."

* * *

"Do you truly think I will simply sit around in London and marry that obnoxious excuse of a man? Do you ladies even know me?" Eden exclaimed, trying to re-pin her hair back into its up-do. She sighed, letting her arms drop to her sides. Her curls never could be tamed by pins.

Aimee and Ivy had finally come to Eden's home, well after noon.

"No, we didn't think you would," Ivy laughed, shaking her head.

Eden's gaze flicked to the window where carriages moved past.

"But we will miss you so much," Aimee pouted, "What will Ivy and I do without you here with us? Who will go shopping for jewelry with me, and who will attend balls with us? We need you." She plopped herself down on the leather-cushioned chair in Eden's parlor room.

"Would you have me marry that insolent cur just so I can

stay here with you, Aimee?" Eden jutted her chin out.

"He *is* an earl, Eden. You know your father needs the money a marriage like that could bring." Ivy placed her teacup back on its saucer on the table next to her.

"And he is quite handsome," added Aimee, giggling and straightening one of the pink bows on the shoulder of her frilly dress.

Eden inhaled a slow breath, the deep, earthy scent of her father's smoking pipe filling her nostrils. He had always smoked in their parlor room after her mother had died even though it was a habit Eden detested. "Now wait just a minute—whose side are you on, ladies? Lord Clive Rutger—" she imitated his low, nasally voice, eliciting a hearty chuckle from her friends"—is nothing but a shallow cad who wants to marry me simply because he decided he fancies the way I look. Despicable monster." Just thinking about the slimy excuse of a man sent an uncontrollable shiver crawling down Eden's spine, especially after what that fiend had tried to do to her. The fresh bruise on her shoulder throbbed. She could not bring herself to think about it, much less speak of it to her friends.

"But what are you going to do to prevent this marriage, Eden? Knowing your father, I hardly think he would want to cancel the deal. You know what a disgrace it would be for you if the engagement is called off. Besides, your father appeared quite happy with the arrangement at your engagement party." Aimee tossed a golden curl from her shoulder as her emerald-hued eyes reflected in the hand mirror she had grown attached to.

"You are right; Father refuses to back down on this marriage arrangement. I already tried pleading with him. The union would be beneficial to us. 'Twould give us the money we so desperately need to keep living as we are." She opened her arms wide, indicating to her only moderately posh surroundings. Unlike her father, Eden cared not for wealth. Especially if wealth meant being chained to a monster for the remainder of her existence.

"So what are you going to do about it, Eden?" Ivy patted her hair, the rich color of fire in the moonlight. Her lovely waves were the envy of the town, along with her eyes, the cloudy blue of the sky before a thunder storm. Looks like that could get her into a situation like Eden's.

"I don't know what to do yet, but I *will* escape the earl. I promise you I will." Eden shifted her feet from where she stood by the fireplace. She would not sit around and live such a life married to a man she did not love. Not only did not love, but despised with all of her heart!

"Only you would be plotting to escape marriage to this man, Eden. Do you know how many women would practically kill to marry a lord, not to mention an earl?" Ivy replied, a stern look on her face.

"I care not if he is an earl. I do not want his title or his money. Oh goodness, all those women who want him can have him! Since Papa won't help me, I *need* to leave. I think I would like to visit the Caribbean. You know how I loved all the stories Adam used to return home with. I know I don't have enough money to pay for a passage across the sea yet, but I will find a way to escape. I can assure you of that."

Aimee and Ivy cast each other an exasperated look. Eden knew her friends could read the expression in her own eyes as a determined one. She could not be stopped now that she had set her heart on escaping this life her father and Lord Rutger

7

had planned for her.

"Why on earth would you wish to set off for the colonies all on your own? I have heard it is quite a wild, dangerous place. Vicious, cutthroat pirates are rumored to run the seas. They kill and kidnap without a thought. You will have to fend for yourself all alone. Do you even understand what kind of trouble you could get yourself into over there?" Ivy asked.

Eden rolled her eyes and leaned back on the edge of the mahogany fireplace's mantelpiece. She had come to her friends for support, not a lecture as if she were some guilty child. They were not her parents by any means.

She sucked in a breath, realizing she would have to escape before her father could catch her. "It is not as if I would be venturing to Tortuga or a place like that. I think Port Royal or New Providence would be pleasant. Adam told me they are quite charming little areas, surrounded by the sea. That was a couple of years ago when he went there, but they cannot be half as bad as what I have heard of Tortuga."

"It still must be quite dangerous. Anywhere is a dangerous place for a young woman on her own. How will you ever provide for yourself? You have to understand, we just don't want you to end up hurt in some way," Aimee reasoned.

"I will be able to take care of myself," Eden huffed, sinking down onto the embroidered footstool that sat next to Ivy's chair. "I do not care what everyone else says. I will *not* marry him! I never want to marry a man. All marriage does is give a man a chance to control a woman. I will not be a part of a union like that, and especially not with Lord Rutger. Have you two not seen the way he looks at me? And he always stands far closer to me than propriety allows." She shivered and glanced away from them, blinking the tears from her eyes.

8

The room was utterly silent for a few moments until Ivy grabbed her friend gently by the shoulders, peering into her eyes. "Has Lord Rutger harmed you, Eden? Tell me. Tell me everything. What has he done to you?"

Eden shook her head. She couldn't. "Not … exactly. But h-he tried to kiss me last night. When I refused, he got so, so angry with me. I was scared he was going to strike me or worse. He claimed that as his fiancée, I had to kiss him. I *owed* him a kiss. It was completely horrible. That night—I wish I could forget about that night. And just to think that soon I will actually have to give the monster a kiss … and once he's my husband …" At least that much was true. Eden shook her head again. She did not wish to tell her friends about how the vile man had hit her, frightened that it would happen again if she told them. He had threatened her a handful of times, if she told anyone what had happened; he would make her regret it deeply. Luckily, her clothing covered the blackening bruise that had spread onto her shoulder and collarbone. The large hand marks on her ribs would not be seen, either. Besides, she did not want their pity. She didn't want anyone's pity. All she needed was their support.

"Why does he even want to marry me? It is not like I have a large dowry or anything. I have the opposite, if anything …"

Ivy studied Eden silently for a moment.

Aimee shook her head.

"I-I don't know, Eden. I don't know." Ivy clasped Eden's hand in her own, and Aimee patted her on the back.

* * *

Captain Caspian Archer sped through the streets of London, dodging city dwellers, merchants, and carriages along the way. A muddy man bumped into him and swore before continuing on his way. Caspian clenched his jaw. If they were on board his ship, he would have the man punished for such impertinence. He shook his head and continued on, avoiding a puddle along the way.

Eager to return to his ship, the *Dawn's Mist,* he quickened his pace. Finally, he had received a Letter of Marque issued in the name of King William to rid the Caribbean of pirates and any of England's enemies. He had a mission now. No longer would he be a despicable pirate himself. Instead, he would stop the same men who had thus far succeeded in ruining his life. Caspian gritted his teeth. Captain Moore would dearly pay for what he had done.

The invigorating, salty scent of the sea washed over him as he rounded a corner, erasing the grimy odor of the streets he had grown to despise. He brightened at the welcome refreshment.

Caspian looked ahead and scanned the docks, which were bustling with sailors of all sizes, shapes, and nationalities. He spotted the *Dawn's Mist* in the distance; the main mast of his frigate standing tall above the sloops and dinghies docked next to her.

"Nice to see you, Cap'n!" Gage Thompson, his first mate, beamed at him from the starboard rail, his straight teeth white against the tan of his skin.

"And the same to you, Gage," Caspian replied, climbing up the ropes to the foredeck of his ship.

"Are we prepared to set sail tomorrow, or are we in need of another day to stock up on provisions?" Caspian squinted against the orange rays of the setting sun.

"Nay, we have all of the needed provisions, and I would say she's been completely repaired from our last encounter. We are ready to set sail at first light, Cap'n." He answered, running a hand through his dark, wavy hair.

"Very well." Caspian nodded at his friend before trudging to his cabin to prepare the charts for their next voyage. He could only hope this one would be successful unlike the many before it.

Chapter 2

"I gave him permission to take your hand in marriage. You are to be married within three months."

Eden found her throat closing. She could not swallow. Her lungs seemed to fail her. Was this what it felt like to drown? Adam had spun tales for her of ships wrecking in terrible storms and sailors drowning when she was a small child and he wanted to spook her.

This could not be real. It could not be happening.

At last, she gasped in a small bit of air.

"I told you to sit down, Eden. Now sit before you faint. Look at how pale your face is. You are a foolish, stubborn woman, just like your mother."

Eden obeyed her father, sinking down onto the plush armchair across from him. She chose to ignore his cutting remark. As of late, she had become accustomed to them.

"Y-you gave ... Lord Rutger ... my hand in marriage?" She managed to lower her voice, using every bit of her resolve not to scream at him like a panic-stricken child. How could he have done this to her? *"Father, you know how I feel about that man! I cannot marry him, Papa. I cannot."*

"You can and you will, Eden. You know full well that we are in need of his money. Lord Rutger will be a respectable husband for you." Respectable, ha! *"We cannot go on living like we do now if you do not bring in money for me soon, you know that. His title will do wonders for our family name."*

Eden could tell just by the way Lord Rutger leered at her that the man was anything but respectable. Besides, he was not even born into his title! The man was a peasant by birth. He had not become a nobleman until later in his life when a foolish earl had taken pity on him and adopted him as his son.

"Father, please, do not make me do this. Do not force me into a marriage with a man who I feel nothing for. I will be stuck in it for the rest of my life, for heaven's sake! Please, Father." Do not force me into a loveless marriage like you and Mother had …

As if reading her thought about her parents' marriage, Eden's father continued, "I let your mother read you far too many of those foolish fairy tales when you were young, didn't I, Eden? There is no such thing as true love, and you should know that by now. You will marry this man and live a privileged life just like the life I have provided you with since you were but a babe. You will obey me and not say another word about it." He slammed his fist down on the table, sending a teacup crashing. *"I had enough of your pig-headed objections when you were a little girl. Your spoiled complaints will not be tolerated by any means in my old age. That is the last I am saying on this subject, young lady."*

The last sentence caused Eden to shrink back. Her father, never one to yell or scream, raised his voice with each word and his tone grew harsh. His face was red.

Eden shook her head, staring intently at a loose thread on her frayed slippers. She knew that some couples had truly found love in real life, however rare it seemed to be among English aristocracy. Arranged marriages were much more prevalent, but Aimee Dawson's parents were in love with each other, and they had found each other against all odds. Aimee's mother was a Frenchwoman and her father a British lord, and they had married despite the war which had divided their two countries.

However, Eden kept her rebellious thoughts inside, because she did not want her father to be cross with her again. He was her only family after her mother's death and her brother's disappearance.

Eden sighed as she leaned against her windowsill, forcing the jarring memory aside. Her conversation with her father had caused so much trouble, but she would avoid it all now. She would not have to marry Lord Rutger nor deal with her father's anger.

But escaping these terrors would cause her to lose her friends. A shiver ran through her and she tried to push the thought aside. If she ran away she would never see Aimee and Ivy again. She chewed on her bottom lip, stood up, and moved away from the window. The brisk night air seemed to follow her to the other side of the room nonetheless. Since they were at least five years old, they had known each other. Their mothers had been close friends before them. Aimee's mother had practically taken over the role of Eden's own mother when she had died. Oh, how Eden would miss them all …

Yet, I must leave.

Leave her family, leave her friends, and leave everything she had ever known. She did not care about what she would do once she got to the Caribbean. And yet would she be able to find work for herself there? Eden shivered at the thought.

Even though she had heard many glorified stories about the Caribbean from her brother, she knew plenty of women had gone to the Caribbean hoping for a new life, but events forced them to become harlots in order to earn enough money to survive. She decided she would die before she did something so demeaning. Perhaps she would have greater luck remaining in England. But then again, maybe she could find Adam over in the colonies. He had adored his younger sister and would no doubt take her in until she could settle on her own feet ...

Yes, she would leave, and hurry, too, for anything was better than marrying Lord Rutger and enduring his beatings for her entire life. Eden had suffered through enough of them by just becoming the man's fiancée. She snatched the sapphire necklace Rutger had given her off of her vanity, realizing it could provide money when she began her new life.

Eden grabbed her valise which contained only an extra set of clothes, a stale crust of bread one of the servants had been about to throw to the dogs, and the few shillings she had been able to gather. She began her descent out her bedroom window.

Eden positioned her valise on one arm and swung her legs over the window sill. She had absconded with a pair of trousers and an oversized shirt from her brother's old bedroom, both of which she was now wearing. The waist of the trousers was cinched in with a rope she had found in the stables to keep them from sliding off, but all together her outfit fit just fine. Her hair was stuffed snugly into a bicorn hat.

How much easier it was to climb down from her bed-chamber in nothing but trousers and a shirt rather than in her cumbersome layers of taffeta! She held back a giggle remembering a year long ago. Adam had convinced Eden to sneak out of the house with him through her window so they could go outside and play while she was supposed to be taught by her poor, confused governess. Oh, how she missed dear, fun-loving Adam.

Eden leaped the final few feet to the ground and glanced around. She paused only to smudge a handful of dirt across her face to disguise her feminine features then sped down the streets to the harbor. Luckily, she knew the way from her stolen days with her brother. He had always dragged her to the docks in the full light of day to look at the ships he was so fascinated with. By the dark of the night, the streets looked entirely different and not nearly as friendly and cheerful. The moon illuminated Eden's path, and the still-bustling docks were infested with grimy sailors who ambled about. Salty, moist air, laden with the smell of fish, hit Eden's face. Ships—too many to count—bobbed up and down in the harbor like children's toys in a small pond.

Which one to choose out of so many? Which one to start her life anew and carry her to the Caribbean?

A loud guffaw caused her to turn, her heart racing. Men, a rowdy group of pirates by the looks of them, sauntered toward her. A bullet of dread shot through Eden. Could they somehow see past her disguise? Was some of her stubborn hair falling down from its confines in the bicorn hat she wore? Panicking, Eden dove behind a stack of barrels, in case the vile creatures realized she was not a boy. She did not need any unnecessary troubles before she even left London.

A look behind her told her it was too late. They were heading toward her makeshift hiding place, laughing drunkenly.

A frigate, her only hope of salvation, loomed tall behind

Eden's back. On the hull of the ship, the name *Dawn's Mist* was painted in black, unfriendly spikes.

She glanced around the barrels again. The group of filthy sailors was still strolling closer, but they no longer appeared to be looking at her anymore. Maybe they had not noticed she was a woman. Maybe they had not even seen her at all. Oh well, this ship behind her had to be as good as any because she had no idea where any of the vessels were sailing anyway. It wasn't like she necessarily had a choice of which ship she was stowing away on anyway.

Please, God, she prayed, *please let this ship be heading toward the Caribbean. If not, some place that will at least be beneficial to me.*

Eden scurried up the gangplank and landed on the wooden deck with a soft thud. She glanced around, taking in her surroundings. Stairs on either side of her led up to a higher level of the ship, called the forecastle and quarter deck, if she recalled from her brother correctly. On both sides of the main deck rested stacks of barrels, crates, and coils of thick rope. An old gray-haired sailor lounged on a barrel, chin rested on his chest, and a bottle of rum in his right hand. Besides him, no one else was in sight. She was thankful she had thought to wear boots, for she knew her flimsy silk slippers would no doubt catch on the deck's many splinters.

Eden tiptoed across the rough wooden deck. The full white moon illuminated her path. The vessel wobbled over a wavelet. Stifling a startled cry, Eden stumbled and threw her hand to her mouth. As she recovered her balance, she spotted a set of stairs, or a companionway, leading down below the decks. Down was the only way to head if she did not want to be discovered by the entire crew. If not for the noise it would make, Eden would have laughed ruefully. The shrouds certainly were not the place for her to go! *Please, Lord, do not let them find me down here.* She silently pleaded with God, hoping He would see past the times before when she had not called upon His name first.

Taking a deep breath, she climbed down the steep set of stairs. These led her to another hallway which led to even more stairs. She passed a door. A crack of light escaped from underneath and the foul stench of urine and rotten food emanated from within. Some deep snores met her ears, but she also heard raucous laughter and shouts. How could some of the men be sleeping through noises like that?

Then, a terrifying thought occurred to her: had she gotten herself on a pirate ship? No, surely it was common for sailors to get into a simple brawl now and then. She had probably just arrived during one.

Eden hurried down another flight of rickety stairs into a section of the ship that was dark and eerily quiet compared to the level above. Good. Although it sent a shiver crawling down her spine, dark and quiet were exactly what she needed to avoid being seen or heard. Her reticule dropped out of her hands, sending her coins clattering to the floor. She quickly gathered its contents and took in her surroundings. A wooden hatch in the floor revealed a ladder that did not look particularly sturdy. She gingerly placed her weight on it, calculating where to step and how hard, terrified it would break and send her plummeting into the bowels of the ship. When she decided the rickety ladder was as safe as anything she would find here, she descended down to what must be the deepest level of the ship. The odor of fish and filth assaulted her nose, and she tried to breathe through only her mouth, but to no avail. There had been unpleasant odors everywhere on the ship, but here she literally could taste the foul stench of it. Black, sludgy bilge clawed up to her ankles, dirtying her clunky boots. Everywhere she looked, nothing but the thick darkness met her eyes.

Should she soil her clothes and sit in the murky bilge? She could sit atop one of the many wooden crates lining one side of the huge room. But then, what if some brave person ventured all the way down here? Not that it was likely that someone would go down to this horrible-smelling hold. What sane person without fear for their life would want to?

She decided against the risk of discovery and crept behind some of the crates, braving the slimy substance that covered most of the floor. The dark shadows seemed to swallow her completely, and the chill seeped far into her bones. What she would not give to have a lantern.

* * *

"Weigh anchor, gentlemen! Unfurl all topsails and topgallants!" Caspian shouted, striding across his forecastle deck. Yelling emanated from amidships. He cocked his head, listening to what was going on. It sounded like two men arguing. What was his aggravating crew up to now?

The afternoon sun bore down on him, causing a droplet of sweat to slide down his back underneath his shirt. He brushed from his face some strands of hair that had escaped the tie at the back of his head. A jarring shout drifted up to where Caspian stood, causing him to scan his ship. He spotted two of his sailors brawling on the deck. His other crew members circled them, shouting and placing bets. The money-hungry men seemed to love every chance they had to gamble.

"Smithy, Kelton, stop that violent nonsense immediately, or I will keelhaul the both of you and hang your carcasses from the yardarm!" Caspian charged down the steps and plucked Kelton from atop Smithy. "Now, men, who started this?" His crew grumbled at the sudden end to the fistfight and their potential loss from the wagers.

"He insulted the character of me wife, Cap'n! I had t' defend 'er honor! What else was I t' do?" Smithy shouted, pointing at Kelton, who glowered at him from across the deck. Caspian easily believed Smithy's testament. Kelton, his master rigger, had a record of such indiscretions. The young man never seemed to know when to hold his foul tongue.

"Mr. Thompson, take Mr. Kelton to the brig, if you please. The pup needs to learn some restraint. I will not tolerate brawls on my ship," Caspian commanded, shaking his head.

"Aye, Captain." Gage grabbed the man by the arms and began to haul him off.

Kelton scowled and struggled against Gage. "But-" Luckily, Gage had the advantage of greater strength and jerked the man's arms behind him.

"Two days without food or water should teach Mr. Kelton not to insult Mr. Smithy's wife again—" Caspian's order was interrupted by Kelton grumbling under his breath "—unless, good sir, you wish to protest further. Yes, I do believe the sharks would enjoy a fresh meal."

Kelton shook his head, jaw and fists clenched in defiance. But he said nothing. He knew who his captain was.

Caspian took a deep breath of the cool, moist sea air and watched his first mate drag the young man away. That insolent whelp would cause a lot of trouble on his ship if Caspian did not prevent it. Kelton had already caused more trouble than he was worth, but Caspian needed him for this voyage. It was too late to hire another man now. However, Caspian planned to dismiss him of his duties once they reached Port Royal and hopefully not have to deal with the constant headache the young man gave him. He did not need to be given any more trouble. No, he would not let anything get in the way of success on this voyage. He would persevere for Isabelle's memory.

* * *

Gage Thompson clasped a lantern in one hand as he dragged the struggling Kelton down the ladder to the hold. He shook the young man by the collar of his grimy, once-ruffled-and-crisp white shirt. The man seemed to have always dressed like a dandy, but he had failed to maintain his appearance.

The warm, dank air of the hold assaulted him as he descended into the ship's depths and had Gage not grown accustomed to the stench over his years at sea, he would have gagged.

"If you refuse to cooperate, I promise you, I will not hesitate to run you through with my sword," Gage threatened, fingering the hilt of the cutlass at his side.

He hesitated. For a moment, he wondered if the foolhardy lad would be crazy enough to fight him.

Unarmed, Kelton chose wisely and cooperated. Gage unlocked the bars of the cell and shoved the young man into it. He slammed the door shut behind him and quickly locked it. Kelton leaned back against the far wall lazily, avoiding any eye contact.

Typical, defiant Kelton.

Gage rolled his eyes and chose to ignore him as well.

A faint moan sounded from the opposite side of the ship.

Gage jerked his gaze in the direction of the noise, scanning the cluttered area with suspicious eyes.

"Hey, what was that?" Kelton asked. "Do you have someone else down here already? Captain Archer truly is a tyrant, isn't he?" He continued spouting useless questions and comments.

Gage chose to ignore the man while he listened intently for a few more seconds, then, convinced he had not imagined hearing something, headed over to a pile of boxes to search for the intruder. Could it have been a rat? *No*, he shook his head, *no rats sound like that. No kind of rat at all.* Anxious to discover the culprit, he pushed one of the large crates aside and uncovered a small, pale hand lying motionless on the wooden floorboards.

He lifted another crate aside and swung the lantern high above the area. The bright light shone upon a boy. No, it was not a boy at all. It was a young woman dressed in baggy trousers, taking on the guise of a boy. But she was far too pretty to be anything close to the male gender. Could they have a stowaway on their hands? A female stowaway? Surely that was a rare discovery. Her long umber hair spiraled down her back and around her shoulders until finally resting on the slimy bilge below her. A bicorn hat perched on the top of her head. Why in the world was a beautiful young woman down here in the hold? How could she have gotten here? She stirred in her sleep, moaning, reaching forward with an open palm.

Gage shot back.

Chapter 2

Without a single look behind him, he sped up the ladder and companionway to report his bizarre finding to the Captain. He had no idea what the man would make of it, but he was anxious to find out.

Chapter 3

❧

Caspian opened the heavy book that had taken residence on his desk the last few years yet had not been touched once. The first few pages were covered in ink, the names of deceased family members Caspian had never met. He flipped the page. There it was. The one name that meant everything was scrawled in Caspian's own shaky handwriting. *Isabelle Wright Archer. Death. August fifth, in the year of our Lord, sixteen ninety-one.*

Slamming the Bible shut, Caspian sank down onto the leather armchair positioned before the porthole and adjacent to his bed. He inhaled the strong scent of the leather, closed his eyes, and willed the gnawing headache away.

With an unplanned late start in the morning and Kelton's insolence in the afternoon, it had been a most trying day. The glass cabinet in the left of the room, lined with port and rum, beckoned to him, tempting him with a reprieve from a stressful day. He had not drunk to drown his sorrows since before Reed was born. But on days like today, the thought held a lot of appeal.

Caspian stood and reached out, his hand pausing at the handle of the cabinet. He jerked his arm away and moved to the opposite side of the cabin.

Isabelle had always hated it when he drank. She had told him only weak men turned to the vile brews in times of trouble. And he supposed she had spoken the truth.

His cabin door suddenly burst open and a mop of sandy blond curls bounced into the room.

"Father, Father, guess what I found!" Reed exclaimed—no, screamed—, skipping over to him, a charming grin on his little face.

Caspian let out a heavy breath. He was not in any mood for his son's incessant cheerfulness. How could the boy be so happy when he had tragically lost his own mother?

Yes, that had happened nearly five years ago. The child had been only a few months old at the time, but it still must be hard for the boy to not know his own mother. Egad, Caspian had certainly missed the dear woman enough for the both of them.

What must Isabelle think of him now, dragging their only child across the Caribbean onboard a pirate ship! Caspian laughed ruefully. What a wonderful father he had turned out to be. Hopefully once they arrived in Port Royal, he would make Isabelle proud.

"What did you find, child?" Caspian leaned forward, his elbows planted on his knees.

Grinning at Caspian, the boy held up a long silver chain that boasted a round, blue sapphire.

"And where might you have found that, Reed? Some poor woman is no doubt missing it back in London."

"I found it on the companionway. It was just lying there on the floor," Reed answered simply, that bright smile still plastered on his little face.

"Well, that is peculiar. We haven't had a … a woman on board since …" Caspian swallowed back a rush of emotion that had snaked its way into his throat,"… since your mother. I wonder where it could have come from."

"May I please keep it, Father? Please?" Reed pleaded, staring in awe at the sparkling blue gem. The lad was mesmerized.

Caspian huffed in resignation. It was probably just a bauble that had been separated from the rest of the treasure from one of the *Dawn's Mist*'s conquests. No one would miss it. "Yes, I suppose, boy."

"Oh, thank you, Father. Thank you so much!" Reed grinned from ear to ear, looking every bit like his late mother whenever she had heard the slightest bit of good news. Poor foolish, optimistic woman.

Reed was bouncing up and down. "And, Father?"

His son's voice was so timid, so thin, and so weak. He did not have the voice of a strong privateer. What could he ever do to make the boy stronger, more of a man? More like him, and less like his mother. It was bad enough he reminded Caspian of the woman every minute of every day …

"Yes?" groaned Caspian. He needed rest; needed to stop thinking about his dear Isabelle. Sleep would work to clear his mind so effectively …

"Will you play with me, Father? We just got that spinning top in London last week." The dear boy's bottom lip protruded out in a pout.

"I am sorry, Reed, but it has been a most trying day. Maybe I will play with you some other time." Caspian could not help but notice the moistness of tears glistening in the child's bright blue eyes.

What is wrong with me?

He always managed to upset the boy some way or another. That probably made him a worse father than his own. Many times, the man had been too busy to do anything with young Caspian and had shooed him away. Caspian knew he needed to do something about how he treated his boy.

A knock sounded on the cabin door.

"Who is it?" he snapped, not eager by any means for another intrusion. With a grunt, he rose and started toward the door to open it—and send away the interloper.

"'Tis me, Captain. It is of most importance that you come out here immediately."

Caspian opened the thick oak door to see Gage panting as if he had just rowed the *Dawn's Mist* across the Atlantic on his own.

Caspian stepped out of his cabin, motioning for Reed to stay behind and inside. "By fire and flame, man; what is the matter with you? You look as though you've just seen a ghost. What is going on?" His friend's tanned face had altered to an unbecoming shade of whitish gray.

"I-I'm afraid we have a stowaway on board, Captain. You must come and see for yourself," he half-chuckled, his face slowly regaining its normal ruddy coloring as his familiar smile once again formed on his mouth. The man always seemed to have something to be joyful over.

Stuffing a pistol into the waist of his pants, Caspian followed his first mate all the way down to the dark hold. He was ready to dispose of the offender and return to his cabin for a good night's rest. Heaven knows, he needed it.

Gage nodded toward a stack of crates in the starboard corner of the ship's hold. Upon examining it further, Caspian identified umber curls spilling out from a bicorn hat and over feminine curves. Men's trousers and a baggy white shirt were unsuccessful in hiding a tiny womanly figure.

A woman. He had a woman stowaway on his hands? If so, this was quite an amusing circumstance.

Caspian leaned forward to study her, wondering if she was asleep or … dead.

A wooden plank beneath his feet creaked rather loudly.

"What is it, *Captain*? What are you two so entranced with?" came Kelton's even louder sneer from the other side of the cabin.

Caspian shook his head and moved closer to their strange discovery as Gage shushed the insolent Kelton.

The woman groaned, a long, low sound, and her eyes snapped open before she scrambled to sit up. Her coffee-colored eyes soon expanded with fear and displeasure. A tiny freckled nose scrunched up in a most adorable pout along with pink lips.

Caspian couldn't hold back a grin. Yes, indeed, he could have quite a bit of fun with this situation.

"Ah, very nice to meet you, milady," he gave her a mocking bow as her disoriented eyes flickered between Caspian, Kelton's annoying shouts, and Gage. "I am Captain Caspian Archer. I cordially welcome you aboard my ship, the *Dawn's Mist*. Do you happen to know what we do with stowaways here, milady?"

She gulped, shivered, and shook her head, but then jutted her chin out stubbornly. She was trembling. Caspian took her by the arm, drawing her up to a standing position. The sweet scent of vanilla and coconut wafted over him, erasing the revolting stench of the bilge.

"Well, if he be a man, we throw him to the sharks ... and, well, a woman ... why, I'd suppose her fate would depend on how pretty she is ..." he scratched the day's stubble that was growing on his chin, grinning and enjoying the appalled expression on her comely face. He liked the way this stranger's cheeks became pink. It reminded him of a sunset over the sea in the Caribbean.

The woman swayed, her eyes slowly drooping shut, and he steadied her by grabbing onto her tiny waist. Her body went as limp as a windless sail. He scooped her up in his arms before her body could plummet back into the foul-smelling bilge. Glancing down at her, he noticed her shoulder was exposed at the neck of the oversized cotton shirt she wore. The delicate, pale shoulder was marred by a large, garish bruise that appeared to be a few days old. Now how could she have gotten that?

"Master Gage, find that wooden tub we used to have for Isabelle, bring it to my cabin, and fill it with water. Then find a dress if there is one to be found anywhere on this ship, if you please," he ordered.

Caspian didn't look back because he knew Gage would obey his orders. With the lady in his arms, Caspian rounded a corner and headed for his cabin. He needed to lay the woman down before she came to, lest she writhe in his grasp and somehow injure herself. Perhaps he should not have teased her so. She had obviously been injured somehow already.

Caspian adjusted the woman in his arms and opened the door to his cabin. He laid the young lady down onto his bed. The second he set her down, Reed found his way to his father's side and began bombarding him with endless questions.

"What are you carrying, Father? What is that? Did you get me a present? Oh, is it a *lady?* Why were you carrying her like that? Is there something wrong with her? Oh, she is *so* pretty, Papa!"

Caspian brushed aside some hair from his son's face and glanced back at the young woman who had not yet stirred from her fainting spell. Isabelle had never fainted. How long should this lady be asleep like this? Should he attempt to wake her? He forced his concerns to the back of his mind in order to stop his son's chattering.

"Yes, Reed, she is a lady. She fainted, is all. Will you stay with her a moment and watch her?" Caspian spun to his desk to find a basin of water. It was good to give a woman who had fainted a glass of water to drink, was it not? He supposed it could not hurt her.

"What does fainted mean, Papa? Does that mean she's dead?" Reed asked. Caspian twisted back in time to see his son slide his little hand into the young stranger's.

Caspian sighed, turning back to his desk and choosing to answer the boy's question some other time. He was not in any mood to deal with the child's bottomless curiosity.

* * *

Eden's mind stubbornly dragged itself back into the unwanted reality of consciousness. She would much prefer to remain asleep, where she would not have to worry about Lord Clive Rutger or about having been discovered by a nefarious crew of pirates. A nefarious crew of pirates …

A young voice shouted, "Father, Father! The lady—she is waking up!"

A cool cloth glided over her forehead, and a small, warm hand grasped hers tightly.

"Milady." Strong, large hands gripped her shoulders and shook them gently. Eden rolled onto her side and groaned, swatting at the hands. She had no intention of opening her eyes and facing that she had been discovered after such a short portion of the voyage. Bitter disappointment made her cringe. She had failed to survive even one short day at sea on her own.

"Milady." The deep voice grew agitated. The calloused hands shook her again, a little more roughly this time.

"What is it?" Eden moaned and managed to open her eyes a crack, however slight it was.

Lamplight pierced her eyes, and she snapped fully awake and flew up into a sitting position upon a rather narrow four-poster bed. She glanced at her surroundings. A large mahogany desk propped against one wall of the cabin. Perpendicular to it, a huge window allowed a view of the endless sea. Two overstuffed leather chairs huddled in a corner.

But what mainly commanded her attention was the man who loomed before her, the most handsome one she had ever seen. His fists were balled at his waist, and he wore a waistcoat of dark sapphire over a puffy white shirt from which a blizzard of lace burst out at the cuffs and collar. She noticed a silver chain around his neck that held some sort of a gold ring or band. A leather tie restrained his dark chocolate curls, cavalier-style, revealing a strong, lightly-stubbled jaw. Crystal blue eyes roved over her from head to toe. Altogether, he appeared quite intimidating. A young child with a mop of golden curls upon his head stood beside the man, wearing a miniature version of his grin. The boy stared at her in awe as if she was some foreign object.

The man's face looked…familiar to Eden. Had she met him before? Oh, yes. She had.

In the hold.

Terror washed over her when she remembered the words they had shared.

"Please, sir, I am so sorry! I know I am a stowaway on your ship! I know I'm a thief. Just please, please don't send me back to London! Please do not take me back there. Drop me off on an island or … or … somewhere, anyplace at all but London! I will find a way to pay for my voyage somehow, sir. Whatever you want, I will pay for it. Whatever price you say. And punish me anyway you want. You can keep me locked up for the whole trip. Please, sir."

Immediately after the words came out of her mouth she shrank back. She should never have said something like that to a man she had never met. Who knew how he would want her to pay? Oh, but she should have specified payment only in monetary form.

"Hmm … I've never heard of a stowaway who begged for his punishment. Calm down, milady. You are all right here," his deep, sultry voice slid over her like soothing honey tea on a parched throat. He ran a calloused but gentle—oh, so gentle— hand across her forehead. Her heart fluttered at the intimate yet calming action. No one had touched her that sweetly in quite some time. Yet no strange men whose acquaintance she did not have *should* touch her like that.

"Please, sir, promise me we will not turn back toward London," she pleaded, brushing his hand away. His touching her 'twas most improper, in all reality.

Perhaps she had been discovered by the crew late enough so they had sailed too far away from London for the Captain to retrace his steps on her account. She prayed that was so, for if she returned, her father and Lord Rutger would track her down like bloodhounds. By now, the authorities must have announced her missing.

"No, woman. Calm down. We sail toward Port Royal in Jamaica," he answered.

Port Royal! God had answered her prayers.

The Captain grabbed her hand but she shrank back. She had experienced far too much of men's false affections. And their painfully real wrath. The fresh injury on her shoulder began to throb and she bit back tears. She quickly moved the fabric of her oversized shirt over the wound, lest the Captain see it and wonder how it had gotten there. Of course, she bore other wounds from Lord Rutger, but this was the most noticeable.

"You have naught to fear from me, milady. I assure you I would never hurt a woman." He studied her face, seemingly shocked at her reaction to him. She glanced down, uncomfortable at how he seemed to see right through her. Could those crystal blue eyes see straight past the cotton of her shirt to the bruise left *so kindly* by her fiancé?

"Of course not. That's why you acted as you did in the hold … and you said those horrible things … about … about what you were going to do with me because I am a stowaway …" she pouted, shivering. Then Eden squeezed her eyes shut, realizing she should not have said such a bold thing to him. She expected to feel his fist pound into her flesh. Any moment now, that chivalrous demeanor would no doubt flee, and pain would singe through her arm or her face or her shoulder or her ribs. Eden refused to let down her guard and fall into his trap like some innocent doe. Experience had taught her to trust no man, and she would not be fooled by one now, especially not one who appeared to be a pirate captain.

Eden rose from the bed lest the man get any false ideas about her intentions. She *was* in his bedchamber. All alone in a man's bedchamber with nothing she could do to save herself. To top that, she had even promised to pay whatever he asked.

What on earth was the matter with her? She had obviously not planned very well to have put herself into a situation like this.

"Hang it, woman! Nay, I was only bantering with you, milady. I had no way of knowing you would swoon as you did," he retorted, huffing and running a hand through his thick hair.

"I was already dizzy because I awakened so suddenly, and you had frightened me … and …" she began to counter, and then looked away from him. She did not want to be thought of as some weak, browbeaten woman, even if she had become exactly that.

"I apologize, milady. Let me introduce myself so we may start anew. As I'm sure you remember I am Captain Caspian Archer. And this is my son." Bowing, he nodded toward the little blond boy hidden directly behind him. The child could be no older than five or six years. He had remained so silent she had all but forgotten he had even been in the room. How foolish of her. Surely the man would not assault her with his own son in the room, pirate or not. And where was this child's mother?

"Introduce yourself to the lady," the Captain ordered harshly. "Where on earth have your manners run off to, boy?"

The child's cheerful grin fell under his father's chastisement and Eden's heart sank. How could someone be so cruel to this innocent little child? The boy bowed before her formally, kissing her hand like a tiny gentleman in a royal palace would.

"I am Reed Archer, at your service, milady," his young voice wavered in shyness and his gaze lowered. Eden gave him an encouraging smile and nodded at him in greeting. What she truly wanted to do, however, was take the boy in her arms and tell him he was perfect and he had done nothing wrong, and he did not deserve to be chastised by his father. There was nothing wrong with being a trifle shy.

"And please, milady, grace us with the knowledge of your name," the Captain demanded, leaning against his desk and crossing his arms over his thick, wide chest.

"Why do you need to know my name, sir?" She speculated and threw her nose up in the air. This man had no right to know anything about her ... except for the fact that he was the Captain of the ship she had stolen passage on. Maybe this man did deserve to know something as trivial as her name.

"Well ... since we are to share such close quarters for a voyage all the way across the Atlantic, I should think we would get along much easier if we knew each other's names. Unless you wish for me to make up a name for you, perhaps. I think you would make a nice ..."

"If you must know, I am Lady Eden Trenton."

"I'm impressed, milady. Just to think, a *lady* saw fit to stow away on my humble ship! Nice to meet you, Lady Trenton." He bowed as he winked at her.

"And you, Captain." She averted her gaze from the man.

Was this the same pirate ship she had boarded the other day? The Captain certainly did not show any intentions of hurting her. He acted nothing like a pirate, either. She was certain that with any other, she would have been hurt or even killed by now. A gentleman pirate? Could that even be possible? *Thank you so much, God, for taking care of me. I certainly would not be safe here without you, Dearest Father.*

A knock sounded on the door. "Enter," the Captain called, moving from his desk.

In strode a tall, muscular young man who carried a tub of steaming water. A frilly rose-colored gown was thrown over his shoulder and his short, light brown hair was slicked back away from his face.

"Thank you, Master Thompson," the Captain nodded and dismissed the man as he set the items down.

With a quick wink at Eden, Mr. Thompson left the room.

"You may take a bath, milady," Caspian offered, "After sleeping in the bilge; I should suppose you would want to wash the filth away."

"But …" she objected, blushing and glancing from the Captain and his son to the water. Surely he did not expect her to … bathe … with him right there in the cabin, watching …

He apparently understood her objection. "I shall post a trustworthy guard for you outside the door. Just knock when you are finished bathing and dressing." His icy blue eyes sparkled in amusement. He faced the boy. "Come along, Reed. We must give the lady her privacy."

She exhaled as both the father and son left, leaving her with a tub of water that was cooling by the minute.

* * *

Caspian frowned as he leaned his back against the sturdy oak door. The salty scent of the sea beckoned him to climb up the companionway but he stayed put. Although he had told the baffling girl he would post a guard, he could not bring himself to leave her, even in the company of a man he trusted like Gage. No, she was his lady to guard and no one else's. Besides, it was his fault she had fainted, and the poor woman had seemed so scared.

Caspian grimaced when he remembered the dark bruise on her shoulder that crept over to her collarbone. He prayed no one had hurt her. Maybe it had just been an accident, and it had not been inflicted by someone else. His thoughts shifted as he felt his son tug on the hem of his shirt, begging for his father's attention.

"Papa, will you please hold me?"

Caspian crouched down so his eyes were level with his son's. The child eagerly smiled at him.

"Aren't you getting too old for that, my boy? You just turned six." The boy actually seemed quite small for his age. Caspian worried if he was raising him improperly. Maybe he wasn't feeding the child like he should. Perhaps a diet of dried beef and hardtack was not the best for a young, growing boy. And yet, Caspian rarely had contact with other children. What did he know about raising children?

He brushed a golden curl from Reed's sweet face. Oh, how he longed for his Isabelle back! She would know exactly when to stop holding their child and when to start teaching him to be a man. Caspian's own father had practically nothing to do with him when he was growing up, which was why he and Gage had left to pursue sailing the first chance they got.

"But you were holding Lady Trenton, Papa!" Reed crossed

his arms over his chest with the same determined look on his face that Isabelle had always worn when she had set her mind on something. That look that had eventually resulted in her premature death.

Caspian sighed. The stubborn boy was correct. He *had* held the woman. Warmth showered over Caspian as he remembered the feel of the lady in his arms when he had carried her to his cabin. "That was entirely different," he said, giving in and picking the boy up. He leaned against the wooden door.

"I love you, Papa," the child whispered, leaning his head against Caspian's shoulder.

"And I love you, too, Reed." Blast it, the boy was the spitting image of his mother! Same blond curls, same loving violet-blue eyes filled with admiration. Caspian still ached even after five long years had passed.

Caspian rubbed one of his son's tawny locks between his fingers. Would he ever do right by Reed?

"Papa, who is Miss Trenton?"

A fresh wave of worry washed over Caspian at the mention of her name. Why did the woman affect him so? Why should he care what would happen to her, or if she was frightened? Certainly, she was quite pretty, but nothing much compared to his Isabelle. Her bone structure was delicate and feminine, but her eyes were brown and her hair the same. Plain, really, compared to Isabelle's golden hair and purple-tinted-sapphire eyes. Why did he feel this unexpected urge to protect this lady and not let anyone else touch her? He had only just met her.

It was probably because of the bruise. He wanted to take care of a weak woman who had nobody to protect her. That was all.

"Papa?"

"Yes." Caspian looked down and then remembered his son had asked him something. Oh, about the lady.

"I'm afraid I am not quite sure yet, son. Mr. Thompson found her sleeping in the hold. She is a stowaway of some sort," he answered.

"A stowaway?" Reed gasped, astonishment lighting up his dark blue eyes.

"Yes."

"On a pirate ship?"

"Privateer," Caspian corrected. "Indeed."

"She must be quite brave, Papa!"

Caspian chuckled at the admiration glowing in his son's eyes for this woman he had just met.

"Aye, I suppose she is. She certainly seems unlike any other woman I have ever laid eyes on."

* * *

Eden stared at the washtub Master Thompson had hauled in. She had no choice, really. The grimy saltwater made her hair crunchy, and the stench from the belly of the ship seemed to be glued to her body. There was no doubt she looked a fright.

She undressed and stepped into the water. It had turned chilly already, and gooseflesh popped up on her arms and legs. Oh well, cold water was better than no water at all.

After bathing quickly lest the Captain and his son decide to change their plans and return early, Eden dressed and wrapped a towel about her hair to dry it. She glanced at the desk, pushed up against one of the walls. If only she glanced at its contents, she would have a better idea of who this captain was. Where was his wife? Did he leave her somewhere at home while he went around pirating with his son? Why, did the woman even know her husband's occupation?

Eden opened the drawer to the desk, but shoved it shut after a moment. She did not want the Captain to barge in on her to find her intruding on his privacy so she tapped lightly on the sturdy door.

"Are you finished, milady?" A deep voice answered almost immediately.

Sucking in a deep breath, Eden answered, "Yes." She opened the door to see the Captain's glistening blue eyes. Eden frowned. The man had said he was going to post a guard, not stand there waiting for her. His sweet, grinning son was balanced on his left hip. Reed giggled and pointed at the towel on her head. Captain Archer smirked as his warm gaze perused her from head to toe. He set the wiggling boy down, and the child skipped across the room and sank down onto one of the armchairs.

"I must say, Lady Trenton, that this dress is far more becoming on you than those trousers were," he smiled, seeming to relish the blush that she knew crept up her neck and reached her cheeks.

"Why, you cad." Eden glanced down at the deep rose-colored dress he had given to her. Lace bounded out from the bodice and the cuffs of the mid-length sleeves. The dress fit her snugly, hugging every one of her curves. She shifted in the gown. Having never worn such a tight dress before, she felt somehow exposed in this.

"Papa, what's a *cad*?"

Captain Archer sighed and shook his head.

Eden stifled a giggle.

"Papa, may I please go up and play on the deck then?" Reed interrupted.

"If you are careful, boy; I don't want you to get hurt. Weatherly thinks we might enter some turbulent waters soon. He spotted dark storm clouds ahead."

"Of course, Papa. I will be just fine." The young child skipped away and after a moment, the Captain closed the door behind him.

Eden sank down onto the bed and Captain Archer rested on the leather armchair across from her. "Now, pray tell, milady, inform me on how you came to be aboard my ship." He raised a dark brow as he watched her remove the towel from her head. His gaze remained fixed on her hair, which tumbled down her back, loose and damp from her bath.

Eden shifted under the attention he was paying her. "And why should I tell you that, Captain?" She jutted her chin out in the air and crossed her arms over her chest.

"Because, as a discovered stowaway, you are now my prisoner and you will do exactly as you are told, milady." He folded his hands in front of him and leaned back in his chair.

She pouted and frowned. "You are simply a beast."

"Ah, milady, your opinion of me would drastically alter had you stowed yourself away on any other pirate ship, I assure you." He grinned.

She sniffed as she attempted to pin her hair up into an elegant twist Aimee had once showed her. "Well, I am here now, and my opinion remains quite the same, good sir."

The Captain leaned forward, his elbows on his knees. He was so close to her she could feel his warm breath on her cheek. His black curls were in a tangled mass and his jaw was scratched with stubble like some ... pirate.

The man was anything but a gentleman, yet he had not raised a hand to her yet. Maybe she was fortunate he was not a London-bred "gentleman."

"I suppose I am sick and tired of 'gentlemen' anyway," she muttered and then froze. Had he heard her statement?

"Ah, the young lady is adventurous!" He exclaimed. "Do you prefer a pirate to a gentleman? Or are you just sick and tired of men in general?" He teased, winking at her.

Yes ... he had heard it. Her cheeks heated, but she raised her chin in defiance. He had no right to wink at her like that ... even if she did enjoy it. What was she thinking? "I am certainly sick and tired of English gentlemen, anyway, at least most of those that I have had the misfortune of meeting."

"Ah, well, I can understand your point. I've met more than my share of scalawags from all classes. But, miss, you are in luck. Standing before you is a man born and raised in New Providence." He doffed his captain's hat and smiled broadly.

"Now please, grace me with the tale of how you have come to be on my ship—without paying for your passage?" He raised a brow.

Eden opened her mouth to refuse but thought better of it and sighed. The man had been gentle with her as of yet, but he was a man, nonetheless. There was no way of knowing how harsh a temper resided behind his handsome face. She had barely just met him. "I was simply escaping a life far worse than death. When I realized I could not garner enough money of my own for a passage to Port Royal, I came to the docks under the cover of night. While I was there, I noticed a group of sailors approaching me. I feared they might have seen through my disguise like you and Mr. Thompson did, so I ran onto the nearest ship, seeking refuge from the men and praying this ship was going to sail to Port Royal. God answered my prayers. He must believe it best for me to start my new life in the colonies there."

He snorted and rolled his crystal-blue eyes, shifting the position of his legs.

Eden glared at him. "Are you telling me you don't believe in God?" She crossed her arms across her chest.

"Nay, milady. I do believe in God; I just know he doesn't care a whit for me. Believe me; God stopped answering my prayers many years ago." He sighed, pressing his large hands together. "And how did you come to be sleeping in my hold? Why did you not come to me and beg or barter some sort of passage?"

"I-I had no way of knowing where you were or what type of man you happened to be. How would I have any way of knowing what sort of payment you would expect? I thought it would be one that would tarnish my reputation, for sure. So, I decided to sleep down in the hold behind the crates. It seemed the safest, if smelliest, place aboard the ship where I would not be seen." She scrunched up her nose, remembering the horrible stench of the hold.

He cocked a dark eyebrow. "And that is your excuse, milady? What on earth was this lifetime worse than death—for a lady of wealth, nonetheless—that you attempted to escape, even hide in a filthy, dark hold to be rid of? I am sure it was never that bad of a life in your little manor in England, or wherever it is. Port Royal is a dangerous city, especially for a young woman who happens to be all on her own, without the benefit of an escort, without money." Caspian countered.

"How dare you suggest such a thing? You know nothing

about me or my life. Such audacity is preposterous, sir." She tugged a lock of her umber hair with her finger.

The Captain huffed. Eden rolled her eyes at his childish behavior. Why, this man's little son had been behaving in a more grown-up fashion!

Chapter 4

C aspian was not accustomed to being denied by a simple girl. Lady Trenton had all but kicked him out of his own cabin—aboard his own ship. Blast, the woman was beginning to grate on his nerves! He was the Captain of this ship, and no matter how pretty she was, she had no authority here.

He sulked, staring at the inky sea. By the smoky look of it, the dark night sky held a storm that would reach them soon.

His mind twisted back to the woman again, against his will. When Lady Trenton had twirled her hair about her finger, the neck of the low-cut gown he had given her shifted and the movement revealed another bruise. This one was in the shape of a meaty fist and on her neck. Someone had hurt her and it had happened recently. Quite recently. Caspian longed to ask her about it, to know who had done this to her, but he thought better of it. She apparently was not fond of telling him anything personal. Besides, he had just met her. In all reality, he had no right to know her personal business.

Gage appeared beside him, the typical grin plastered on his face. "Any news on the woman, Captain? Who exactly is she?"

"Aye, she relinquished some information. It certainly was hard enough to get it out of her. Her name is Lady Eden Trenton. She boarded my ship in an attempt to escape what she claims is 'a fate far worse than death.'"

"Egad, what could a well-off lady like her be running away from that is worse than death?" Gage asked, frowning.

"She refuses to tell me. All I know is she is absolutely terrified of returning to London," Caspian replied, gripping the aft rail of his ship. The sturdiness of the wood grounded him from the oddities that had occurred in the past few hours.

"Well, of course. I suppose she simply got into an argument with her papa over buying a dress or some frilly ribbons and ran away over it." Gage leaned forward and rested his forearms on the rail.

"Nay, I believe she isn't so frivolous a woman. I think this is something more significant than a ribbon or a dress. Lady Trenton seems terrified of me. She recoiled from my touch. What I'm thinking is she was hurt by someone in London and is running away from that person," Caspian reasoned, speaking slowly as he thought.

"Aye, the poor girl. I saw how she fainted in the hold when you were simply teasing her. But she is quite a beauty, isn't she, Captain?" Gage's face lit up with a grin.

"Yes, my man, and you will stay well away from her if you know what's good for you. If I am correct and she has been hurt by a man, we do not want you to give her any further fear."

"Yes, Captain," he smiled, "I was just commenting. Besides, you know how I prefer red-heads to brunettes any day."

Caspian chuckled and shot a glance in his friend's direction.

Reed skipped up to the two men from the other direction. "Papa, where will Lady Trenton sleep tonight?"

Caspian's breathing halted for a second. He had not thought of that. Since his wife had died, he had not been around many women, but he knew how improper it was for the lady to be in the same room, alone with him, at night. But as long as his son was there, he supposed it did not matter. However, because it was only polite that the woman sleep on the bed it looked like their journey would be filled with rough nights until they reached Port Royal.

"Lady Trenton shall sleep in our bed, Reed. We shall sleep on the floor tonight."

"All right, but Papa, may we go to sleep now? The door is locked to the cabin so I can't go in." Reed informed him with a yawn.

"Yes, of course, Reed. It is by far past your bedtime, anyway. We have had a long day. Good night, Gage." Caspian nodded to his friend. "Bid the man good night, Reed," Caspian ordered his son.

"Good night, sir."

Gage flashed a smile and ruffled Reed's hair, eliciting a giggle from the boy.

Caspian shrugged his shoulders and led his son toward their cabin. He took a deep breath to steady himself before he knocked on the door.

"Who is it?" He heard Lady Trenton's voice trill sweetly.

"The Captain."

After a moment, she opened the door, giving him a doubtful look. Reed rushed inside and sat in one of the leather armchairs. Caspian strode to his glass cabinet. The glistening bottles of port and rum clinked together as the *Dawn's Mist* plunged over a particularly large swell. He jerked the door open and snatched a carafe from the shelf before he plucked a glass off of his desk and poured himself a draught of the sweet liquid. Caspian raised it to his lips.

No.

He slammed the glass down onto his desk with a thud.

Isabelle would be quite angry if she found out her husband was guzzling down spirits like a common drunkard. She loathed his drinking habits and Caspian knew that. Then why did he continuously feel the urge to return to a despicable lifestyle?

"C-can I ... help you, Captain?" A soft voice stammered.

The lady.

Caspian spun to look at her, and his breath stopped short in his throat as he looked at her for the first time since she had opened the door from him.

The woman was backed up against the bulkhead and dressed in a lacy white nightgown that was absconded from a merchant ship in the years when he had taken to pirating. If he remembered correctly, the gown was made of silk from China and intricate lace from Paris. It was positively lovely on her.

Caspian let the image soak into his mind, how her curves filled out the gown, how the lace frothed against her creamy skin. Even though she was anything but tall, the gown stopped at her ankles, scandalously revealing two tiny feet and ten perfect toes. He swallowed back a burst of longing to touch those little feet and do a whole lot more. Fire and thunder, what was wrong with him?

He had to look away; he knew it.

He could not bring himself to. She shivered and her eyes shifted to the floor underneath his intense perusal. Yes, he knew it would be best to divert his gaze, although, at the moment, looking away from the beauty was the least of his desires. *Say something, man, or you'll frighten the poor lady to death.*

"Where did you get that nightgown, woman?" He snapped, sounding far more aggravated then he had meant to.

"I-I ... found it in that big trunk over there; I hope it is all right for me to wear it. I'm sorry ... I should have asked you first, before I put it on. That was horribly presumptuous of me. Oh, I will find something else immediately. Why, I had no idea that you ... that you and your son would come back here," she stammered, her hand hovering at her pale throat.

Caspian could not help but notice the bruise there, marring her pretty skin. She took a step toward the trunk she had pointed to.

He gripped her elbow, preventing her from turning her back to him. The moment she flinched, Caspian released her and took a step back, bumping into his desk. "Nay. 'Tis ... fine, Lady Trenton. I just ... was startled to see you in it. And nay, milady, I simply came to go to bed." He explained, grabbing a pillow and a bundle of blankets from a nearby teak trunk.

As soon as he finished his sentence, the young lady's expression altered entirely. "And where, pray tell, shall I sleep?" She asked incredulously, resting her hands on her hips.

"Why, you will have the bed, of course. I am not so much of a cad that I would make a lady sleep on the floor," he answered, lowering himself onto the deck next to the bed. He really did need some sleep. Upon her look of utter shock he continued,

"I apologize, milady, but this is the only available cabin I have on board. You will just have to tolerate my company and my son's. Unless, of course, you wish to sleep back in the hold with Kelton. That I definitely would not recommend." He lifted a brow at her. He knew he was feeling far too mischievous.

Lady Trenton huffed. She glanced around and then said, her voice sharp, as if she were waiting for some way to condemn him, "Where is your wife? Does she even know you are captaining a pirate ship, frightening poor young women? What about Reed? He should be with his mother. A boy as young as him should not be away from his mother on a place as dangerous as a pirate ship."

Caspian froze. Of course a lady like her would wonder why he had a son but no wife. He had not talked about Isabelle to anyone but Reed or Gage for years. "My wife is … gone." He gave her a piercing look.

Lady Trenton took in a sharp breath and shifted her gaze down.

Caspian ignored her and glanced over at his son, who was staring at Lady Trenton, wide-eyed. "Come along, Reed. It is bedtime. We are sleeping on the floor tonight, remember?"

"Nay, Captain. The boy will sleep on the bed with me. I will not be the cause of depriving a child as young as Reed of comfort. You won't mind sleeping up here with me, will you, Reed?" She sank down on the bed.

Reed nodded drowsily, grinning up at her through eyelids dragged down under the weight of sleep. "I like you, Lady Trenton. We shall be the best of friends. I am certain of it."

She smiled back at Reed. The lady did have a gorgeous smile.

Caspian felt a twinge of jealousy traipse into his heart

without any form of invitation. Surely he did not feel it because … because the woman got along with his son so well while he—the child's own father—could not. Nay, who could blame Reed? A lady was a rare treasure to uncover on the seas, and this one in particular was being especially kind to the boy. And Caspian knew he felt no jealousy because of how sweetly the woman smiled at Reed while she glared so hatefully at Caspian. There was no reason for him to care if she liked his company or not.

Caspian watched silently as his child curled up beside the woman on the bed. She turned to face the bulkhead, robbing from him the sight of her comely face. All he could see now was her back, shielded by the thin coverlet.

How could his son automatically adore this woman whom he had never met, this stowaway? Reed baffled him. Besides, how could Lady Trenton be so kind to a shy little boy?

Caspian tried to shake the woman from his thoughts. He failed. Her soft breathing washed over the cabin, tickling his ears.

'Twould be a long night.

* * *

No. No. Not again, Lord, please. Please do not force me to go through this torture again, I beg of you.

Eden felt Lord Rutger's arms grip around her waist harshly. His lips crushed over hers but she swatted him away.

"Come, come, my little flower. We are to be married in a month; I should think you would be more than willing to give me something as simple as a little kiss," he huffed, fingering a lock of her hair.

51

Eden yanked her hair out from his unwanted grasp. The man may be well manicured, but to her, his hands felt filthy. Every touch from the monster made her want to scrub her skin raw.

Why had her father left her alone in the house with this man? Why, even the servants were off work today.

"Please, sir, I have no desire to kiss you." Eden glanced at the door anxiously, longing to escape from him.

"But you have no choice, my flower. You must do as I tell you, as my fiancée." His green eyes seemed to read every single thought that passed through her head. "I will not be denied by a simple wench. As your husband, I have a right to a kiss and far more from you, Eden!" he exploded, handsome face growing red with anger, a color almost the exact shade of the auburn hair that fell in disarray around his narrow shoulders. She wished he did not have the right to even call her by her Christian name. "For heaven's sake, I have every right to take you up to my bedchamber! I may just have a mind to yet!"

"You are not my husband yet, now are you, sir? Why, you have no right to anything at all from me," Eden cried. Tears stung her eyes. No, she would not give him the satisfaction her tears would bring.

How could she escape this man?

Lord Rutger backhanded her. The sharp sting burned her face, and she almost lost her balance as her vision blurred with tears. She refused to cry in front of the monster.

He dug his hands on her waist and planted his lips on hers in an aggressive kiss. Eden threw her face to the side. She gasped for air, desperate to escape his hounding lips, and twisted in his arms to break away from his audacious grip. Raising her hand, she smacked his insolent face although he deserved much more than a simple slap. Turning, she fled to her room and latched the door shut *before she could face the consequences her actions would bring.*

Heavy footsteps clomped behind her. The doorframe shivered under Lord Rutger's pounding fists. A louder banging commenced. He was kicking in the door.

She knelt behind her bed and squeezed her eyes shut.

And then she woke. Eden took a deep, calming breath.

Just a dream. She opened her eyes. And discovered a tall man looming above her.

Eden shot out of bed. She searched for a weapon, anything she could use to protect herself from the man. Finding nothing, she fisted her hands and swung about to face her attacker.

Captain Archer smirked down at her. From the moonlight that filtered in through the porthole, she could identify amusement sparkling in the man's eyes. Eden spotted a pistol on his desk. She seized the weapon and pointed it at the Captain. Finding the foul handgun too heavy, she held it with both her hands although she was still shaking. How in the world did one work these wretched things?

* * *

Caspian chuckled. He must admit he had never had a woman point a pistol at him. Even most of the men he knew were too frightened to threaten him. They knew the consequences of confronting Captain Caspian Archer.

This girl was quite plucky indeed.

He took a slow, calculated step toward her as if she were a young doe he was terrified of frightening off.

"Milady, you have naught to fear from me." Caspian held

his hands up in an innocent gesture and glanced over at his son, who was sleeping peacefully on the bed. The child could sleep through just about anything. Yet another way the lad took after his mother.

Eden fumbled with Caspian's pistol and he chuckled yet again.

"You don't even know how to shoot a gun, do you, Eden?" He realized he had called the lady by her Christian name, but he could not stop himself. She was so frightened of him, and he wanted to reach through the haze of terror that clouded her eyes. By thunder, he had only been waking her from her nightmare, but now he realized the exact same nightmare may have made her even more frightened of him.

He edged nearer to the woman, intent on snatching his pistol away from her before she injured either herself or him. Or both.

"Don't you touch me or take another step toward me or I promise I *will* shoot you!" Her small hands trembled.

Her fingers fumbled and she cocked the gun. Tears streamed down her face. Something dreadful must have happened to this poor woman. Such horrible nightmares had to have been triggered by some terrible event.

"It is all right, Eden. I promise I am not going to hurt you. You are perfectly safe with me, I assure you." He gave her what he hoped looked like a comforting smile and reached a tentative hand out toward her.

The lady jerked away, back out of his reach. She let out a startled cry as the gun fired with an earsplitting crack.

A stabbing pain ripped through Caspian's left shoulder.

The acrid smell of gunpowder filled the air.

Reed jumped straight up from his position on the bed.

Caspian glanced down to find blood gliding from his shoulder down his left arm.

He shifted his gaze to the lady in shock. "You shot me, woman."

* * *

Eden dropped the smoking gun and flew to the Captain's side. Had she truly just shot a man? Would he kill her now? Surely he would at least strike her. Not many men took kindly to a woman harming them. At least she knew Rutger would never take kindly. But the Captain's blue eyes flickered in amusement and something else she couldn't quite place. Perhaps it was just anger and she misread his expression.

"Papa! Papa, what has happened? Wha-what was that noise, Papa?" Reed was sitting up, looking as if he had just jumped out from a dead sleep.

Caspian twisted to face his son, shock still painted on his face. His right hand clutched his wounded shoulder. "Nothing, Reed. Go out on the deck for a moment; I need a moment alone with Lady Trenton. I will call you back when we're done, all right, boy?"

Reed moved toward the door, his wide, sleep-filled eyes shifting from his father to Eden. Finally, he left.

The second the door shut behind him, Eden spun to the Captain, fighting to hold back the tears in her eyes. Was the man dismissing his son so the child's young eyes did not witness what he had in store for Eden?

Her shoulders shuddered when she realized her fears were probably true.

"I-I'm so sorry. I didn't mean … will … you … are you going to … s-strike me now?" Eden felt certain her voice rose in pitch with each word she spoke. The blood flowing from the Captain's shoulder distracted her. Careful to keep her body well away from the man, she pulled out her handkerchief and gently pressed it to his wound with an outstretched arm. She refused to look him in the eye and instead studied the hole she had put in his arm with the gun. But then she noted, with a spark of relief, that the bullet had barely grazed the flesh of his arm.

Well, she had had no idea the wretched firearm would truly fire that time. When she had pulled the trigger mere seconds before, nothing had happened. She had concluded that the gun was not loaded. How was she to know she would actually hurt him? He took the handkerchief from her and pressed it against his shoulder on his own.

She stumbled away. "Please, just get it over with now, sir." Eden stared fixedly at a splinter protruding from the wooden planks beneath her.

Her words finally seemed to sink into the man when he cried out with what sounded something like alarm in his deep voice, "Never!" Captain Archer wrenched the handkerchief from his wound and took a step closer to her. "I would never strike a woman. Never. What kind of man do you believe me to be?" He glared at her so hard, she felt it almost the same as a blow. "Besides, I am not gravely injured, milady. The bullet barely grazed my arm. It is nothing drastic by any means." He placed a finger underneath her chin, nudging her face up gently. A callus on his hand brushed against her skin, but his touch was anything but rough.

Eden felt a surge of heat flood over her at his touch. He tied the cloth that remained in his other hand around his wounded shoulder, studying Eden as if he had never before seen her. Why was his mouth curled up in a smile? For goodness's sake, why wasn't he upset with her?

* * *

Why had the dear woman even considered the thought that he would strike her? Egad, he could never do anything even remotely near striking her. Caspian now had confirmation where that garish black bruise had come from. But who had done it to her? Who would have the gall to harm such a precious creature? He certainly should not ask her now. Now, she was too vulnerable, too fragile, and somehow, too fearless.

Even now, she cowered against the bulkhead, her lower lip trembling.

"Faith, woman, you are quite brave to shoot me like that." He felt one side of his mouth curl up in a smile.

Eden shook her head repeatedly. "You would never say such a thing if you had seen what I did in my nightmare. How terrified I was. How I ran away." She chewed on her quivering, plump bottom lip and gazed intently at the ground.

"Ha! I daresay I have never seen a woman with enough daring to simply point a gun at a man, nonetheless shoot him. A pirate captain, even so." He chuckled.

Eden trembled and leaned back against the bulkhead. She swayed.

Caspian leapt to her side and engulfed her in his arms. He winced, but the pain from his bullet wound did not last long with an adorable woman in his embrace. A sweet scent of vanilla and coconut teased his nose. Had he truly just met this girl? By the urge deep in his gut to protect her, it almost seemed as though he had known her for years.

She was as stiff in his arms as a bowline caught in the wind until he set her down next to him on one of the leather armchairs. The poor girl melted against him and onto his lap, and then she began to sob.

"Milady, will you please tell me about your dream … your nightmare? Who is it who hurt you, sweetheart? What did they do to you? I want to know who struck you and gave you that bruise on your shoulder." He gently touched her delicate shoulder. The heat of her skin bore through the thin silk of the nightgown she wore.

She shook her head and covered her face with both of her hands. "It matters not, Captain. As long as we do not return to London, I shall be safe from him. I have vowed it will never happen again."

Tears pooled in her doe-like eyes and soon began to pour down her face in little rivulets. Caspian felt a sudden surge of protectiveness and anger sweep through his body. By all that is great and good, if he ever laid his eyes on the man who had done this to the poor woman, gave her these terrible nightmares, he would kill him. By all that was right, he must make certain the lady was safe from this monster and others like him. He would see for certain that once in Port Royal, she had a safe place to go with as much money as she needed to survive.

Perhaps she was thinking similarly.

"Can I get you anything, Lady Trenton? Is there anything I can help you with once we reach Port Royal?" Caspian inquired, longing to remove those dreadful tears from her pretty eyes.

She nestled her head against his chest and remained silent so long that for a moment, he wondered if she had fallen asleep. Finally, she answered, "No, thank you." She released a shaky breath.

Caspian stroked her umber curls, relishing the fact that she didn't stop him, didn't recoil from his touch like he had expected from the lady and her skittish ways. He was enjoying how soft and silky her locks felt beneath his fingertips.

After a few moments, the lady's breathing altered from ragged sobs to quiet, even snoring. Caspian could not hold back a grin at the sight of such a pretty little thing snoring. He scooped her up in his arms and laid her down on the bed before going up on deck to retrieve his curious son.

Chapter 5

⚬⚬⚬

C aspian gazed out at the sea. Oh, how wonderful it felt to be at sea again, to smell the salty, moist air! When he was here, he was in full control. He had proven himself more than capable of overcoming even the greatest pirates of the Spanish Main, and he could destroy those who had destroyed him.

He rubbed his tender arm, still healing from the bullet wound and smirked. Well, he was capable of destroying these men, but maybe not controlling the little woman in his cabin.

It was barely fathomable that it had only been a week since he had met Lady Trenton. She had grown on Reed by the second, and yet stayed far away from Caspian. He wondered if she would ever be anything but cold and distant to him.

Caspian squinted at a point on the horizon. Was that the bright white of a billowing sail? He trained his eyes to focus, but after a second, all he could see was the churning, gray waters.

Moments later, a cry rained down from the shrouds. "A

sail!"

Caspian whipped out his telescope. There was a ship off their western horizon, sailing toward them. Just as he had suspected.

He recognized the colors. Gray and red. The colors of *Neptune's Poison*. Moore. There was no way it was not Moore. Caspian had been told the man was in the Caribbean, miles away off the coast of Jamaica, but it seemed that information was incorrect. After running into the man a couple of times over the years and never actually getting close enough for another battle, the time had come for Caspian's revenge.

Gage walked up beside Caspian. "Captain, who is she?"

"Moore."

Gage sucked in a breath. "I suppose you plan to take her, Captain?"

"Aye, Master Thompson. Prepare the men."

Caspian could accomplish his goal before even arriving in the Caribbean. Moore would get what he deserved once and for all after all the pain he had brought upon Caspian and Reed.

* * *

Gage watched as Captain Archer ran a hand through his curly black hair. A feeling of foreboding washed over Gage, and he hesitated to do the Captain's bidding. Did they truly want to pick a fight with a ship that could easily best them? The ship appeared to be more heavily gunned than the *Dawn's Mist* as Moore's had been, true, but what were the chances this ship belonged to Moore? There were plenty of other ships flying those same colors.

Caspian spun around, his fists clenched. Gage lowered his gaze. He did not want to ignite his friend's anger, but he wondered if it was a good idea to approach this ship.

"I told you to prepare the men, Master Thompson … what is keeping you?"

"Well … uh … Captain, do you truly think it is Moore? That is to say …" Gage stammered, wringing his hands as he stood in front of his captain. For some reason, he felt there was something terribly wrong with this situation. If this ship really was Moore, the last thing Gage wanted for his Captain was to let his emotions control his actions and make a mistake. Besides, if something happened to Reed during the imminent battle, Caspian would never, ever, forgive himself.

Gage did not know if he could forgive himself, either. Children were a precious gift from God. Everyone would be much better off if they high-tailed away from this ship with the gray and red flag.

"Master Thompson, you were given an order by your Captain … I don't care if you are my friend; there will be a consequence if you disobey me." He paused and spoke more calmly. "Yes, it has to be Moore. Those are his colors. Don't think I do not remember every blasted detail of that day."

Gage recognized the anger coiled in his captain's eyes and the bite to his words, but Gage knew they were not directed at him. No, it had to have been reserved for Moore and what he had done.

But Gage also noticed something else in Captain Archer's eyes … something like … fear.

"Captain, is this truly the time for a battle with your old enemy? We have the lady below, and really, should we risk harming her? Besides, think of Reed. What if something were to happen to him?" Gage knew if they did not avoid this battle, many of their men would die and Moore would no doubt best them again.

Besides, revenge was a bitter thing to seek. Gage had learned that lesson long ago from his parents' actions.

Something passed through the Captain's eyes, and for a moment, he did not speak. Gage glanced out at the horizon, where the ship was approaching them by the minute.

"Reed will be fine. Lady Trenton, well, she might be ... no. We must do this. We cannot allow Moore to escape when he is just within our grasp."

"Captain ..." Gage warned.

Captain Archer rotated away from him, fury the dominant expression on his face. He addressed the crew, who had stopped in front of them, awaiting orders. "Prepare the guns and keep your weapons at the ready! We will take her!" Caspian lodged his fists on his hips. "Tanner, make haste!" he ordered the man behind the wheel.

"Really, Captain, are you certain we should ..." Gage interrupted with one final plea.

"If you wish to defy me, Master Thompson, then go below. I will not have you up here. This man has bested me once; I will not allow him to slip by without a fight."

"My apologies, Captain." He glanced at the men milling about the deck, strapping weapons onto their bodies. Foul words spewed from their mouths.

Gage nodded at his captain, truly regretting being so defiant to the man who had been his friend since early childhood. But what was wrong with the man? Was his thirst for revenge outweighing even his sense for protecting Lady Trenton and his son?

* * *

Caspian let out a groan, frustrated that his first mate and best friend was being so contrary today. He retrieved his spyglass, glaring at the ship that had ruined his life five years earlier.

He squinted to make out the familiar gray and red. It appeared to be in the shape of an hourglass, not Moore's trademark skull.

Caspian backed away from the rail, shaking his head in disbelief.

That was not Moore at all; in fact, he recognized the colors as Captain Harden's, a fellow privateer.

It took him a moment to swallow his pride, but he did it in haste, before Captain Harden caught sight of them approaching. "There will be no battle today, men! She is a privateer. Turn her back to starboard, Tanner!"

Caspian looked at his first mate. He could not read Gage's expression, but he thought he saw disappointment in his eyes. Not disappointment in Caspian's decision to avoid a skirmish, but disappointment at Caspian's lust for blood. Moore's blood, to be exact. Well, the man did not understand what he had gone through at the hands of Moore, and he hoped he never would.

Caspian would rid the sea of all of these wretched pirates like Moore.

He frowned when he remembered how much his Isabelle had abhorred piracy. How could he have remained a pirate when he was with her, during their short-lived marriage? Well, he was not a pirate anymore, and he *would* get revenge for the dear woman.

Countless whistles and bawdy catcalls assaulted Caspian's ears. He whirled around to see Lady Trenton parading across the deck, huffing indignantly at the pirates, her face flushed to a becoming pink. The forecastle deck gave him a good vantage point to study her from. She had changed into a fresh coral-colored gown and pinned her umber curls into a loose bun at the nape of her neck. He snapped his thoughts away from admiring how pretty she looked. What on earth was she doing out here, in full sight of the crew, without his permission? Foolish girl.

The full crew had not even realized she was on the ship with them yet. Caspian had planned to explain the situation to his men later, but this was a lot more trouble. Now they would all assume the worst. Why else would a beautiful lady be emerging from the Captain's cabin?

The moment Caspian saw Kelton eying her up like she was nothing but a common trollop he leapt from the forecastle deck and ran amidships. He never should have let the insolent man out of confinement in the hold the day before. He should have known the young man would cause trouble.

But Caspian's intended rescue was no good for Kelton struck before he arrived. The man approached her as if he had not seen a woman in years. He grasped her by the waist, a greedy look in his eyes. She screamed and slapped him in the face. Kelton roared and shook her by the shoulders.

What a foolish young man! Did he not realize his captain was right there, in front of him? Nay, the man no doubt realized that fact. He was doing this purely to defy his captain before the whole crew.

"Help! Captain? Captain Archer!" Lady Trenton screeched, searching for him, a shaken and helpless look on her pretty face.

"I am right here, Lady Trenton. No need to worry." Caspian glared at the whelp, clenching his jaw tightly. "Kelton, you will release her immediately if you know what's good for your useless carcass," he barked.

Growling, Kelton obeyed and shoved Lady Trenton away from him as he did so. Relief washed over Caspian and he slowly unclenched his fists when the whelp released her. Caspian did not want to resort to violence in front of the woman. It appeared as if she had experienced too much viciousness in her lifetime already.

The lady stumbled, swaying for a moment before regaining her balance.

Kelton glared up at his Captain. Caspian noted the small, bright red hand mark that stained the young man's face. He chuckled. The woman was brave. And quite strong.

"I do believe the young lady has adequately punished you physically. Thank her, for she has spared you a long lashing. Now be gone with you. The sight of you sickens me," he ordered.

Kelton begrudgingly minded his captain.

"I trust you are unharmed, milady?" Caspian held a hand under Eden's chin to examine her profile for any newly acquired wounds. Thankfully, she appeared unharmed. He grimaced when he remembered the bruise on her collar bone that was no doubt turning a shade of yellow-green by now.

She nodded and shriveled away from him. Caspian sighed. Why did she fear his touch? *He* had never hurt her. For goodness's sake, he had given her no reason to fear him! Why, he had given her every reason to *trust* him.

She noticed him looking and moved some curls from her

coif, attempting to cover the bruise from his sight. Too late.

"What brings you up on deck unescorted, milady? It is best for you to stay below in our—my cabin."

"Well I-I simply … I needed some fresh air, Captain Archer. I hate being cooped up in a place where I can barely move around," she stammered, backing away from him.

"Next time, all you need to do if you want to go for a walk is ask me. I will happily escort you on deck so you will not be harassed by Kelton again."

Anger coursed through his veins like boiling hot oil when he looked down at her; when he noticed the delicate curve of her chin and the graceful tilt of her dark eyelashes. How dare Kelton scare this precious girl? Even a fool would realize she had been abused by a man quite similar to him before. Men like him deserved to rot in hell for their actions.

Blast it, why was Caspian so protective of this blasted woman? The only other woman he had ever desired to protect and cherish and comfort like this was Isabelle, even though that had felt a little different. And that had ended in nothing but disaster. He might as well have not even been present to defend her against Moore.

Lady Trenton chewed on her bottom lip, drawing his attention to it. He pulled his gaze away, knowing it was rude to stare.

"Now, if you please, Lady Trenton, go below and be safe." A cool breeze drifted onto the deck from the ocean, only slightly cooling Caspian's anger.

"No! Please—please, let me stay up here! It is terribly boring and stifling in the cabin." She folded her hands together and looked up at him through those pretty lashes of hers.

He let out an exasperated breath.

He did not need her to be hurt and in truth, the woman was a distraction to both him and his crew. She was quite fetching in her coral-colored dress, her dark curls cascading down her back like a delicious waterfall of the cocoa he had once drunk in Jamaica. Those curls could not stay in that bun of hers for long with the wind and humidity of life at sea.

He shook his head. The lady had distracted him yet again. Yet how could he refuse something as simple as fresh air and a stroll to that beautiful woman? "Yes, I suppose you can. For now."

She smiled sweetly, and then strutted over to the rail in triumph. Caspian followed closely behind her, enjoying the gentle sway of her shapely hips despite his efforts to ignore it. He cleared his throat. "Well, you have been on my ship for nearly a week now, milady. Are you enjoying life at sea?" He asked, stopping beside the lady. When he spoke to her, his voice cracked nervously. Like he was nothing but some weak little schoolboy with a hopeless infatuation. He certainly did not take a liking to the feeling.

She nodded cheerfully, not seeming to notice his indiscretion. "I don't know how anyone could be happy living on land after they have experienced life on a ship. I love the feel of the waves beneath me and the smell of the salty air. I suppose I get it from my brother."

He flashed a grin at her. "I completely agree with your sentiments, milady. Was your brother a sailor, may I ask?"

"My father is an owner of a trading company centered in London, and he expected Adam to become a wealthy businessman like him. When I was twelve and Adam fifteen, Adam hopped aboard one of the ships heading to the Caribbean. He paid his way as a cabin boy, not telling the sailors he was the son of the owner of the company. When he returned home, boasting of the beauty there, Father nearly disowned him. Father said no son of his would be a common sailor, but Papa's anger cooled down after a few weeks. Adam fell in love with the sea and soon worked his way up to becoming a first mate, all against our father's will. I have not heard from him for a year or so. I wonder what he is doing now." She looked away wistfully, chewing on her bottom lip.

"It sounds like your family has a propensity for running away from home, Lady Trenton," he teased, tweaking her nose playfully. He delighted in the grin she rewarded him with.

The ship plunged over a swell and Caspian instinctively placed a hand on the small of her back to keep her from faltering. She scooted away from him once she was righted, a gorgeous shade of pink staining her cheeks.

What did he expect from a proper lady?

"That—that reminds me, Captain. I apologize for my brazen behavior the other night. I know this is no excuse at all for me sitting on your lap and letting you hold me and … and falling asleep in your arms, but … I was just so frightened and … well, there is no excuse whatsoever, sir. I know not why I am trying to manufacture one. My sinful nature, no doubt. I am deeply sorry, sir."

"There is no need to apologize, milady. What you did was completely understandable given the circumstances."

Their conversation came to a quick halt when Reed skipped up to them, the usual grin plastered on that little face of his. That little face that was just like his mama's. "Lady Trenton! I have been looking for you for so long! When I saw the men grab their weapons, I was worried for you. They told me to stay below, but I came up because I was scared for you."

Caspian knew he had been a terrible father to Reed. He longed to take the child in his arms and change that but was afraid of his reaction. The boy might not want a hug from the papa who paid little attention to him. Why, Gage probably spent more time with Reed than Caspian did! What kind of father was he? Besides, the child had called for Lady Trenton, not him. Reed was looking for the lady he had met only a week ago and not his father.

Lady Trenton hugged the boy in his stead.

"See what I found, Lady Trenton?" The boy exclaimed, holding up the sapphire necklace he had found the same day Lady Trenton had been discovered in the hold.

It dawned upon Caspian that the trinket most likely belonged to Eden.

* * *

Eden recognized the pendant as the one Lord Rutger had *so graciously* bestowed upon her as a token of their one-sided *betrothal*.

"Oh! That used to belong to me, Reed. I must have dropped it when I was … when I came aboard the ship a couple of days ago."

"Oh." Reed lowered the bauble slowly as his lashes lowered over his eyes.

"Give the necklace back to the lady, son. It does not belong to you," Caspian commanded, his eyebrows drawn close together.

Reed glanced down, a despondent expression on his adorable little face.

Eden had to stop those tears from welling up in his violet-blue eyes.

"Nay, Captain, Reed may keep it. It was simply a gift from … from a man. I certainly do not need it. Reed will enjoy it far more than I ever will, I assure you." A wave of nausea washed over Eden at the memory of Lord Rutger's overly familiar hand, the night he had clasped the necklace around her throat. His warm, sickening breath had washed over her shoulders and he had pressed a lingering kiss beneath her earlobe. Before she could control it, a shudder shook her whole body.

Her thoughts transferred when the child grinned up gleefully at her. "Really? May I please, Lady Trenton? Please?"

"Ed—Lady Trenton, surely you can use it more than Reed. He will no doubt have it lost within the week. You can't get rid of something like that with a simple shake of the head," Caspian objected.

Eden softly placed her hand on the Captain's arm but removed it the second she realized how improper her action was. "I truly do not care for the bauble. Honestly, I am much happier without it."

"But even if you don't like how it looks, it must be worth a fair amount of money. You could use it when we reach Port Royal; you could sell it so you have a place to stay and food to eat."

"No." She honestly did not want to even touch something the monster had given to her. The mere sight of it made her feel sick. "God will provide for me. In truth, I want no memory of my life in London. It was terrible, and I do not need to remember it when I begin anew in the Caribbean."

Reed glanced up at her with grateful eyes. "Oh, thank you, Lady Trenton. Thank you!" He wrapped his little arms around her waist, smiling appreciatively.

"You are quite welcome, my dear." Eden patted his back gently. After his hug, the child skipped away once more.

The Captain moved closer to her. "That was quite kind, milady. You did not have to give my boy the necklace. Thank you. I promise I will pay you back for it somehow," Caspian said, staring into her eyes.

She backed up slightly, keeping a decent space between her and the intriguing man. "Captain, I assure you, it was fine. I have no need for that frivolous necklace. Consider it as a payment for my voyage."

"Milady, I would be leaving this bargain with much more value than you would. I will not be counting it toward your voyage. Thank you, though. Reed seems to be quite fascinated by that little sapphire." He chuckled.

Eden could understand. The only thing she ever did like about the necklace was the sparkling blue gem. But now she realized it was not very pretty, after all. For she peered into Captain Archer's eyes and saw they were a far more beautiful shade of the color. His masculine scent of salt and leather wafted over her in waves like the ocean on the seashore.

He offered her a sultry grin, and she realized she had been caught staring at him.

"I-I," she stuttered, "I'm sorry ... I do not know what went over me ..." Her cheeks heated.

"Nay, milady. No need to apologize to me. I only assumed you would find it most improper for an aristocratic lady such as yourself to be gaping in such a manner at a pirate like me." He winked at her.

Was it possible for her entire body to turn pink with a blush? "I do not care a whit for high society's rules. Why, I suppose I can look at whomever I wish now that I am no longer within view of London's prying eyes."

He smirked. "I didn't think you did care. You are not like many other ladies I have met. Although I admit I have not met a fair share of them."

Was that a compliment or an insult to her? She didn't want to know, unsure which one she would prefer.

"Well, sir. Good day. I feel a … need to lie down for a moment out of the sun." With one last glance at Captain Archer, she fled to the cabin before she had to face either his admiration or his condemnation.

* * *

Ivy sank down like an anchor onto her soft bed. How irrational could Eden be? Why had she not told her and Aimee before she had actually run away? Eden should have asked Aimee and Ivy for help before going. For all Ivy knew, Eden could already have been attacked by some sailor when she was by the docks. Even as she sat here now, her friend could be lying in some alleyway, dead or close to dying.

She wrung her hands together, praying her friend was safe. Ivy glanced at the other side of the room, where her little brother slept in a cradle. With her mother's ailment, Ivy only trusted herself to care for Will, so he slept in her room and she did not mind it at all. William was practically an angel. Assured the boy was settled in for the night, she finally leaned back down against her pillows and felt the cool breeze from her window flow over her body. The aromatic scent of the sweet gum trees outside drifted in, soothing her tension somewhat. Soon, Ivy fell asleep from sheer exhaustion.

* * *

Her curtain swayed. Dim moonlight sprinkled in through her window.

Ivy bolted upright, her heart pounding. What was that noise? She blinked. Strange. There was no wind. Had she been so daft as to leave her window wide open when she fell asleep?

Suddenly, a hand smashed firmly over her mouth. Who would be in her room at this time of night, without intentions of harming her? Or William! A terrible feeling brewed in her belly. She tried to scream, but her voice came out too obstructed for it to have any affect. The man stuffed a piece of cloth into her mouth and then she felt the cold press of metal against her neck. A ... knife?

"Let me go!" she tried to cry, but only managed to utter a strangled yelp. Ivy struggled to remove the cloth that muffled her every sound.

She finally twisted around enough to glance up at her captor.

Chapter 6

❧

Caspian sat on the edge of his deck, his legs dangling out over the expansive ocean below him as he laid his forehead against the rail. After he had told the woman she was unlike any other lady he had ever met, a compliment in every sense, she had run away from him and to the cabin. What had he done wrong? He had thought she would like a compliment; he had always thought all women liked to hear something good about themselves. Isabelle had. Apparently Eden did not. She was unlike any other woman he had ever met.

Now he heard the soft trill of the infuriating woman's voice drifting from somewhere on the ship. It was followed by his son's giggling. How could she get the boy to laugh in that gleeful manner with her when Caspian could barely force a smile out of the beloved child?

He shook his head.

* * *

Lord Clive Rutger.

What on earth was Eden's fiancé doing in Ivy's bed chamber? With a knife pressed to her throat?

Instinct flooded her after the initial shock that had paralyzed her body. Ivy kicked and clawed at him, desperate to escape his tight hold. She jabbed his gut with her elbow. He shoved her to the floor. A soft whimper drifted from the other side of the room. Ivy's three-year old brother, William, sobbed in his cradle.

Lord Rutger immediately stuffed a handkerchief into her brother's mouth and transferred the knife to the tyke's throat. He kicked Ivy in the stomach so she could not stop him. Ivy doubled over in pain and clutched her belly. She did not blame Eden for being terrified of this man. Everything made sense now.

Then she realized her baby brother's life was at stake. Why was she wallowing on the ground in self-pity and not doing something?

"No! Please! Don't hurt him, I beg of you! He is just a child! Please, sir. Show some mercy." Her screams were stifled by the cloth over her mouth.

Lord Rutger chortled at her useless attempts. Ivy regretted ever allowing, even slightly encouraging, her dearest friend's engagement to this wicked, heartless man. She had nothing he could want from her, and yet for some reason, he was here. Threatening her. And William.

"I will unbind you if you vow to remain silent."

She nodded fervently. Really, she would do anything he asked just to remove that knife from little William's throat.

"And if you make a single noise without my permission, I swear I will kill the baby. The child means nothing at all to me.

"Now, you will be a good girl for me, will you not?" he threatened in a demeaning tone.

She nodded again, her eyes wide as he removed the cloth from her mouth and dragged her up to a standing position. She was tempted to scream, but she knew from the hard look in Lord Rutger's eyes that he would kill William without a second thought. What could he want so badly from Ivy that he would visit her in the middle of the night and threaten her and her brother like this?

"I am aware that you have been one of my fiancée's closest friends for many years."

She nodded hesitantly. Eden. Her stomach tightened into a nearly unbearable knot of dread. A droplet of cold sweat slid down her back beneath her nightdress and stopped between her shoulder blades.

"And I assume she has graced you with the knowledge of all of her deepest, darkest secrets," he continued, grabbing one of her red curls and squashing it between his manicured fingers. She jerked away, disgust boiling within her. Had she truly, foolishly, once thought this man handsome?

How she wanted to smack away the malicious grin that was plastered on the face that she certainly no longer found attractive.

She remembered his question and nodded again.

"Tell me where she has gone," he demanded, tugging on that lock of hair brutally before releasing it.

"I don't know." Ivy felt her face redden as it always did when she told a lie.

He smacked her across the face with the back of his hand, sending her flying onto the floor. "You filthy, lying little wench!"

* * *

Eden leaned over the Captain's son as she tucked him into bed that night. Captain Archer was nowhere in sight to do so and it seemed like the child was far too accustomed to staying up late. Well, she would have no more of that. Reed needed a responsible mother figure to help him grow up to become a good young man. She would have to scold the Captain for neglecting the dear boy.

"Lady Trenton, I'm glad you are here. I am so happy that Papa didn't throw you to the sharks like he did with the other stowaways we have found on other voyages." The child's hand found hers and squeezed it gently.

Eden gasped, surprised to find that the Captain's claims of tyranny were true. "He actually did that, Reed? Captain Archer … your father threw some poor, helpless person into the ocean like that?"

The little boy paused, a frown tightening his small face. "I can't remember, Lady Trenton. He always told me that is what we do with stowaways on board our ship, but I remember one time when we found an old man down there. Papa did not do anything to him; he just let him join the crew until he had paid for his passage on the ship."

"That was kind of him." Eden hid a satisfied grin. Maybe the Captain wasn't so harsh behind the gruff exterior he portrayed after all.

"Yes, it was, Lady Trenton. He's the best pirate captain in all of the Caribbean!" The boy's voice beamed with pride for his father.

Eden grinned down at him. "I am sure he is, Reed. By the way, darling, there is no need to call me 'Lady Trenton.' Please, you may call me Eden; I insist."

A smile spread across his little face.

A smile that was an exact replica in miniature of his sire's. "I would like that very much, Miss Eden." She stifled a giggle at the polite title of "miss" he had given her. It seemed that his father was actually teaching him some manners even though they lived on a barbaric pirate ship. Eden stepped away, preparing to sit in the leather armchair for a couple of moments before sleeping in the bed herself.

"Miss Eden?"

Eden stopped. "Yes, dear?" A surge of motherly longing swept through her when she saw his mussed blond hair and those purple-tinted blue eyes. She had never realized how much she longed for a child of her own. Well, there was no way she would have one because she had vowed to herself she would never marry. There was no way she could ever promise herself to a man. Never again would she allow another man to control her life like she had in the past.

"Miss Eden, I wish you were my mama." Pity welled up in her heart at the boy's sweet, innocent words. From what she had understood from the Captain, Reed had never known his own mother.

"Oh, Reed, darling, why would you say such a thing? I am certain your own mama loved you dearly," she replied, pressing a gentle kiss onto the child's forehead. She inhaled his innocent scent of childhood and the fresh, salty sea air.

"But my mama went to heaven without me before I even knew her, Papa says. She never tucked me into bed at night like you do."

Warmth swept through her veins at the thought of the boy liking her so much. It was such a sad thing that he would eventually grow up to be what she despised most: a man.

"Well, I will be more than honored to act like your mother for this voyage, darling, but I don't ever want you to forget you had your own, real mother. Your Papa seems to have loved her a lot, so I am sure she was a very special woman."

Chapter 7

E den closed her eyes and counted to ten. "Here I come!" she called.

Reed had persuaded her into playing a game of hide-and-seek with him in his father's cramped cabin while the Captain was away commanding the ship. He was hardly ever around to spend time with Reed. The poor boy deserved much more attention.

Eden put a hand to her stomach. Since she had woken that morning, it had been upset and she felt rather weak. The Captain had told her it was probably just an unusual case of seasickness but she had not realized it could hit her after well over a week of sailing. But she pushed her ailment aside, enjoying the chance to play with Reed.

She opened her eyes and almost immediately spotted the child lying down flat under the bed. To make him think he had found a great hiding spot, she wandered about the cabin, feigning the search for him.

"Hmmm, where did Reed go? Where on earth could he be?

I do believe he has turned invisible," she mused, brushing a lock of her hair out of her face. Her words were answered by a fierce giggling. She knelt down next to Reed and tickled the child underneath the ribs.

He laughed all the more. Finally, out of breath and shaking with amusement, both stood. She put a hand to her forehead to fight off a thick wave of dizziness. The cabin moved around her more than it normally did on the rocking ship. Was that her dizziness or had the waves grown more choppy?

"It's your turn to hide now, Miss Eden!" She simply could not make herself say 'no' to those eager blue eyes that were a darker and younger version of his father's.

"Oh, really, Reed, I am far too big to hide in this tiny cabin. Why, I am over twice your size!"

"Please, Miss Eden, please?" He pleaded, wrapping his little arms around her waist.

"Very well." She sighed as she finally gave in to the young boy's pleading tone.

"You have to count to *twenty*, Reed. Miss Eden is not as good at hiding as you are." She shivered, though she had no idea why. After all, she was having a good time, and if her memory served her correctly, it had been rather hot in the cabin just moments ago.

"All right!"

He covered his eyes, and she frantically searched for a nook large enough to conceal herself in. Eden squeezed her eyes shut to dismiss the black that was edging into her vision. She had never known that seasickness felt like this. With a shake of her head, she continued the hunt for a hiding place. The Captain's sturdy wooden desk appeared in the corner of her vision. If she did not find her hiding spot soon, she would be spotted by the boy the second he opened his eyes, so she slipped underneath the piece of furniture as quietly as she possibly could despite her swishing skirts. Reed counted all the way up to twenty.

Just then the cabin door burst open.

* * *

"If you do not tell me where that blasted trollop ran off to, I swear I will kill your sniveling, whining little brat over here."

A shiver of terror convulsed Ivy's entire body. The monster of a man would truly kill her poor little William.

"Please, sir," she whimpered. He struck her again, ruthlessly. Had he beaten poor Eden like this?

Oh, God, please keep Eden safe wherever she is. Please don't let this horrible monster find her.

"If I tell you, you will leave me and my family alone and safe? You will never harm us again?" she whispered, too afraid to look at his clear, emerald green eyes that she once had thought were handsome. She most certainly no longer held that opinion.

"Yes."

Ivy bit her lip. She considered screaming for help but thought better of it. First, her brother would be dead the instant she made noise. Holding back a sob, she looked into the child's trusting, wide blue eyes that were just like their mother's. Second, her father would run in the minute he heard a cry. He was a small, thin man who was no match at all for Lord Rutger's tall, bulky frame.

She took a deep breath, trying to calm her rattled nerves.

It did not help one bit.

She prayed Eden would find it in her to forgive her for this.

"She told me and A-," she had better leave Aimee out of this, she decided, "she told me she wished to catch a ship and head toward the Caribbean. Port Royal, possibly."

* * *

"Aimee, wake up." An anxious voice jarred Aimee awake from a peaceful dream. "Wake up this instant!"

"What?" She moaned, rolling over onto her side. Her soft embroidered coverlet squished underneath her. Reluctantly, she cracked her eyes open to see Ivy leaning close over her.

"It is an emergency, Aimee. You must get up and dress immediately."

She rolled over once more, and then rose from the comforting warmth of her cocoon of blankets to begin dressing. "What is it that was so important that you had to come all the way up to my bedchamber this early in the morning?" Aimee groaned, stepping behind a curtain in the corner of her bed chamber. She called a maid in and waited until the young lady who did not meet her eyes came forward, pretending to ignore her mistress's conversation. The woman tightened Aimee's stays near to their breaking point as Aimee always demanded.

"It took a quarter of an hour to get past your grumpy old housekeeper. She did not want me to come up here and I was almost ready to climb through your window! Lord Rutger has set sail in pursuit of Eden."

Aimee poked her head through the curtain. Ivy was sitting

at Aimee's vanity, sorting the jars and bottles that cluttered it. The strong, fragrant scent of lavender perfume filled the air.

"And ...?" Aimee sighed the tired question. Lord Rutger was Eden's fiancé. He possessed every right to seek his runaway bride.

"*And* he happens to be a horrible, wicked man who will stop at nothing to obtain what he wants, no matter what the cost. He snuck into my bedchamber last night when I accidentally left my window open. First he threatened me with a knife, and then he threatened to kill little William if I did not do exactly as he said."

Aimee gasped at this news. So Lord Rutger was every bit as terrible as Eden had hinted to them. Why, then, had Aimee and Ivy refused to believe their poor friend's claims?

"Whatever did he do that for? What would he want with you and your little brother?" Aimee inquired, frowning. She dismissed her maid and emerged from the curtain.

"He threatened me and my brother until I was forced to reveal to him that Eden had planned to head for Port Royal. I ... I was so frightened."

"Egad," Aimee whispered strongly, not caring about her unladylike language. Her mother was not in the room to correct her, anyway.

Poor Eden.

"And now I am utterly terrified he will catch her and hurt her, and it will all be my fault because I told him where she was going." Ivy's eyes sparkled with unshed tears.

"What can we do, though, Ivy? We are simply women; we're no match for Lord Rutger and whatever he could do to her."

"I know, but perhaps we can get someone to aid us in her rescue. We have a few merchants and privateers in our congregation who hopefully might be headed toward Port Royal." Ivy didn't add that she wondered who would ever agree to help them find a young woman who had run away.

* * *

Lord Clive Rutger stood in his bedchamber and glared at the light flickering in the fireplace. It reminded him of the fire he saw in Eden's eyes when he hit her. He needed to extinguish that fire. A woman should learn how to obey the men in her life without question, and the little flower still had not.

He paced about the room, his fists clenched tight.

So, the little disrespectful woman had run away. Did she not realize he would not let her go so easily? She was promised to *him*.

He sank down onto a chair, rubbing his face with his hands.

The Caribbean.

Of course she would run off somewhere far away, somewhere exotic where she thought he would never find her. Well, she was wrong. He could hire a ship to take himself to find her.

He would *not* let her get away.

* * *

"Hmmmm, what have we got here?" Caspian chuckled, tossing his baldric and weapons onto an armchair rather than putting them away. "Why, I do believe that I have a beautiful young lady hiding out under my desk. Now, is that not a strange occurrence, Reed?" Caspian asked. The child giggled, his eyes sparkling in amusement. "I daresay this has not happened to me before."

Lady Trenton's face flushed to a comely pink. She clambered to her feet, but tripped on her voluminous gown.

"Blast these skirts!" She muttered. Caspian chuckled at the word "blast" coming out of those pretty pink lips.

"Shame on you, Lady Trenton. A lady such as you should not use such loose language. Surely 'tis most improper." Caspian suppressed a grin at her reaction.

Lady Trenton gave him a deadly glare. The woman ceased struggling with her skirts and tried to rise quickly. In the process, she whacked her head against the corner of his desk.

After a moment of looking dazed, she crumpled to the floor in an unconscious heap.

Caspian immediately sobered and stooped down to take her limp form in his arms.

After a second, her head jerked up and she struggled against his grasp. Caspian gently laid the woman on his bed. She moaned and curled onto her side, mumbling something incoherent.

He placed his hands on her shoulders to keep her in place lest she injure herself. "Stay still, milady." He ran a hand over her head near her wound and was horrified to find that a portion of her brunette curls was already matted down with slippery blood. An all-too-familiar metallic scent slithered its way up to his nose. Blood. No, no, no!

"Papa? Papa, what is wrong with Miss Eden?"

"Reed, now is *not* the time for your questions. Go get the surgeon."

The child ran out the door, his face white.

Caspian followed suit and sped out of the cabin. Memories flooded back, haunting him. Memories he had tried to push aside throughout the last five years. Isabelle lying in his arms, the blood from the wound on her chest dripping down her neck into her honey-colored hair. He hated blood.

Caspian snapped out of his thoughts like a sail snapping in the wind. Lady Trenton.

"Davis! Come at once!" The ship's surgeon was definitely needed. "It is an urgent matter, Davis!"

He huffed when the surgeon did not come instantly at his bidding. Why could the man not hurry for his Captain? There was an injured lady who needed his assistance immediately. Caspian ran a hand through his hair.

Finally, Davis eased up the companionway. Reed was trailing behind him, clear tears running down his face.

"What on earth took you so long, man?" Caspian hurried Davis down toward the door of his cabin. "By all rights, I should have you punished for such sluggishness."

"Sorry, Cap'n. Johnstead was sick and I was tending to him. A fever seems to be spreading among the men."

Caspian grunted. Johnstead would live. Eden was hurt. He could only hope she would fare the same as Johnstead and not sustain a permanent injury from his own idiocy. His youthful impetuousness had injured another young woman in his care before.

Once they reached the cabin, Caspian stepped aside in order for the ship's surgeon to enter first so he could tend to the lady. A look of bewilderment crossed Davis's face when he saw Lady Trenton resting on the bed. Her eyes were closed. Caspian assumed she had fainted again or simply fallen asleep.

"I-I wasn't aware I'd be tending a lady for you, Cap'n.

Besides, she shouldn't really be aboard. Don't you know 'tis bad luck?"

"Yes, you will be tending her, you insolent jackanapes. She is not bad luck at all, and you had better see to her immediately and ensure that she is all right, or I will personally throw you overboard for the sharks to feast upon your carcass. Then you may be able to spare a moment to consider your luck!" Caspian regretted being so harsh with his crew, but he was upset and worried over what would happen to Lady Trenton.

Reed stood next to Caspian, unusually silent.

"Aye, Cap'n. What's happened to 'er?" Davis scratched his chin as he studied the woman. He seemed relatively unaffected by his captain's strong words.

Caspian decided Reed should not stay in the room. "I will tell you what Master Davis determines." He nudged Reed toward the door.

"But, Father, Miss Eden …" Reed lifted his tear-stained gaze to his father's.

"She will be all right, Reed. Go above while Master Davis examines her."

Reed squeezed Lady Trenton's limp hand and reluctantly walked away.

Davis began to examine the woman's wound. "What 'appened to 'er?" He repeated.

"I would assume any simpleton could see she has hit her head, you fool. She fainted afterwards."

Caspian watched as the surgeon shook his head but cleaned her wound and wrapped a pristine white bandage around her head.

"It doesn't need stitches, but she does have a nasty cut. I think if we change this bandage every day or so she will be all right. The cut will hurt terribly for her, though. And it will feel worse if she touches it, Cap'n."

A red spot blossomed on the cloth, marring its immaculate white color. Caspian grimaced at the sight. The cloth was tied firmly against her tender wound. He was glad the woman was unconscious while being examined, for he knew it would hurt a great deal if she were not.

* * *

Ivy watched as churchgoers, all dressed in their finest, passed by her. This was one of the few places the wealthy and the poor came together. She gazed at all of the peasants exiting the church down the stairs, their clothing drab, plain, and worn. Even after her father's poor business investments, she had never been dressed in anything but the finest silks and satins to church. She closed her eyes, trying to imagine what life was like for those unfortunate people but yet could not. It was a blessing to live like she did.

A man who she recognized as a merchant sailor moved toward the pew she and Aimee were resting on. The pungent smell of fish seemed to be attached to the man even though he was on land.

Ivy stepped toward Aimee. "Should we ask him?" She whispered, leaning near her friend's ear.

Aimee nodded, and they both rose. This was the fourth time they had asked a man to assist them in helping find Eden and each time they had been rejected.

Ivy prayed this time would be different.

"Good morning, Captain Hall!" Aimee exclaimed, as if the

man were a long-lost friend and not a mere acquaintance. She touched her golden blond hair that was swept up into an elaborate coiffure.

The poor man appeared startled as he glanced from the women to the line of people behind him, waiting to exit the church.

"The same to you, ladies." He turned and started to walk away. Ivy threw a panicked glance at Aimee, who jumped to set her hand on Captain Hall's arm.

"May I help you, ladies?" He tugged on his cravat.

"Oh, yes, please, sir!" Ivy nudged the man out of the line of church-goers so they did not block the crowd's flow. "You may have heard, Captain Hall, that our dear friend, Lady Trenton, has gone missing." She paused, waiting to gauge his reaction. He appeared quite bored.

"Yes, milady, I heard of it. 'Tis most unfortunate. But why, may I ask, are you informing me of this?" Captain Hall's gaze shifted to the door of the church as if he were itching to leave.

"Well, sir, Lady Dawson and I were wondering—hoping—if you would assist us in finding her. We wondered, since you have a ship, if you could search for her? If you wanted, we would come along, and we would pay you handsomely, I assure you. We think we know where she was going," Ivy supplied.

"I'm sorry, ladies, but I think it is pointless. A pretty, wealthy girl like her can't have gone far. Certainly you'll find her on your own. With my business, I'm far too busy to be wasting my time with things like a little lady who got herself kidnapped. Someone should offer a ransom soon. Now, I have work to do, so if you will excuse me, please."

The man ducked back into the line and was gone before either Aimee or Ivy could respond. They sank back down onto the pew.

"What are we going to do, Ivy? No one will ever even take us seriously. We *need* to find her." Aimee seemed close to tears. Ivy took her friend's hand.

"It will be all right, Aimee. Look, there is Captain Emery coming towards us. Surely he will be able to assist us. Eden has known him since she was a babe."

Chapter 8

"So, as you can see, sir, we are in desperate need of your help." Lady Shaw's brow crinkled as she talked.

Captain Matthew Emery sighed. He did not like to get himself involved with women and their problems. The majority of the gender, from what he had witnessed, was deceitful and only cared about acquiring wealth.

"Please, sir. Don't let Lord Rutger harm her. You are the only one who has even been willing to listen to our pleas. Help us find Eden, please," begged Lady Shaw.

Lady Aimee Dawson leaned toward Matthew, fluttering her fan. Her sweet lavender fragrance wafted over him.

He could not resist a glance down at the woman's glossy golden curls. How could he say "no" to those sweet jade eyes and that pink pout? Besides that, he truly wanted to help Eden. She was a good, kind woman and did not deserve to be treated cruelly by an unwanted suitor. What made it all the worse was that the suitor was Lord Clive Rutger—a man Matthew knew from personal experience could be rather inhuman and uncaring. The man hated anyone who did not have a title or who was not as wealthy as him. Matthew had been treated coldly by the earl more than once. Eden deserved far better than a man like that.

And, perhaps, just maybe, once he found her dear friend for her, Lady Aimee Dawson would reward him just a little bit instead of looking down her snooty, upturned nose at him.

Matthew jerked away from her. What was wrong with him, allowing such traitorous thoughts to pass through his head? He did not want to have anything to do with Lady Dawson, spoiled little brat that she was. Besides, he needed to have his ship careened. It was past time to do so, and if he went much longer without it, the *Cross's Victory* would be sailing a lot more slowly. But he knew the right thing to do was to help the women find Lady Trenton. He did not want her to be abandoned and abused like he was as a child. She did not deserve that. No one deserved that.

"Yes, I will gladly assist you. Where were they heading for?" His merchant work would be requiring him to sail to the Caribbean sometime soon anyway. He might as well help the women while he did so.

"Thank you so, so much, Captain Emery!" Lady Dawson cried, nearly leaping up and down. It looked like she was about to give him a hug so he stepped away quickly. Matthew remembered when he had first attended the church and seen Lady Dawson, her golden hair in braids. He distinctly recalled an occurrence where she had selfishly ripped her doll out of another child's hands, refusing to share. Matthew had always been mesmerized by her beauty and yet appalled at how spoiled the young woman was.

"They were going to Port Royal, Captain Emery. We must

set sail immediately; I heard Lord Rutger started off on the voyage last night. We need to hurry if we wish to find Eden before he does." Lady Shaw pushed a tendril of hair behind her ear.

"We?" Matthew questioned. He had not agreed on the women accompanying him. It could be dangerous, and they could be a distraction to his sailors.

"Yes, Aimee and I must join you, of course," Lady Shaw explained patiently, glancing over at Lady Dawson.

"I will not have it." Matthew crossed his arms across his chest. A merchant ship was no place for two lovely ladies.

"Please! We must be there for Eden." Lady Dawson's pretty pink lips formed to make both an adorable yet ridiculous-looking pout.

Mathew rolled his eyes.

"I will not put you women in danger aboard my ship." A deep, sudden sadness weighed on Matthew's chest. It upset him to refuse to take these ladies with him, but he did not want them hurt.

"Please, sir, we will pay for our way. You truly can't refuse us." Ivy held out her reticule and cocked an orange eyebrow.

"No, it is not about the money, Lady Shaw. Besides, I own a merchant ship, not a passenger ship. You ladies—" he truly meant Lady Trenton and Lady Shaw; he did not know Lady Dawson besides what he had seen from her while he stood in the background, "—are practically my family, you have helped me so much. I have none of my own." Lady Dawson was never one to help or care about anyone other than herself.

How could Matthew refuse to try to help save Lady Trenton from Lord Rutger? She had befriended him far more times than he could count. He knew the right thing to do was help, and the ladies were not going to take no for an answer. Surely nothing dangerous would happen if they went on his ship just this once. Besides, they would be helpful in assisting him to search for her. Well, Lady Shaw might. So far, he was not yet convinced of Lady Dawson. Nonetheless, he knew his answer, whether he liked it or not. "You women are welcome any day onboard my ship."

* * *

Caspian sat in the armchair he had pulled up next to Lady Trenton's bedside, elbow planted on his knees, chin resting on his palms. His late wife's Bible was perched on his lap. He had uncharacteristically taken to praying for Lady Trenton days ago. The little lady was always so certain her God was with her constantly that Caspian thought he had better check in with her heavenly Father, just to make sure He was remembering her. Caspian glanced over at the angel sleeping on his bed. Umber curls cascaded down her back. She groaned and rolled over in her sleep. Her dark, thick lashes fluttered.

He dropped his arms and raised his head, depositing the Bible on his desk. Her pretty brown doe eyes opened and then soon grew wide with fear and shock.

Thank you, God, if this was truly Your doing.

"Where-where—" she stammered, struggling to rise. "Are you going to … to …" She gave up and finally sank back down onto the bed.

"Shush, sweetheart, it's all right."

She was either in an extremely groggy state or did not notice the endearment he threw her way, for she gave no objection.

From the frightened look in her eye, all her old fears of being beaten had made a resurgence. He decided to placate her, "I would never hurt you. You are in my cabin and you have hit your head on my desk. It might take a while for you to remember everything." He gently took her hand in both of his. The softness of it almost made him smile.

"Oh, Captain," she whispered simply, holding out her other hand. He gladly took it.

"Yes, Eden—Lady Trenton, 'tis me. You are perfectly safe," he assured her again, just to be certain she would not forget it.

He gazed at her as realization flickered in her coffee-colored eyes and the cloud of confusion lifted from them.

"How long have I been sleeping, Captain?" she asked, chewing on her plump bottom lip.

"At first, you were sleeping only as long as it took the surgeon to bandage your wound. But you have had a fever the past three days and you have been sleeping on and off. You may thank that God of yours that it has subsided now." He ran a hand across her forehead softly. He had found himself praying more than once during the last three days.

"And have you been sitting here with me the whole time?"

"Yes, except for when I was needed above decks, my dear. Then I saw to it that either Reed or Master Thompson stood guard over the sleeping beauty."

Her face pinked and she suddenly stared down at the coverlet.

"May I have the audacity, milady, to ask precisely what you were doing hiding underneath my desk?" Enjoying how she squirmed under his stare, he arched a teasing eyebrow. He hoped she did not take offense, however, at his question.

Luckily, she giggled rather than becoming angry with him

like she seemed fond of doing. "I suppose I did look quite strange, didn't I? Well, I was playing hide-and-seek with Reed. He insisted it was my turn to hide. So I was hiding under your desk."

Ah, so it was his son's fault that the poor woman had become injured. He would have to chastise the boy.

"I-I also remember feeling sick that day. You said it was seasickness but I also felt horribly dizzy and cold. I think maybe I had a fever even then," Eden stated.

Caspian found himself loving to watch her pretty brown eyes.

He had thought it was strange that the woman had developed seasickness so far into the voyage, but he had experienced some odd cases in his years of sailing. Her being sick with some type of fever that day explained a lot.

"Where is Reed?" She moved to sit up but Caspian eased her back down.

"Reed is up on the main deck. He was very concerned about you, but I did not want him underfoot while the surgeon was examining you."

"Thank you, Captain," she murmured.

Did she still have some sort of a fever? Why on earth was she *thanking* him? Surely not for keeping Reed at bay; she was far too attached to the child.

"What are you thanking me for, milady?" He put a hand on her forehead. No. It was smooth and cool.

"For taking care of me. Heaven knows, you did not have to." She glanced shyly up at him.

"You are on my ship now, so we are stuck in here together, milady. Besides, I cannot ignore the angel who is lying in my bed, unwell."

The woman blushed. Caspian did have to admit she was quite pretty, especially when her cheeks were painted pink with a blush.

She huffed. "I assure you, I am not an angel, Captain." A frown creased her forehead as she swung her legs over the side of the bed to sit up and swayed. Caspian wrapped an arm about her shoulders until she was steadied.

"You look like one to me. And from what I have seen, you act like one."

Eden laughed.

* * *

"You seem to forget that this is the angel who shot you two weeks ago." Why did he insist on making her sound like such a good person when she was horrible inside? Could he not see that? Was the man blind?

He chuckled, sitting back down and running a hand through his dark, curly hair. His masculine scent of salt and leather filled her nose, teasing her senses. She smiled at how she had grown to love that smell in such a short time.

"What makes you smile like that?" the Captain inquired lightly, brushing a lock of hair from her eyes. Eden almost let herself lean against his hand, almost responded to his gentle touch, but no; she could not. He was far closer than propriety allowed and he was just a man. She decided to just frown instead.

Certainly it was most improper for him touch her in such a manner, also. No, there was no question about it. It was more than improper. Eden pushed his hand away.

He grimaced. "What can I do to get you to smile like that again? You never smile when you are near me. Why, you always frown around me, and you get a little line right here when you do it," he mused, leaning over to touch the spot between her eyebrows, just above her nose, gently with his thumb.

She made a face.

He *certainly* should not be touching her face like that. And she should not be liking it so much. Yet he had the audacity to lean down and plant a soft kiss on her forehead.

Eden drew back across the pillow, stuttering, "A gentleman would never … t-touch … or … or kiss a lady like …"

The Captain chuckled. "Well, if I recall correctly, you have said you are 'sick and tired of gentlemen.' I thought you might enjoy being treated in such a manner." He winked.

"Why … you … how could you?" Eden reached up to slap the infuriating man, but he caught her wrist mid-air. She tried to jerk her hand away but he held fast.

Why must he continue smirking at me in that annoyingly cocky manner?

He kept her hand in his and kissed it. She shrank away from him, terrified of what he might do next. Memories flooded back. Memories from nights she longed to erase.

The Captain groaned and shook his head. "What must I do to prove to you that I will … that I … could *never* ever hurt you?" he inquired, standing and pacing the tiny cabin.

"It's just … I-I was … No, there is nothing you have done to me. It is just that a man … abused me once, and I am afraid I have not warmed up to that gender quite yet. I am sorry. Really, I am, captain. You have not harmed me in all the time I have known you."

He stroked her cheek tenderly with the backs of his fingers. "That's all right, milady. I am the one who should be apologizing. For what happened to you. That I wasn't there to protect you from that horrible, cruel excuse of a man, whoever he was …" His warm blue eyes gazed straight into Eden's. He took her hand in his again, gently. "You have my absolute word that I will never, ever harm you. I could never lay a hateful finger on you."

She looked into his clear, sparkling blue eyes. They were filled with nothing but kindness, sincerity, and something else. Something that baffled her and looked … indescribably warm. How she yearned to believe his kind words.

"Believe me, Eden. I promise you can trust me," he murmured, staring at her carefully as if she were a terrified deer that would run off in an instant if he moved in the wrong direction.

She shifted her legs in an attempt to rise. "Don't you dare run off like the little hart that you are. You could hurt your head again."

"I wasn't *planning* on going anywhere." She glared up at him. "Did you just compare me to an animal? To a *male* deer?!" She cried indignantly. Really, the audacity of that man!

"Aye, I apologize, milady. I guess I meant a doe." He grinned sheepishly.

Eden sulked. She did not at all appreciate being weighed up against a wild animal, male or female.

Captain Archer rose from his position on the armchair that had been situated next to the bed and moved to sit beside her on the bed. He put his arms around her and held her against him tightly. Gently, he cradled her head so the part that was hurt was not jostled.

At first she tensed, but she had never felt so comfortable, so safe, with a man before. She slowly laid her head against his strong chest. Really, she should not have. What would Ivy and Aimee think of her?

"No. Let me go." She spun suddenly in his arms and banged her fists against his chest in an effort to free herself, panicking suddenly.

"Lady Trenton, I promise …" His face fell as he released her from his arms. She had hurt the poor man's feelings.

Eden stood abruptly. "No, it's not that I don't trust you, Captain. I'm sorry; I-I do trust you, it's just that … well, it simply is most improper. Isn't it? I should not let you hold me like that … people would think me … I don't know. A … an immoral woman." Just thinking about it made her head injury throb.

"Nay, milady. You are nothing of the kind, believe me," he chuckled, shaking his head, "in fact, you seem to be quite the opposite. You are a perfect lady. Besides, no one can see you at the moment to gossip. No one besides me, that is." He winked and planted another gentle kiss on the top of her head.

"Please, let us stop talking about this. It makes my head hurt all the more." She glanced away, startled at what she saw in those blue eyes. For a moment, they sat that way, him peering into her eyes and her moving away. Finally, she spoke, "Thank you so much for being so kind to me. You are the … I think you are the kindest man I have ever met."

Captain Archer chortled. "I think you certainly need to rest now. I am not the nicest man you have ever met." He tucked the coverlet around her shoulders as if she were nothing but a child and he, a loving parent. Why did he not tuck Reed in at night like this? She would have to speak with him some other time about neglecting the dear five year old. The child needed a loving father who spent more time with him. But she could discuss his parenting choices another day. Right now he was being kind to her, and she did not want that moment to go away.

"But you really are kind," she murmured, feeling her eyelids grow heavy. Before she knew it, she tumbled back into a restless sea of dreams.

* * *

Ivy marched across the deck of Captain Emery's ship, the *Cross's Victory*. She leaned over the rail of the boat and pressed a hand over her restless stomach in a weak attempt to calm it.

Uggh! She hated the sea. Hated it! Before she could control it, she felt the contents of her belly spill out into the roiling ocean.

A gentle, brotherly hand settled on her back. She looked up to see Matthew leaning over her, a grim look on his handsomely structured face.

"Mayhap we should not have brought you along, milady. It seems as if your body does not agree with sailing." He handed her a handkerchief to wipe her mouth with.

"No, sailing does not agree with my stomach. Right now, however, I feel quite better. I pray it will last." Six days of vomiting the little Aimee had convinced her to eat had begun to take its toll on her.

"Well, I promise I shall keep you in my pray-"

Their conversation was interrupted by a shrill scream.

"What on earth was that?" Matthew glanced around the

deck of the ship, appearing rather frightened.

"I believe that was Aimee," sighed Ivy, hurrying down the companionway.

What on earth had Aimee gotten herself into?

* * *

"Are you quite all right, Lady Dawson? May I enter?" Matthew shouted, pounding his fist on the door of Aimee's and Ivy's cabin. Whimpering sounded from the cabin. Terrified whimpering.

"Yes—come in. Please." His heart sank at her trembling voice. What could have frightened her so?

He burst open the door and sped in, Ivy on his heels. The scent of lavender erased the saltiness of the sea outside. Aimee was standing on the top of her cot, her pretty face pale white in terror.

"Whatever happened?" Instinctively, Matthew grabbed her waist in his hands and lowered her to the floor. After he realized what he had just done, his hands dropped to his sides as he felt a heated blush creep up his neck and across his face.

"There-there was a … a rat," she sobbed, reaching to go into his arms.

Matthew side-stepped her grasp. He had to hold back a grin at her childishness.

Lady Shaw moved forward and took the frightened young woman's hand. "Shush, Aimee."

"Shall I get rid of the ferocious beastie for you, my princess?" Matthew chuckled and rolled his eyes.

The girl glared up at him. "You couldn't anyway. It escaped

down … down that little hole right there." She pointed to a crack in the deck and a shiver rattled her shoulders.

Matthew glanced at Lady Shaw, who was staring at her friend, a deep frown in her forehead.

"Do you wish me to cover up the hole so no more devious monsters creep their way in to harm you, princess?"

"Well, what if it had come in during the night and crawled over me while I was sleeping? Just to think … ugh!" She shivered, looking away.

He could not help but laugh at Lady Dawson's foolishness. "Well, it shall happen no more, I promise you. I will send a man in to fix it when the time comes. Now, I am needed above, milady. Good day to you, then." He left with a nod for Lady Dawson and Lady Shaw.

Chapter 9

⚜

Aimee Dawson sat on the edge of her cot, wary of every miniscule sound that reached her ears. Where had the rat gone? Oh, goodness, this rodent would be the loss of her sanity.

The ship creaked and she nearly jumped out of her skin. This had to stop. Truly, she despised life at sea. Back home in her comfy little bedchamber or parlor there would be no rats, and she would have nothing to worry about. A maid was at her beck and call and she had nice food and the best fineries. Now, she was crammed with Ivy in a room she could barely stand upright in. She was missing her home and her family more than she had ever thought she would, and the added worry of rodents was no comfort at all.

A visit to Captain Emery would solve the problem entirely. It had been a few days since her encounter with the rat, and he had not done anything about the hole in the floor of the cabin. Far too long. She trudged her way up the companionway to the Captain's cabin and knocked on the door tentatively, nervous of his reaction. The man had never seemed to like her.

"Yes?" He opened the wooden slab.

"Ah, princess, do come in." He stepped aside for her to enter.

Aimee glowered at him for calling her by that wretched nickname. She was no princess. Just because he was poor and jealous gave him no excuse to belittle her.

"What is it that you want, Lady Dawson?"

She took a deep breath. Why should she care if he thought her to be a frightened little brat? Matthew—Captain Emery already believed she performed that role. *Insolent cur.*

She sighed. That was not the right way to act toward the man, no matter how annoying he could be, and she knew it full well.

"I am sorry, sir-"

"What have you done with Lady Dawson?" He interrupted. "I do believe I never expected to hear the words 'I am sorry' uttered from the vain princess' lips before."

Aimee glowered up at him, anger equal with her blood shooting through her veins. How was she supposed to be kind to him when he acted like that to her? "As I was saying before I was rudely interrupted by you, sir, I am sorry, but I believe it has been over two days and the hole in my cabin floor still has not been repaired yet. What if another rat crawls in?" She cringed, barely able to speak the words. "I simply could not bear it."

He laughed. He possessed a deep, hearty laugh. A musical laugh.

She hated it. Hated *him*. He was *mocking* her.

He stood up, and his scent of cedar drifted over her. "Ah, I knew the princess had *graced* me with her company today out of reasons purely for her own pretty self. You see, I understand you. We would not want a rat bite to scathe that faultless complexion of yours."

Aimee drew in a deep, stuttering breath. Why, she had never been insulted in such a demeaning way. What had she ever done to Captain Emery to make him loathe her so? She had no memory of the action, whatever it might be. Before she had known the man well, she had thought him quite handsome and ... charming, but even now, she hated to admit she still liked the look of his features and how his broad shoulders filled out his coat and the way his golden blond hair curled at his pure white collar. The man simply was infuriating.

"Just because you are a blasted man and I am not ... and you can protect yourself and I cannot ... just because I am rich and you aren't ... simply because you are not frightened by a freakishly big rat ... doesn't mean I am not! Rats terrify me!"' Aimee threw her hands in the air and stood up to her full height. She was a short woman, but she could look into his face without straining. "When will you stop constantly belittling me in this wretched way? I am—I am simply sick and tired of that arrogant, pious grin of yours that is always planted on your face when you are talking to me! I truly cannot stand you!" She smacked her hand across his insolent, charming face before she could control herself.

He grabbed her arm, pure anger burning in his eyes for a split second. But then his eyes—the stark color of a midnight sky—softened into shock.

"Forgive me. I should not be so cruel to you, milady."

She glared up at him, pulling out of his stunned grasp. Rather than replying, she focused her attention on a splinter in the wooden floorboards.

Chapter 9

Silence consumed the room before he finally spoke first. "I will go with you to repair the hole immediately. I apologize for letting it slip my mind, Lady Dawson," he declared.

"Nay, send one of your men—your sailors. I do not wish for your presence in my cabin. I cannot stand the mere sight of you." As she began to turn away, he firmly grabbed her by the elbow.

"So am I to understand that the flawless princess prefers a simple sailor—one who is hardly God-fearing, I am sure, one who has no respect for ladies like you—to me, the merchant Captain preparing to become a missionary?"

"I am certain they would not be half as arrogant as you are." Before she could explode into an outburst of anger—which she knew she would do in any minute—she rushed out of the cabin without a further word to Captain Emery.

* * *

Matthew sank down onto a wooden chair in his cabin. He was *not* arrogant. It took all his self-control to not go out the door and stop Lady Dawson.

If she was not so concerned about her appearance every second of the day, maybe she would notice he was far more than what she thought she saw.

Foolish woman.

Matthew gazed out at the sea through his porthole. They still had a few weeks left before they reached the Caribbean, and there was still no sign of Lady Trenton. An overseer at the Port of London had given Matthew a list of all of the ships sailing for the Caribbean, so Matthew had told all of his crew to be on the lookout for those vessels. They also were warned to be searching for a privateer ship rented by Lord Rutger.

Matthew was eager to visit the churches in the Caribbean, once they reached the area with Lady Trenton safely in their care. He had been fascinated by the mission work that was happening in the exotic islands the last time he had been in the Caribbean.

During his years being raised by Reverend Dobbs, who had taken him in when his mother had left him on the doorstep of the church, Matthew had always longed to join in spreading the Gospel to the far edges of the world.

He hoped to plan another expedition to the Caribbean to personally participate in a mission once he got the ladies on his ship home to safety in London.

* * *

Caspian sat on the steps to the top of the forecastle deck and sighed.

It had been a trying day. Three of his men were below deck with a sickness, probably what Lady Trenton had been under the weather with, and he had almost put Kelton back in the brig again. The man—boy, really, although he was only a couple of years younger than Caspian—had been lurking outside of Caspian's cabin, no doubt trying to catch a glimpse of the beautiful Lady Trenton in a compromising situation. Caspian had given the rude man a flogging for his insolence to the sweet Lady Trenton. Then, he sent the man below deck before the fool could do anything else to frighten the poor lady.

Once they arrived in Port Royal, Caspian planned to rid the crew of this man. He was proving to be far too much trouble than he was worth.

A fierce giggling came from behind Caspian. He turned to search for the creator of the noise he had barely heard on his ship since Isabelle had died. Lady Trenton was by the railing, leaning over while Reed whispered into her ear. Caspian strolled over to the lady and leaned over her other ear as his son had.

"I believe the young lad is making me quite jealous," he whispered, breathing in her intoxicatingly feminine scent of coconut and vanilla.

She jerked her head to the side away from him, a baffled look twisting her comely features.

"How could little Reed possibly make a man like you jealous?" She worried her bottom lip like he had begun to notice she did a lot.

"Well," he rubbed his chin and took a step closer to her. She stepped back. "You allow him to get so close to you, and you giggle when you talk to him ... and with me, well, I get nothing ..."

"May I remind you he is your own offspring, Captain?"

Caspian grinned, delighted with the hint of the compliment she paid him. He laughed. "I suppose so, but I fear you hold no affection for the child's papa."

The beautiful woman offered him an alluring smile that caused heat to rush over his body, all the way down to his toes and the tips of his fingers. "Whatever would make you think such a thing, Captain?"

He could not contain his smile, realizing that in the past few days she had become far less cautious of him.

After winking at her, he moved to face his young son. "Reed, my boy, will you please help Master Clarion down in the galley?" Caspian asked, intending to steal some time alone with Eden.

"Of course, Papa." Caspian watched as his son skipped away joyfully.

Eden's smile faded slowly as her eyes followed the child who was hopping off. Caspian wondered if she wanted a child of her own. By the look on her face, it would seem so. Maybe he would ask her sometime. Later.

The woman rotated back toward him. "Captain, I think you should spend some more time with Reed. He is a good boy and he deserves more of his father's time."

Caspian let out a loud breath. Right now he did not want to talk about her questioning him as a parent. He was far too distracted by the way her beautiful hair curled and was tossed around in the wind ... he did not wish to become upset with her when she was looking up at him so sweetly.

She rubbed her head, obviously waiting for his answer. He did not wish to give one.

Instead of replying, Caspian moved her fingers aside to run his fingers over her wound. It was healing nicely and had become only a scar now. He was glad she had not had a concussion and there was no permanent damage done.

He found it hard to believe that anything could feel as soft as her umber curls.

"How is your head, milady? Does it hurt much anymore?"

"It has been recovering quite well and only hurts when I touch it. I suppose it has been three weeks now. As you can see, Mr. Davis allowed me to remove the bandage."

"I am quite glad." He privileged himself with the liberty

of running his fingers through those dark tresses. When she smiled up at him, the light smattering of freckles that appeared only on her nose scrunched up.

"You get a little dimple in your cheek when you smile. Did you know that?"

She shook her head. "No."

The dimple was quite pretty.

She frowned and he leaned forward to lightly kiss the tiny line between her eyebrows. "What makes you so sad, sweetheart? Why do you frown like that?" He brushed a lock of hair from the girl's face.

"Oh, I was just wondering, how far are we from Port Royal?"

"We're about a week and a half—possibly a fortnight away. Why?"

"It's nothing, really. I just shall miss Reed. And ... you very much once we get there ..." she answered, looking away. The ship plunged over a rolling swell and Caspian caught her by the waist, drawing her close.

"Who says it will be good-bye for good once we reach the port, milady? I shall see for certain that you are safe in Port Royal before the thought of leaving you even passes through my mind. Besides, we can write letters. I'm sure Reed will insist on that. Maybe I will visit you in your new home, wherever that might be ..." He put a finger under her chin and turned her face to make her look him in the eyes.

She smiled again. Caspian felt a sudden longing to kiss those perfect, smiling pink lips. He tucked his hand under her chin and leaned closer to the woman until he was only mere inches from her mouth.

She placed her hands on his shoulders and suddenly he realized he had drawn her all the way against himself. Something tugged on his pant leg as he lowered his mouth to hers. A tugging on his pant leg …

What?

"Papa! Are you going to *kiss* Miss Eden?"

Reed.

Caspian glanced at Lady Trenton, who had jumped out of his arms the second she heard Reed's voice. She was hiding her face behind her hands, her skin a brighter shade of red than he could have imagined.

"You *should* kiss Miss Eden, Papa. I think she would like it if you kissed her. Wouldn't you, Miss Eden?" The young boy peered up at Eden innocently, obviously not understanding what he was saying. She looked positively mortified, and Caspian had a hard time holding back his laughter.

"Yes, 'Miss Eden', I think you just might like that, wouldn't you?" Caspian grabbed the young woman's hand in his, pulling her closer to him.

She jerked away. "You helped cook our meal, Reed? Did you enjoy it?"

"Mr. Clarion allowed me to stir the batter for the biscuits. He told me they'll be the best biscuits the crew has ever tasted!" Reed moved toward the woman in Caspian's place, tugging on the skirt of her dress.

"I am sure Mr. Clarion appreciated the help you gave him. You will make a fine cook someday. I am certain of it!" Eden hugged Reed.

The boy pulled himself from her arms, a concerned frown on his sweet face. "But I will *not* be a cook. I shall be the fiercest pirate in the whole Caribbean. Just like Papa!" Reed announced, violet-tinged blue eyes shining bright with pride.

Well, at least the boy seemed to like Caspian as he never had before. It must have something to do with Lady Trenton. Her presence seemed to be working magic on the both of them.

"Now, Reed, you know I am not a pirate," Caspian corrected his son, frowning. He should never have been a pirate. Isabelle had hated it. And it had been the death of her.

"You aren't a pirate? Really?" Eden inquired, a deep frown forming across her forehead.

"Nay, milady. As I am sure I have told you before, I am a privateer," Caspian explained.

"But aren't they the same thing? I always thought they were." As Eden spoke, that cute little nose of hers scrunched up tight in thought.

"Well, my dear, that sailor brother of yours must not have taught you much about life at sea. Reed here just likes to think I am a pirate, don't you, Reed?"

Reed nodded, his wide eyes studying Eden while his father spoke.

"Nay, privateers are commissioned by the king to raid and attack enemy ships like the French and to rid the Caribbean of pirates. In fact, that would make me quite the opposite of a pirate, would it not?" He smirked at her.

She gazed up at him, wide-eyed. Caspian laughed. He longed to know exactly what was going on inside of that pretty little head of hers.

"Yes, I am afraid I am not the complete rogue you believed me to be. Forgive me, milady." He winked, delighting in the pleasant expression on her face.

"I never would have guessed the difference."

They were interrupted by the shout from the shrouds. "A sail, Cap'n! A sail!"

Chapter 10

Eden shielded her eyes to see the boy in the crow's nest. His hairless chest was bare as were his feet, and his head was covered by a mess of tangled auburn curls. The young man could be no older than thirteen or fourteen. A sudden pang of worry for her brother, Adam, tugged at her heart. When he was younger and he had first run away, had he worked up in the shrouds like this boy, climbing from sail to sail like a little monkey? Was Adam even alive anymore? She prayed her dear brother was all right.

She glanced over at the Captain. He had plucked a spyglass out from his belt and was now gazing at the western horizon. "What do you see, Captain?" Eden asked, sidling up next to him, following his gaze with her eyes and squinting at the far-away ship. "It is not another—I mean—it isn't a … a pirate ship, is it, Captain? Will they attack us?" A spark of both fear and excitement coursed through her at the thought of a battle at sea. That feeling soon died down when a sudden trepidation sped through her. Could it be Lord Rutger?

Could he have found them and was he here to take her away from Caspian, take her back to London where he would marry her and beat her for the rest of her life?

Suddenly, Eden had trouble breathing.

Caspian handed her the spyglass to look through. "Milady, it—it … I think …" He sighed and ran a hand through his black hair.

Eden frowned at the way he stuttered. That was not like the powerful Captain Archer at all. She peered through the glass and spotted a tiny gray and red flag hoisted atop the main mast. "We—we aren't going to attack them, are we, Captain?" Eden breathed, chewing on her bottom lip in terror.

"I am afraid we might have to, milady," he muttered, tearing his gaze from the fast-approaching enemy to her face. "I pray all goes well."

"Pray?" She threw her hands on hips. "And you had me believing you did not believe in God. You said He does not care for you, did you not?"

He huffed. "I apologize for the confusion, milady. Hope. I meant to tell you I hope all goes well." And with that, he turned his back to her and joined his crew on the forecastle deck.

Eden paused, placing her hand on her chest and worrying her bottom lip. Why was Caspian so worried about attacking this ship, when it was what he was paid to do by the king?

"I say we take 'er, Cap'n," one member of the crew yelled as he dared a defiant step closer toward his captain.

"Aye, we haven't in far too long!" Another grimy man cried, raising his hairy fist in the air.

"No, we can't," Caspian said quietly as he shook his head, looking sick.

"Ah, the Captain says 'no.'" A wicked leer was spread across Kelton's face. He winked at Eden. She shivered and glared back at the jackanapes, as Caspian had called him once in passing.

"We must take her!"

"If you object with your crew, why do you hesitate on putting them in their place, *Captain*? I'm beginning to doubt yer made of captain material anyway, with that little bit of fluff around. Nay, I take that back. I doubted your captaining abilities long ago." Kelton sneered and jabbed a finger at Eden.

She shivered, remembering clearly the day the man had tried to take her below when she had first stepped up on the main deck. Thinking of that brought back even more jarring memories of what Lord Rutger had done to her.

Annoyed by the gnat of a man, Caspian sighed. "If you doubt my abilities as your captain, by all means, man, challenge me to a proper duel. May I remind you I have yet to be bested in swordplay?"

"Nay, *Captain*," he snarled.

Eden glanced at the ship that was growing closer by the second as the men argued.

"We should take her, but …" Caspian started.

The muscles in Caspian's broad, strong chest tightened and flexed underneath the cotton of his shirt. His handsomely firm jaw clenched in anger. Eden would have normally been frightened, but she knew he was upset with his contrary crew and the anger was not directed at her. She had nothing to fear from him, as he had told her many times in the past.

"Captain?" Gage approached Caspian, who was staring at the ship as if he was transfixed by it.

"Yes?"

Chapter 10

"If you don't mind me saying, it should be an equal fight. I think we are better off doing what the crew wants, as long as there is a good chance we'll win. The crew *did* sign your articles saying that if a disagreement arose, then they could take a vote," Gage reasoned.

Eden felt pity for their enemy course through her body at those words. What if something like this had happened to Adam's ship? What if he had been attacked and … and that was why he had not contacted her or her father in so long?

"I do not recall inquiring as to your opinion, Master Thompson!" the Captain spat as he violently whirled about.

"I apologize, Captain," Gage mumbled, studying a wooden floorboard, the usual smile no longer brightening his face.

"Very well." Caspian whirled around and barked orders to his crew and then took one of Eden's hands in both of his and squeezed it as Gage relayed the orders. The men sprung to action.

"You must go below, milady."

* * *

He knew without a trace of doubt that it was Moore this time. No mistake about it.

Caspian kissed the creamy skin on the girl's forehead, trying desperately to shake the thought from his head that she could come to harm this day on his account.

She frowned. "But why must I? I wish to stay up here, Captain. Besides, why must we attack them? They have done nothing to harm us."

"I am the Captain of this ship, woman. They are pirates and

119

therefore our country's enemies. You will do as I tell you," he reprimanded sternly, brushing away a stray lock of hair that had been blown in front of her face by the brisk sea wind.

She pulled away from him, an expression of pure defiance written on her face. He hated nothing more than that look at the moment. Foolish woman.

"Can I not stay just for now? It is not like we are in the midst of a battle or anything. We are not even close to them. I can hardly even see any of the people on it." She crossed her arms over her curvy chest in defiance.

"I suppose you are right. But you can only stay up here for a little while." If she caused any trouble or distracted his men, however, he vowed to carry her to their cabin and lock her below even if it was against her will. He had already lost one precious woman to a battle at sea. A battle with this exact same man.

He took her delicate hand in his. "Stay safe for me, all right, milady?"

She nodded and took a deep breath. Caspian saw they were almost within firing range of Moore. His heart pounded with a violent force.

The woman would not be safe all on her own, however brave she was. He had already lost one precious lady to Moore.

He intended to exact revenge, not harm another woman.

Caspian's eyes scanned the deck for Reed. The child was amidships, watching the gunner prepare the cannons. Reed was young himself, but at least Lady Trenton would not be all alone this way.

"Reed, come up here immediately! I warned you not to wander about on the gun deck by yourself. You could be hurt! What kind of fool are you?" Caspian barked.

Caspian regretted his harsh tone when he saw the grin on his son's face drop. It was about time he learned to be a better father. Surely he should not just yell at him like that. He did not want to be like his own father.

Eden laid a gentle hand atop Caspian's arm, the smoothness of it almost unbelievable. "That is no way to call for the boy, Captain. There is no need to be so harsh on him. Reed was not causing any problems down there. Please be gentler with him. He is only five years old!"

Caspian frowned. He had already realized he treated Reed too harshly, but what right did the girl have to question his skills at parenting? Lady Trenton had no children of her own. She probably knew nothing about youngsters at all. Who did this young woman think she was?

"I will do as I wish when it comes to the boy, Lady Trenton. You are not his mother." Although the thought did hold some appeal ...

Caspian shook the pleasant thought from his mind. What was he doing, allowing himself to think of such things, especially with a battle that threatened their lives fast approaching?

He moved to face his son. "Reed, I want you to stay with Miss Trenton at all times. You must keep her safe and give her your company. Do you understand me? And I don't want either of you on the main deck during the battle. Take her right down to the cabin if I tell you you need to. I can't afford for either one of you to become hurt." Or worse.

Reed nodded and grinned at Eden as Caspian placed the woman's hand inside of his.

"Now I must go see to my duties as Captain." He paused, realizing he was giving his five year old son a hefty responsibility. Well, he would send a sailor he trusted with Lady

Trenton rather than leaving everything on the young child's small shoulders.

* * *

Gage Thompson strode about the deck, relaying his captain's orders to the crew as they were being given. His gaze reached the starboard rail. Lady Trenton was leaning on it and Reed was loyally standing next to her like a little dog. The woman's curls flew around her like a coffee-colored halo in the wild gusts of wind. She giggled like a child when sea spray drenched her. A woman did make the ship a much homier place. He could see why Caspian seemed to admire her so.

In the past few weeks she had seemed to grow even more the beauty. Gage could tell Caspian had taken some sort of a special liking to her by the way he looked at her and spoke of her. She was truly a special woman.

Gage had heard his crew gossiping like a bunch of hens. Most were convinced the woman was Caspian's mistress, but Gage knew his captain and best friend better than that. He would never do such a thing to any woman.

Ever since his wife had died in a tragic accident, Caspian had hardly so much as looked at another woman; he had been so drowned in his grief. But since Lady Trenton had come aboard, the man had changed. He smiled more and he interacted with little Reed more often. The lady had changed his captain for the better.

Gage's thoughts were interrupted by a cannon being fired. Their guns replied, fracturing Moore's hull. He sucked in a breath, fully realizing they were attacking Moore, which had been Caspian's goal for the past few years.

Again, Gage's thoughts were jarred back to reality. Lady Trenton. He had to get her and Reed below to safety before they were harmed!

His captain seemed to share the same thought. "Mr. Thompson! Take Lady Trenton below immediately. I want you to stay with her to keep her company so she is not frightened during the battle. Make sure she remains safe," Caspian ordered. By the desperate look in Caspian's eyes, Gage's suspicions were confirmed. Clearly the woman held a special part of Caspian's heart.

"Aye, Captain."

Caspian nudged the beauty forward. She glanced back at Caspian, obviously reluctant to move below with a man she barely knew.

Captain Archer nodded to her reassuringly and then turned to his son.

"Come along, milady." Gage tugged on the young lady's arm. She followed him, shrinking away from his tight grasp. He softened his grip when he remembered Caspian had told him she had been abused in some way before. "I am not going to hurt you, dear. Caspian would never have placed you in my care if he did not trust me with you. I'm not the kind of man who would assault an innocent woman, I assure you. Now come on. Reed can join us if you want. That's what the Captain wanted anyway, I'm sure." He motioned for Reed to follow them below.

* * *

Eden smiled warily up at Mr. Thompson as he opened the door to the Captain's cabin. A glance behind her told that Reed was following right behind them, a scowl on his little face.

He most likely had not wanted to go below, and she did not blame him one bit. Not only did she not want to go below because she did not want to be stuck below if the ship were to sink, she wanted no part in being ordered around by Caspian. Who did he think he was to tell her where to go and when to do it?

Fuming, Eden sank down onto one of the leather arm chairs at the rear of the cabin and Gage sat across from her. Reed plunked himself down on the bed.

She frowned.

"What is wrong, milady?" Gage moved to sit in a chair next to her.

Eden glanced around the darkened room, not able to control the shiver running up her spine. If something terrible happened during the battle she would have no way out. She hated being cornered. Finally she realized her solution to everything had always been to run. Well, she had nowhere to go in this little cabin, on this little ship, in the center of this vast sea.

And Caspian had forced her down here.

She had no doubt if she had refused to go below at his bidding, he would have carried her over his shoulder and locked her up in the cabin himself. Even when she had vowed to never let another man control her life, or have any part in her life, for that matter, she had just let the Captain dictate her.

Eden held back a growl. "I absolutely hate being down here.

What if the ship sinks? I can't stay down here and drown! Oh, but I hate being so helpless!"

* * *

Caspian watched as Gage led the pretty lady below decks, Reed trailing along behind them.

He prayed she would remain below unlike Isabelle. Because he knew Gage would restrain her, he had no need to worry about her coming up on the main deck.

The battle would be tougher without Gage by his side, but Caspian could not trust anyone else to take care of the lady. Besides, he needed someone strong enough to protect her if the ship was breached in battle.

What concerned Caspian, however, was that there was a real danger of taking a shot to the hull of the ship, and a hit like that could damage the Captain's cabin where Lady Trenton and his son were. He shuddered to think about it.

Caspian shook his head. His mind needed to be clear during this battle. There was no chance he would let Moore defeat him again.

* * *

Gage chuckled at the frightened young woman. He could see she was angry, also, by the deep line of a frown in her forehead and the way her little fists were clenched.

There was nothing to be afraid of. "I can assure you, Lady Trenton, we shall not sink. Now quit your talk like that. You are worrying little Reed. Besides, I have known Caspian since we were little boys. The man is a wonderful captain." Gage took a good look at the woman and could not help but wonder what the Captain did with her. "That reminds me … I wondered what has gone on between you two." He glanced over at the young child whose blue eyes had grown wide with fear of their talk about sinking ships and pirate battles.

"Whatever do you mean? Nothing at all has gone on between us two. Nothing in any way. What do you mean?" She raised a perfectly arched brow. Her voice got faster and higher-pitched with each sentence, disproving her innocent questions. He suspected the lady knew full well what he was asking her. She just wanted to deny it.

"Well, I can tell that he … likes you quite a bit. He has not been like this—especially this protective—around a woman since his late Isabelle. And he was quite young then. I know you two haven't known each other for long, but … I just was wondering if you two have … uh … feelings for each other." Gage felt like a big, bumbling idiot. He had no business at all talking to a lady of such things, and yet he had hoped to take her mind off of the battle outside by doing so. Instead, her cheeks were a bright pink and she looked distraught. What kind of idiot was he?

Reed moved over to the porthole where he stood on the tips of his toes and peered out, no doubt watching what he could of the battle.

"He does not like me." She laughed nervously. "I can tell he does not. In his eyes, I am merely a stowaway, a criminal. He probably would not even consider me his friend. There are no feelings between us."

The lady pouted. She was quite a beauty, but, of course,

Caspian had some sort of claim on the woman already.

"Ah, but I am afraid you are incorrect in that, milady. I have never seen him like this, not even with Isabelle. Caspian practically worships you when you are around … He speaks so well of you all the time. The man has fought duels with the crew before to defend your honor. I do not know if he has told you of that, but I do know he truly likes you. Really, I would not be at all surprised if it is love. And I suspect you might have similar feelings for the man yourself." Oh, how he missed teasing Addie, his sister about such things growing up. Until he left to sail with Caspian and she was married off to the highest bidder.

Her face grew pink, making her even prettier than before. He could see why Caspian loved her.

"He-he truly doesn't like me, Mr. Thompson …" She objected.

"Ah, milady, what is the sense in lying to yourself? Anyone can plainly see he holds affection for you."

The ship shook from yet another cannon being fired, and he heard the crack of wood. Lady Trenton shivered.

Gage took her warm hand in his and squeezed it. Normally, he would never touch a lady in such a forward way, but she needed comforting and he viewed her like a younger sister. The corner of his eye caught Reed scooting over to sit beside Eden.

"How old are you, Lady Trenton?" Gage inquired. A brotherly urge to brush away the dark lock of hair that was in her eyes made him move his hand to do so, but he quickly stopped it. He was used to brushing hair out of his younger sister, Addie's eyes, but it would not do with Lady Trenton, although the young woman reminded him of his Addie.

Gage removed his hand from hers. Caspian would be furious if he knew Gage was taking such liberties with his woman, even if he was only doing it to comfort her. She appeared quite flustered.

"I am eighteen."

He felt his heart sink for this poor dear. She was so young, far too young to be running away to a foreign island all own her own, even if she was a year or two older than his sister.

A terrible *crunching* of wood sounded, followed by the roaring of men. They had been hit.

Neither spoke for a moment. Then Lady Trenton broke the silence, "But what has happened to you, sir? How has a gentleman like you ended up as a first mate on a pirate ship?" The lady was sweet to ask a question like that. She would get along well with Addie if the two ever met.

The girl jumped when another cannon boomed. Reed wrapped an arm around her waist and laid his head on her shoulder.

Gage sighed. The lady would not want to hear his life story but he decided to pour it out to her anyway. Perhaps it would take her mind off of the blasts and screams all around them. "Well ... let us just say I did not have the best of beginnings. My home was not a loving one. From the start, my parents had an arranged marriage. Father left us after my mother found out she was going to have another child. Apparently, after knowing me, he didn't want another baby. When Mama died a few years after giving birth to my sister, Caspian's family found me wandering the streets with a little girl and took us in."

Gage stopped. He had not met a true lady before. Well, not counting his tough little sister. But by the shocked look on Lady Trenton's face, he realized he probably should not speak of such matters in front of a refined woman like her. The lady probably could not even imagine what life had been like for him. She most likely did not know anything but her pampered, well-provided life in her English manor where she had countless servants at her beck and call. She would not understand what life was like for him and Addie in the colonies, adopted by a family where the father disliked him and the mother only took pity on him, never truly loved him. The only family he had ever had was little Addie.

He stood abruptly. "Forgive me, milady. I should not speak of such things to you. Surely it is a most improper thing to speak of. I apologize." The abrasive sound of men cheering and yelling sounded above. Gage suspected his reliable captain had just garnered another victory. This time, though, it was against Moore. Caspian was no doubt ecstatic.

She glanced up at the ceiling, her eyebrows drawn together, but she continued speaking, "Nay, sir; it is perfectly all right. It is not your fault that that is what happened to you. I am sorry your life was so rough-" She was interrupted by a knock sounding on the door.

Gage tensed. He did not want trouble from one of the sailors. Finally, he reached for his cutlass and approached the door. "Enter," he called.

He opened the door to discover Johnstead. A grin lit his wind-cracked face.

"Cap'n wishes me to inform ye that we defeated 'em." Johnstead announced, licking his lips when he caught sight of Lady Trenton.

"Captain Archer defeated them?" Lady Trenton leaned forward to look at Johnstead from where she sat.

"Aye, milady."

Lady Trenton smiled and Reed cheered. Gage could not stop a grin from spreading across his own face.

"Thank you, sir." Gage pushed the man out the door and then assisted the lady to her feet and led her up the companionway, little Reed trailing behind.

Chapter 11

N o. He was not in his room. Where on earth could William be? Ivy prayed Lord Rutger had not returned. Egad, what if the horrible man had come back and taken William ... or ... worse? What if he had killed him like he had promised he would just a fortnight ago? She chastised herself for even thinking of abandoning her dear brother. He was only three years old!

Where could he be? If she could just find where Lord Rutger was, she was certain she could find William ... If she could just find where Lord Rutger had taken him ...

"Ivy. Ivy ... wake up!" Aimee's startled, sleepy cry broke into Aimee's nightmare. She felt her friend shaking her.

"I'm awake ..." Ivy muttered, forcing her groggy eyes open. Aimee was leaning over her, a worried look marring her perfect features.

"Are you all right, Ivy? You were screaming and then you started to cry. I thought something was terribly wrong. I was so frightened."

"Oh … I am fine, Aimee." Ivy had to put up a brave front for Aimee. The girl had always been the baby of the friends, and Ivy did not want her to be worried. "Well, I had a nightmare, 'tis all. About Will. I should never have left him alone like that. I'm horrible. What kind of older sister am I to him?"

"William is fine, Ivy. You left him with your parents. He will be all right."

"Yes, but once Papa hears I have run away to find Eden without even asking him for his permission, he will be furious." He knew little about children. Her mother had become sick a few months after the child's birth and Ivy could not help but wonder if anyone would take care of little William without her there. She shuddered, praying for her darling brother's safety. Ivy truly was the only person who could be relied on to keep her younger brother out of harm's way. "And Mama is sick, Aimee. Mama will be too worried about me and too weak to take care of him properly. Oh, I should never have done this, Aimee. I was not thinking properly when I decided to come along." Ivy threw her hands out in exasperation. She jumped to her feet and moved to look out the cabin's tiny porthole.

"You just have to trust your family, Ivy. William will be perfectly fine without you there to watch his every move. He will be all right."

* * *

As soon as Eden placed a foot on the main deck, Caspian rushed over to her with a brooding expression on his face. He lifted her chin with his index finger as if searching for something on her face. "I trust that you remain unharmed, milady?"

Reed ran to the railing and leaned forward to look at the sea rushing past their hull.

"Yes. Yes, of course I am perfectly fine. I am not some weak little thing that needs to be checked on every couple of hours and then hidden away at the first hint of danger," she snapped, slapping his hand away. The Captain had had no business in sending her below earlier! Eden could fend for herself. She did not need any man to protect her. She never would, ever again.

"Good." He frowned at her and then nodded for Mr. Thompson to leave. Reed followed him. Once the man and boy were out of sight, Caspian leaned toward Eden, lowering his voice to a whisper. "Mr. Thompson treated you well? That is what I meant when I asked if you were unharmed."

"He was a perfect gentleman, sir." She flicked a long curl of hair from her face as if it were an annoying insect.

"I trusted he would be. I apologize I didn't go below with you myself, but as the Captain, I was clearly needed above to guide the men in battle."

"But why did I even have to go below? It looks like there was no damage done to the ship. I would have been perfectly safe up here. You were here, Captain. Why couldn't you protect me if I am such a weak little thing in so much need of protecting?" All she ever had been was a small, weak woman who needed to be protected by the men in her life. Well, one of the men in her life who was put there to protect her had done just the opposite. And the other one had promised her life to that very monster.

The Captain's face blotched red with anger and his jaw twitched to some rhythm she could not hear.

"Because, woman, I will not have you dying on my account!" he yelled, garnering the attention of a few crewmembers.

They stood and gawked while Eden chewed on her bottom lip, trying to ignore their prying stares. Moisture filled her eyes and she knew she was trembling.

She squeezed her eyes shut tight, preparing to feel the impact of a fist on her cheek or her shoulder.

She should have never evoked the Captain's temper for she realized it must be just as potent as Lord Rutger's or worse, reasoning he was a rough pirate captain. What a fool she was to ever think he would not hurt her. After all, he was a man. The muscles on his arms were twice the size of Lord Rutger's and his chest was much more powerful. Why, he probably would not think twice about striking her the same as he would a disobedient sailor. Indeed, she should not have made him angry. Oh, why did she always fail to keep her big mouth shut?

What a foolhardy mistake!

He shouted something indistinguishable at his crew, and Eden pried one eye open when she was not struck. She flinched when the Captain reached out to touch her arm. "No, milady, you are quite safe. Let's move to the cabin. We are causing a scene." He wrapped his strong arm around her waist and practically dragged her to his cabin until he set her gently on the bed. Eden scrambled to a sitting position and drew her knees tight to her chest. It would not do to have her lying there, defenseless.

She wanted to be prepared for the coming beating even if she would be unable to protect herself against a powerful man like Captain Archer. She never had been able to before.

* * *

The fact that Moore had run away like a scared dog with its tail between his legs before a real battle had even begun did not matter to Caspian anymore. After he had seen Eden cower when he had raised his voice, nothing mattered but making her realize she was safe with him.

He took up a pace in front of the endearing girl. Why on earth was she just sitting there, crying?

Finally, she spoke. "P-please just s-strike me now, sir. I know you are cross with me. I cannot bear to sit here in silence knowing what will come in any instant. Do not prolong it. J-just get it over with, I beg of you."

Caspian flew to her side and engulfed her in his embrace. He needed to end her confusion. Instantly. "Nay, milady. I assure you, I do not lie. By now, I had hoped you realized I never lied to you. Blast it, how could you think such a horrible thing of me? By fire and thunder, I have never hurt a woman in my life and I never will. I had hoped that I had changed your opinion of me with how I have treated you thus far. Please, tell me who has hurt you, sweetheart."

Those dark, gorgeous eyes of hers opened wide and she shook her head wildly, sending loose pins sailing from her hair. He removed the rest of the pins from her hair by running his fingers through the silky chocolate strands. It was an audacious and most likely improper thing to do, but he found he did not care and he hoped she didn't either.

Caspian leaned his forehead against hers lightly, letting out a deep sigh. He realized the poor girl was trembling under his touch with what he guessed was fear. And he had reignited that fear by screaming at her as if she were but a man under his employ just moments ago. And she certainly was far from even resembling a man.

With a groan, Caspian leapt up immediately.

He took up a pace about the tiny room and decided to explain why he could not let her stay above and why he was headed toward Port Royal. "My late wife, my dear, sweet Isabelle, died in a battle at sea. It was entirely my own fault. If only I had kept her below, kept her safe, she would still be alive right now. She would not have lost her life.

"We'd been attacking another ship. *Neptune's Poison*, it was called. The same ship that just sailed away as we were attacking them today. This ... incident happened when I was still a pirate. Isabelle wanted to stay above decks. She was never afraid, but she always hated being stifled down in our cabin with no fresh air. Just like you, my dear." He paused, studying her face as he spoke. "So, being the stubborn girl she was, Isabelle stayed above against my warnings during the battle. My ... my wife was so young. We both were so young and Reed was only a couple months old. He lost his mother that night. He only got to know her the first few weeks of his life." Caspian swallowed down a burst of emotion that had seized his throat. "She ... she was hit by a cannon ball. In the chest. I-I could not save her. *I* should have been the one who was hit. It should *not* have been her. Isabelle did not deserve to die. Reed did not deserve to lose his mother before he even knew her! There was nothing I could do to ease her pain, Eden, nothing to help her. She died there, lying on the deck and in agony. I remember h-holding her, Eden ... kissing those lifeless lips one last time, pleading with God to bring her back to me. But she was gone. He took her away from me. She was only a girl. She was seventeen years old, Eden. So young. We were both so foolish.

"So now you see why I would not let you stay up on the deck.

I could not bear to lose you, too." He had failed his dead wife again. Moore had escaped. The monster was still running free. Caspian wiped the stubborn moisture from his eyes and studied Eden.

Tears were streaming down her cheeks, and she was watching him intently, fidgeting with her dress.

Then she seemed to break free from her unmoving state and gasped. "Oh, Caspian, you poor, poor man! I had no idea it had happened like that! I am so sorry for your loss. It must have been horrible. It wasn't your fault in any way, I assure you. No matter what you may think, your wife is the one who chose to remain above, not you. You did not force her to do it. In fact, you did much the opposite." She rose and threw her arms around him.

He longed to believe her precious words.

"Thank you, Eden. But it truly was my fault. I should have forced her to go into our cabin. I should have dragged her down there and locked—no, barricaded her inside here. I should have saved her life. I should not have failed Reed." He started to pull away from her. If he let her touch him like that, he would become too attached to her. And he did not wish to become attached to a woman whom he could not protect.

"Nay, Caspian. If God wanted to take her home to Him, He would have done it whether she was in front of a cannon or safe in your bed."

The use of his Christian name flooded every nerve of Caspian's body with warmth. She crinkled his shirt with her fist and buried her face in his chest. He had to catch his breath at her sudden closeness. Since when had she decided she liked him? Maybe he should have told her of his wife's death much sooner. He would have, if he had known it would goad a hug

137

out of this sweet lady.

"Thank you, milady, for caring enough to even listen to my sad tale. I had received word that Edward Moore, the captain of the ship that … that caused her death was in the Caribbean again. We were going to search for him in Port Royal. If he had been there already, I was certain I could have found out from somebody there where he was going off to. I planned to find him and make him pay dearly for Isabelle's death. But he found us first, just now. The idiot out-sailed us and ran away before I could do enough damage. We will have to search for word of him when we reach Port Royal like I had planned originally. But never you mind that." He tweaked her nose lightly, smiling when she giggled at him, her tears slowing. After a moment he grew sober. "Surely I am boring you to death. And I don't want to think about what will happen when we arrive in Port Royal. I do not want to think of never seeing you again. I shall miss you dearly. You are a wonderful woman, and I know I will never forget you in my entire lifetime, Eden."

Bright, clear tears were welling up yet again in those pretty brown eyes. "I-I'm afraid I do not feel well, Captain. I am going to take my leave. I-I think I need some fresh air. Forgive me, please, Captain." And with that, she rushed out of the cabin in a whirl of white lace and umber curls.

Chapter 12

A timid knock sounded on Matthew's door.

"Enter," he called, expecting to hear the heavy tread of one of his crew members. But the soft pitter-patter of a woman's slippers filled the air.

He spun around to see an angel in the doorway.

That was the only way he could describe the woman standing there. Soft, golden tresses haloed her perfect face. Jade eyes glistened in the soft candlelight that sent a warm glow across her delicate features.

"Captain Emery."

Trouble was the soft voice belonged to anything but an angel. It was Lady Dawson's.

"Yes, milady? Come to cry about little mice invading your precious cabin?" He chuckled and glared at her.

She shot a venomous look that made him feel a twinge of guilt for being so cruel to this girl. In all reality, what had she done to him to make him so mad at her all of the time?

"Nay. I ... I came to discuss Ivy," she explained, her voice wavering. With what, though? Fear? Anger? Hate? From his past experience with the lady, it was most likely the latter.

"And what is it about Lady Shaw that you wish to discuss, Lady Dawson?" He folded his hands across his stomach. Was the girl actually concerned about something besides herself and which dress she would wear to the next ball? That was doubtful. She was just like his mother and nothing would ever change her.

"Well, Ivy's been having these … these *horrible* nightmares. She's frightened sick about her baby brother, William. She wakes up sobbing every morning. I am just worried about her." She jutted her chin back up where it belonged.

"Ahh, well then I shall pray for her, Lady Dawson. You should, also." He rose and led her to his door.

She stubbornly stopped in her tracks, causing him to scramble to a stop in order to avoid toppling her over. "That's it? You will *pray for her*? That is all you will do for your 'dear friend'? I might as well have not wasted my time here with the likes of *you*." She slammed her fists onto her hips, further showing her obvious fury with him. He could not help but notice the feminine roundness of her figure.

* * *

Aimee slammed her fists on her waist, trying her hardest not to let them fly at the infuriating little man.

"What?" he scoffed, "prayer will help her more than anything I could do. You know that. At least you should, since I see you in church every Sunday. Or are you just like most of the other silly girls I have seen in there? Do you see the Sunday service as merely an hour or so to plan your outfits for the next week and what the next thing you will embroider will look like?"

"You, sir, are daft!" Aimee threw her hands in the air with a shake of her head and stormed from the cabin.

How could he accuse her of some awful thing like that? How dare he? She paid attention just as much as she could to the sermons every Sunday. Who was he to judge her? He hardly even knew her. Aimee ran back to her cabin and slammed the door shut with the loudest *bang* she had ever heard.

* * *

Gage walked up to Caspian, who was standing on his deck, gazing up at the stars. "How did the battle go, Captain?" He moved to stand beside his friend and leader.

Caspian turned to Gage. "There were some flesh wounds, but nothing deadly, and we took a few hits, but we didn't even have to resort to hand-to-hand combat. The fool of a man ran away with his tail tucked between his legs. Imbecile. We will have to continue to track him down. I am *not* going to let that man go free."

"Oh, I'm sorry to hear that, Captain. I know how much this means to you. I know that man should not be free after what happened."

Caspian glared at the sea before responding, "We will get him in time, Gage. There is no way I will let him go without justice doing its part. I will not let another man like him affect me or my son ever again."

"Aye, Captain. You should not have lost your wife. Reed did

not deserve to lose his mother before he even knew her." Gage shook his head at that thought. The boy needed a mother to nurture him as he grew into adulthood. Which made him think ... "Captain, do you realize Lady Trenton believes you don't care about her?"

"Ah, Master Thompson, the matter of Lady Trenton is a dilemma altogether. That woman is a puzzle."

"Aren't most, Captain?" Gage flashed a grin.

Caspian chuckled. "But this lady is so sweet, and someone has truly abused her in the past. I don't know if she realizes what I feel for her, and I don't know if she should. It frightens me sometimes. Besides, I do not think she is ready to trust yet, after whatever happened to her. Ah, but she is a baffling little creature!"

Gage laughed. He wasn't even sure Caspian realized how much Lady Trenton seemed to care about Caspian herself.

* * *

Caspian sat on the edge of his deck the next day with his feet dangling out above the water and watched his crew frolic in the ocean below him. He had given the whole crew a few hours off because the weather had grown so harsh with the hot air and the rare blazing winds. They had ended up reaching the Caribbean in the peak of the summer months. But, in truth, he had never stopped his ship like this in all his years as a captain. It was always more important for him to reach the port in good time.

No, it was not the weather at all that had led him to take a reprieve from sailing. Gage had even teased him about it. It was the beautiful young lady who was sleeping in his cabin at the moment. He could not bear the thought of reaching Port Royal and having to bid her goodbye so he was putting that dreadful day off as far as he could.

After he had complimented her, the woman had fled from his presence, bursting into tears and running out onto the main deck. Caspian had immediately followed and tried to comfort the dear, perplexing girl, but she had refused his attentions and protested vehemently by hitting and screaming at him. He had surrendered at last and let her return to his cabin because she was causing yet another scene that his crew was enjoying far too much. When he had returned to the cabin to retrieve the pistol he had left on the desk, the blasted woman had been sound asleep, curled up on top of his coverlet.

She was beautiful when she slept. When she was silent and was not yelling at him or giving him one of those nasty glares. He knew she held some affection or something of the like for him, however, because she had not refused all of his attentions. The lady had never actually told him to leave and stop spending time with her. She liked it when he was close to her; he could tell that. Maybe she did not despise him after all.

Why she acted like that, so unpredictable, when he had done nothing offensive to her, he had no clue. She was much more confusing than Isabelle had been. If Isabelle had a problem with something he had done, she straight-out told him and they solved it together.

"Come and join us, Cap'n!" Jack Collie, his boatswain, shouted from below. Caspian glanced down to see the scrawny man cupping his hands over his mouth to yell.

"Yes, Captain! Come on and have some fun for once!" Gage

urged.

"Please do come in, Father!" He heard Reed's little voice cry up. The boy was half-swimming while Gage held him. No doubt the child thought he was swimming on his own.

"I will." Caspian nodded acquiescence and stripped down to his breeches before leaping into the blessedly cool turquoise ocean. The refreshingly chilly, salty water energized him. He grabbed his giggling son from Gage and threw him up into the air. Reed chuckled and latched back onto his father after he landed with a splash in the water. Suddenly, a commotion sounded from up on the main deck.

The gentle lilt of Eden's voice from above made his heart sing.

"Pray tell, where are the Captain and Master Thompson?" Her voice held a desperate tone, as if she was afraid the crew had mutinied overnight and tossed Caspian and Gage to the sharks.

Caspian smiled that she had inquired after him, but then bristled. Why had she asked for Gage also? He could not help but feel a twinge of jealousy.

"Er, miss, they's swimming out in the ocean. Cap'n gave all o' us the day off," the gruff voice of a sailor answered. Before long, Caspian was blessed with the sight of her creamy face leaning over the rail, those chestnut curls of hers looking tousled and tumbling over her shoulders. The woman always wore pins in her hair, but the stubborn strands never failed to escape their confinement after a few moments in the sea's winds.

"Come in, Eden! You can swim with us down here!" Caspian teased, gazing up at her and winking playfully. He did not expect her to actually come down into the water but he thoroughly enjoyed seeing her flustered.

She bit her pink bottom lip. "I am afraid I cannot swim, Captain."

He had not expected her to take his request seriously but now he did want her in the water if only to hold her.

"Well, come on in, and I will teach you how to swim. If you will want to live in Port Royal, or anywhere in the Caribbean, for that matter, you will need to know how to anyway." That at least was true.

"Yes, please come in, Miss Eden!" Reed shouted up at her.

Caspian prepared to tell the boy that she would not come to swim with him, that it would never happen, and that it was certainly most improper. But how did he know for certain? Maybe all the ladies in London swam in their leisure time. Perhaps Eden would join them after all.

Caspian looked to his son and then glanced out at the rest of the ocean. All the sailors excluding Gage had already left the water and were back on the ship, dripping wet. Some of them shook the moisture off of their bodies in the same manner as dogs.

His men had been in the ocean for hours and so had Reed. Surely the boy should not spend so much time in the water. But what did he know? Caspian had done nothing like this with his father and had no example of how to be a father to a young boy.

"By the bye, Reed, you should go back up on the deck and rest. You have been in here for hours."

"But must I, Papa? I just got in here!" He looked every bit like his late mother when he pouted. She had always had a stubborn tilt of the chin and used to cross her arms across her chest just as the boy did now. Caspian felt a pang of hurt remembering his dead wife. Were his feelings for Eden betraying Isabelle? He hoped not. Reed let out a loud breath, gathering his papa's attention once again.

"Yes, Reed. You should obey your father without a question; you know that. Now come on up." Eden beckoned for the boy to join her on the ship.

The poor child reluctantly climbed the ladder. After a long glance between Caspian and Eden, Gage followed the boy right up the ladder, grinning from ear to ear like some crazy fool. Which he did quite often.

After they had left, Lady Trenton stammered, "H-how do I get in?"

"Jump!" Caspian said simply, laughing. "But first, you must remove your dress." He winked at her.

"My *dress*?" She shrieked indignantly, her face growing a dark shade of pink.

"Well, you may leave your … your … undergarments on, of course …" He smirked. In all reality, she would do much better at swimming without all the heavy layers of fabric dragging her down, but he supposed she would not take kindly to the idea.

She glared down at him. "If I had known this was some sort of trick, I never would have agreed to it. You, sir, are a horrible cad and I will be bidding you good day, now! Here I had thought… I had thought … oh, never mind!" She exclaimed, clenching her fists in frustration and turning away.

He had not meant to upset her. He had never meant to upset her.

"Ede-Lady Trenton!" He called, willing her to stop and to listen to him before she stormed away like she always did when she got upset with him.

"Now what?" She whirled around.

"Why, jump in, of course. I suppose you could just leave your dress on. Please, don't leave, Eden! You may leave your dress on, but I will not promise to keep you from sinking anymore then. The dress might weigh you down quite a bit. And I was simply joking before." He was enjoying teasing the poor lady far too much.

"Are you mad? How could you say such a thing? I certainly will not jump in now, with you acting in such a childish manner," she objected, straightening.

"You will be perfectly fine, Eden. I promise I will catch you. I'll not let you drown, I assure you. And I already apologized for what I said, milady."

She glanced away, frowning yet again.

"Trust me just for once, 'Miss Eden.'" He hoped she noticed the wink he offered when he called her by the same name his son always did. Maybe she enjoyed answering to that name. She certainly liked the boy much more than she liked him. Maybe she would like him more now, too. It could not hurt to try. "I will take care of you. Let someone besides you take care of you for once. You may find that you enjoy it, milady."

Eden took a deep breath, that little worry line forming between her eyebrows like it always did when she frowned.

She leaned down, out of sight for a couple of moments. Two small thumps told him she was removing her shoes. Finally she stood and then bravely flung herself over the rail, her arms flailing.

Caspian caught her before she even touched the water. The trembling woman clung to his neck like he was a lifeline, which he probably actually was to her.

He found he liked someone depending on him like this.

True, Reed depended on him, but it was not quite the same. Reed was his son, not a beautiful young woman. Caspian held her closer to him than propriety allowed, he was sure, but he didn't care and he suspected she didn't, either. Really, he adored the feel of her soft curves pressed tight against him. Their bodies seemed to be made for one another with how perfectly she fit against him. Maybe they had been made for each other.

"Look at me, Eden. Just look at me, dear. I do not want you to be afraid. You should have a good time when you first learn how to swim." Although he had not. Just after he had first learned how to walk, his father had thrown him into the ocean and expected him to learn for himself, which he actually did.

Caspian's fingers brushed the hair from her face like a reflex. He found he enjoyed doing that, and he would miss it when they reached port and he had to leave her there to fend for herself. Well, he certainly could not take her with him to search for Moore in taverns and all sorts of rough places. No, that would not do at all. And he definitely did not want her to be with him when he confronted the man once again. He would not let that cur take the life of yet another woman he … loved. No, he could not be certain it was love yet.

But he was certain he would never let another person under his care be harmed.

Her wide, coffee-colored eyes slowly met his as he requested.

"I've got you, sweetheart. You are safe. There is no need to tremble as you are now," he whispered, kissing her forehead gently. She shivered, and he hoped she was trembling from something other than the fear of drowning. He could not resist a grin. "Do you want to learn to swim now?"

"No," she gave him a shaky smile he found entrancing. "I … I think I will learn to swim some other time. I-I am almost too frightened to now I am actually in the water."

Caspian sighed with relief. He truly did not want her to leave his embrace, even if it meant teaching her a new skill. "Do you wish to stay in the water though, milady?" He gently stroked her hair, praying she would answer "yes".

"Yes. For now," she answered, curling up against his chest as he treaded water to keep them both afloat. Caspian knew his legs would soon start burning from the exertion, but he did not care. As he held the woman tight against himself, he realized just how deep his feelings for her ran. He actually did love her: the feel of her soft curves, the delicate features on her creamy skin, her wild mass of brunette curls, her kind, loving spirit, how gentle she was with Reed; how brave she was inside although she never believed him when he told her she was courageous. Could he tell her he loved her, ask her to marry him instead of abandoning her to fend for herself once they arrived in Port Royal? The precious lady needed to be taken care of, to be cherished and respected, and he was the only man he trusted for the job. Some man had hurt her in some way and he almost did not want to know how they had done it. The thought of this dear woman being abused by a man sickened him. How helpless the poor sweetheart must have felt. He just wished he could have been there to protect her.

His thoughts were snapped back to reality when Eden slipped from his arms. She let out a shriek as she sank into the water.

Caspian noted her fear and caught her by the waist before she sank any further into the deep ocean. Panting, the woman smiled up at him. She recovered quickly from the scare.

Caspian looked down at those full, pink lips that were curved into a smile and his whole body ached with the need to kiss them. He lowered his mouth to hers slowly, and she actually did not object but kissed him back. He tilted his head and deepened their sweet kiss as she tightened her arms around his neck, making a soft noise from the back of her throat.

An obnoxious catcall met his ears. He reluctantly pulled away from the lady and noted that one of his crewmembers had not gone back up to the ship yet.

"Go up, Mr. Hansen, or it will be a lashing for you, I promise."

The man obeyed, grumbling.

Caspian turned back to the girl in his arms and smiled. Her face was as red as her slightly swollen, parted lips, and she was gasping for breath. Manly satisfaction swept through him. Before she could bound away like the little hart she was—which actually could hurt her, since she didn't know how to swim—he held her tight and kissed her hair, inhaling that familiar scent of coconut and vanilla.

"I-I ..."

"What, Caspian-er, Captain?" She inquired, looking up into his face, a serious expression contracting her features.

"First of all, Eden, please call me Caspian. I would think it is proper after all that we have been through. Second, I think that … you are … a wonderful woman, Eden." He held back what he was going to say about loving her, for fear of frightening her. Surely it was far too soon in their relationship to tell her something like that, if they even had a relationship. He was not even sure. Why, he had not even properly courted her yet!

But what did he know of courting a lady like her? He was just a pirate cad, worthy of the ladies who worked at the taverns in the worst sections of cities, not a lady like Eden who hailed from a posh manor in England and had never worked a day in her life. Isabelle had only been a plantation owner's daughter he had known growing up in New Providence. She had loved the idea of adventure and eloped with him quickly. No, he was not worthy of Eden. As soon as he could, he needed to stop whatever was going on between them. It was of most importance.

He glanced down at her. She was staring at him so sweetly from underneath those thick, dark eyelashes. No. He could not do it. He would not be the one to end what they had.

He cupped her face in his hand and stroked her cheek with his thumb. The precious girl's skin felt like the silk he had taken from an enemy's ship once. Her wide brown eyes searched his in unbelief. She finally frowned, shaking her head and causing those beautiful coffee-colored curls to bounce left and right.

"Believe me, sweetheart. You are very precious to me. I think you are the best woman I have ever known. I-I do not want our arriving in Port Royal to be good-bye for good, darling." Caspian's breath was coming hard from the effort it took to keep them both afloat, but if Eden enjoyed staying in the water, he was willing to swim until he breathed his last.

"No one has told me something like that before, Caspian," she whispered, tears filling her eyes. He loved hearing his Christian name come from those beautiful little lips.

And then she began to cry. Caspian's heart sank. He had brought this sadness, wherever it had come from, on her. What was wrong with him?

Well, he could not rightly blame himself when he had no idea *why* she was crying. All he knew was she had done it after he had spoken. If just his speaking had triggered it, he would never utter another word in her presence. He had always hated it when women cried in front of him but it made him feel even more terrible to see Eden upset.

"What's the matter, sweetheart? Please, don't cry. Everything is all right."

She pushed away from him, flailing her arms and legs in an attempt to stay above the water, and clambered up the ladder.

What had he done wrong? Had he offended the dear girl?

He prayed not.

And yes, he did pray. He suppressed a grin when he remembered how Eden had scolded him for saying he prayed while he had no faith in a God he thought cared nothing about him.

How Caspian loved the woman's spirit, her bravery. He believed Eden had led him to trust in this loving God of hers as he had in his childhood. Maybe the Lord had taken Isabelle away from him just so Caspian could meet Eden. To begin with, he never would have been in London and heading for Port Royal if it had not been for Isabelle's death. Even if he had somehow met Eden, he could never have fallen in love with her while he was married to someone else. No, it appeared only God could have brought them together. And he certainly was grateful it had happened. He might even visit a church when they stopped at the port.

Chapter 13

Eden stripped off her soaked undergarments and replaced them with dry ones and a simple yellow dress she had found in the back of the armoire. She assumed most of the dresses she wore came from other ships or perhaps the Captain's dead wife. A pirate ship did not seem to be a place to find miscellaneous dresses lying around.

She wrung her damp hair out and tied it up into a tight bun, all the while trying to put a stop her sobbing.

Why she had fled from Caspian like that, she was not sure. The poor man certainly had not done anything to hurt her or make her act like that. He did not deserve her childish reaction. But she was so … so touched that someone would say something like that … say that she was special, that she had simply not known what to do. So she had run.

As she always did to escape anything that troubled her.

A knock sounded on the door. Startled, she leapt up. Should she open it? It was probably just Caspian, coming in to console her. Again. Did the vexatious man not understand that when she left him like that it meant she wanted privacy, and not to be hunted down by him? Why could he not just leave her be?

She shook her head and opened the door a crack, lest he become worried because she failed to answer the door.

But the door was forced open upon her touch, sending her scrambling against the bulkhead to regain her footing.

Caspian would never be so rude to her. That much she knew for certain. Who could it be on the other side, forcing his way in?

Kelton's leering face met hers. His sun-streaked blond hair hung in disarray around his shoulders and his black eyes sparkled with lust.

"What is it you want, sir? The Captain is not here. I am afraid I must ask you to leave." Egad, she should not have said that! She wanted to get rid of him, but she did not want him to realize she was all alone without Caspian to protect her. How foolhardy could she possibly be?

By the look in his eyes, she had divulged exactly what he wanted to know.

He gave her a lecherous grin that sent a tremble all the way from her spine to her feet and confirmed her fears.

"Good. I do not want that prissy little man here anyway. And isn't it perfectly obvious what I do want, my little trollop?" Placing both hands on her waist, he shoved her backwards in one sharp swoop.

"I am most definitely *not* yours, and I am certainly no trollop!" She tripped on a bit of the bulkhead that jutted out before stumbling downward.

Eden's head struck the bedpost as she fell and she cried out in agony. It seemed as if she had hit the same exact part of her head as when she had bumped into Caspian's desk earlier in the voyage. Her vision swirled and she took several long, deep breaths as she struggled to maintain consciousness.

"So, the Captain has left his little mistress unattended? What a pity. How foolish of him. It is about time he shared his precious treasure with the rest of the crew. It is about time I show you what a real man is, unlike your feeble, diminutive *Captain* Archer." He laughed wickedly.

Eden did not have the strength to rise so she remained on the floor, whimpering and ignoring his jabs at Caspian. He was just trying to make her angry. Maybe he wanted her mad at him so he had an excuse to beat her. A bit like Lord Clive Rutger.

But maybe he was different. Would shameless begging work on him? "Please—please, sir. I have done you no wrong; please do not hurt me!" She prayed for someone, anyone, to come to her aid.

"Ah, believe me, lady; you will be begging me for more by the time I am through with you! You will see I am entirely different than your current lover. Now get up!" He chortled at her weak struggles to rise and move away from him.

"No! He is not my lover, and I can already see he is nothing like you. Caspian is a … a *gentleman* and you, sir, are nothing of the kind, I assure you of that! You will never even live to be half of the man that Caspian is!" She refused to be a part of this. This could not be happening again. There was nowhere to run this time. He would beat her just like Rutger had and quite possibly do much worse.

He slapped her across the mouth, hard. Ahh. Here was the beating. "I'll teach you not to be disobedient to me, you wench!" He shoved a handkerchief into her mouth and, grabbing her by the waist, threw her over his shoulder like a wretched sack of potatoes.

Eden kicked and clawed at him and tried to scream but found her throat was constricted with terror. She could not acquire her freedom. She could not overpower him. Just like she could never overpower Lord Rutger.

Kelton led her down, down, where she could smell the foul bilge. That familiar bilge which she had slept in on the beginning of this voyage before the Captain had discovered her.

He finally stopped before a door, opened it, and threw her down upon a pile of burlap sacks. She clawed the handkerchief from her mouth and screamed, wishing desperately she could just remain calm despite what was happening. Men like him loved panic in their victims.

He struck her again, this time square in the abdomen and with his clenched fist. Probably so no one would be able to see it later. So Caspian would not believe her about what had occurred. Just as her father had not.

Eden gasped for breath at that blow.

Maybe Caspian would believe one of his crewmember's words over those of a hysterical woman such as her. Just like the man she had run away from back home. Rutger had been efficient at that. He somehow knew where it would hurt her the worst without being visible.

Eden doubled over after another painful kick. She wasn't sure if her arm would move again anytime soon with how horribly her shoulder hurt.

He turned, no doubt to shut the door they had entered the room through. It simply would not do, for him, at least, if her screams were heard by the Captain. But Eden did not have time to think of this. He lit a lantern that was hanging from the bulkhead.

The second his back was facing her, she ran, desperate to escape this fate. Running was her only escape from many things, and she was determined she would escape this harrowing event in much the same way.

She dove behind some crates—it was difficult to see anything in this wretched darkness—and tried to silence her ragged breathing. Perhaps he would not catch her here. Desperate to find a weapon, something, anything she could use to protect herself against this monster, she pushed open a heavy crate that was behind her. Even a sharp piece of wood would do. After a moment, she located a short knife. It was no match for all of Kelton's weapons, but surely it would be better than nothing.

A slim chance was better than no chance at all. She took a deep breath, desperate to calm the frantic racing of her heart.

A hot hand pressed against her shoulder, gripping her tightly. This was her only chance. She spun around, jabbing the knife.

But it only hit cold, empty air.

She tried to realign her aim and hit some flesh. The man roared in pain but she soon realized she had done close to no damage. He clutched his arm, where she had wounded him, but then charged at her in a mad fury.

She dropped the knife before she hurt herself accidentally or he got a hold of it.

He pushed her down to the floor, her back leaning against one of the crates. He grabbed at her dress, tearing most of her skirt off.

"Please, sir ... I'll do anything, just please, please, please ..." her voice cracked and died down, betraying her. She flinched when he ripped the remains of her bodice off of her and splinters from the deck beneath her cut through her chemise, piercing her skin.

She tried to struggle but her shoulder hurt from his kick.

He chortled at every whimper.

"Caspian!" she wailed for help, even though she knew full well no one could even hear her. Why had she left Caspian, in tears? If only she had not run away, she would be safe with him.

At her rebellious shout, Kelton smacked her head against the crate behind her. An ache throbbed in the back of her head, and she had to blink to keep the tears that were pooling in her eyes from spilling over onto her cheeks. She could not move.

She prayed for death.

So this was it. This could not be happening. This had gone further than last time. Last time she had managed to escape before she had been violated.

She closed her eyes tight, finally accepting her horrible fate. This was actually happening. Was God even with her anymore? Surely He had abandoned her. He would not let a horrible thing like this happen to her if He loved her, would He? No, He could not.

She felt Kelton's weight press down against her and his foul, moist mouth on her exposed neck.

She felt sick.

"Open your eyes, wench. Lemme see that pretty shade of brown the Captain gushes so about to Master Thompson."

It seemed as if she was in a nightmare and this was not reality. "No!" She moved her face away from those probing fingers that were forcing her eyelids opened.

* * *

Caspian stood on his deck, gazing out to sea. Reed sat, cross-legged on the deck, playing with the sapphire necklace Eden had given him. Caspian sighed as he watched the turquoise waves beat against the hull of his ship, resulting in a white froth.

What could he have done wrong? Egad, the woman was fragile and yet so, so brave and so strong. She was quite baffling.

Caspian wiped sweat from his brow and looked down only to discover a frilly, lacy little square of white cloth lying on the ground. It seemed so out of place there, so at odds with the grimy, wet wood it sat on, that he could not help but think of Eden. She, a wealthy English lady, was out of place on this rough privateer ship, just like her handkerchief on his deck. In fact, she was completely at odds with him, the Captain of this wretched ship.

Although they did not seem to be made for each other by any means, they had to have been put together by God's hands.

Even so, perhaps he should not try to venture any further with their relationship. It was probably for the best he abandon her in Port Royal just like she wanted.

Like she had always wanted from the beginning.

Yet he smiled to remember how angry she had been with him when he had told her she had to take off her dress to jump into the ocean. He had never actually expected her to take him seriously.

But she had.

He had never expected her to actually jump into the water and trust him.

But she had.

The woman was a mystery.

Caspian stooped down to retrieve the little handkerchief and take it to his cabin so Eden did not lose it. He had no idea how many the woman had. Maybe it was her only handkerchief left after running away from home. It would not do for it to be swept away with the ocean breezes.

When he arrived at the cabin, however, his door swung wide from its hinge. In her fit of anger, Eden had probably forgotten to close it.

"Listen to me, Eden. I am sorry about whatever happened out there. Really, I never meant to upset-" He quieted when he saw the room was completely, utterly empty.

Something echoed from somewhere in his ship. Was that a scream?

He could not quite tell what it was or where it was coming from.

He rushed amidships.

Another terrified cry, louder this time. From farther below? A feminine scream.

Lady Trenton.

Someone was assaulting his Lady Trenton. Caspian sped down the companionway as fast as his legs could carry him toward the sounds of an intense struggle.

Chapter 14

Suddenly his weight was lifted from her. Eden opened her eyes to see Caspian pounding Kelton's face with his fist.

It had all happened so suddenly.

Caspian paused in his assault only a fraction of a moment to glance at her.

She held her breath as Kelton drew his sword.

Caspian kicked the cutlass out of the young man's hand. He grabbed Kelton by the collar of his shirt and began pounding his head against the wall.

The rage on Caspian's face told Eden he would kill this man if no one stopped him. Even though she knew it was terribly wrong to do, she almost wished him success. She had to stop this. She needed to stop this before someone was killed, but she could not even lift her head.

Just then Master Gage burst through the door. He stared at Kelton's battered head slamming against the bulkhead over and over again. Kelton's body began to go slack. She had no way of knowing, but surely he would die soon.

"Uhh … Captain? Should I take him to the hold for you?" Gage intervened.

Caspian paused his assault and instead of ramming Kelton's head again, he grappled the man's neck in a fierce chokehold as if Gage had not even spoken. Finally, he tossed the vile man to the floor.

"Yes. Post a guard this time. I do not want the man escaping again." Caspian wiped his sleeve across his face, whisking away the sweat that had formed there. His curly black hair fell around his handsome face in disarray, and his white, loose shirt clung to his muscles because of the dampness.

Gage assisted a shaky, disoriented Kelton up but stopped before he left with the young man. He nodded toward Eden.

"She all right, Captain?"

"Don't know yet. Take the mongrel to the hold. Leave him there the rest of this voyage. We will dispose of him when we reach port."

Gage nodded and dragged the man away.

Caspian sunk to Eden's side. "Are you unharmed, milady?" He inquired, searching her barely clad body for injuries. To think she had been unwilling to take off her dress to swim only hours ago. Now, Eden did not have the strength to be embarrassed he was seeing her in such an improper state.

* * *

"I-I-" she stammered. The poor girl was clearly still frightened out of her wits.

"It's all right." Caspian saw her falter and reached out to

enfold her in his arms. "I've got you, Eden. I've got you, sweetheart."

She was shuddering so he quickly removed his waistcoat and wrapped it around her. He hoped she was just shivering because she was cold and not because she was frightened of him.

He carried her up to the cabin and set her on his bed. Then he rested on the chair next to her.

After a moment of studying her face, which was oddly void of emotions, he rose suddenly. "I-I should get you some water, milady … or-or something proper for you to wear. Surely it is m-most improper for me to be seeing you like this. I should just leave you be."

"Caspian, please … don't go … do not leave me alone." She stretched out her hand.

He carefully cupped it in his. How he longed to stop those tears from speeding down her freckled cheeks.

Caspian leaned over her and covered her lithe body with a spare quilt that was lying across a trunk. A dash of blood contrasted the white on the sleeve of his shirt. He had gotten sliced by Kelton's sword before he'd knocked it out of the foul monster's hands.

Her eyes followed his down to the small wound. Tears flowed anew from her eyes. "I'm sorry … I am so, so sorry, sir …"

"Whatever would you be sorry for, love? You have done nothing wrong. There is nothing to be sorry for." Caspian felt himself frown at her strange statement. How could she even have said such a thing? He clenched his fists at his sides.

"You-you … got hurt … because of me. It was … it was my fault, Caspian …"

"No, sweetheart. Not at all. This is just a little scratch. Besides, I should be the least of your worries right now, love." He leaned down to kiss her hand, his eyes searching hers. "Milady," he swallowed, "did I … did I come too late for you? What did Kelton do to you? Did he …?" He tried to stop his voice from trembling but found he had failed. *Please, Lord, have her say "no". Please, I do not know how to control myself if Kelton did more … I may not be able to stop myself from killing him down in that hold …*

Eden shook her head.

Thank the Lord.

"You arrived just in time and I thank you deeply for that, Captain." She averted her gaze and gnawed on her bottom lip.

"I thank God, milady. I was so … worried … when I saw …" He sighed. It was indescribably hard to get the words out of his ever-tightening throat. When he had seen Kelton's body on top of her barely clothed one, he had most certainly feared the worst.

"I do, also, Caspian. I was so terrified … and I thought … I had thought … Egad, but it is too terrible to say aloud! I-I cannot say it." She lowered her head, her face pink.

"It is perfectly all right, milady. You can tell me anything you want anytime you want, and I promise you will not regret it. Sweetheart, you have my word." Caspian stooped down and planted a gentle kiss on her forehead, brushing some of that gorgeous hair out of her face. He decided he much preferred this woman's glossy dark curls to his late Isabelle's straight blond locks, however beautiful they had been.

However, it did not seem to be beauty that was the main concern. He liked Eden quite a bit without just her looks. And his heart broke that something had happened aboard his ship to give her such a fright while she was under his protection.

He had to learn to keep those he loved near to him at all times.

Except for when he was in the middle of a battle.

Eden stared into his eyes for a couple of moments, scrutinizing him, probably to see if she could tell if he was lying, before she responded. "I … I had thought that … that … I had thought God had abandoned me and He did not love me anymore. I didn't understand how He could let what was happening happen to me. Now I know how you feel, how you think that God doesn't care for you because of happened with … with your … wife."

"Aye, milady. You know how I *felt*. Recently my beliefs have changed. A while after I met a certain beautiful young stowaway, to be clear." He winked at her and her face transformed to a gorgeous shade of pink. "I realized God must love me for letting me meet someone as special as you. And what about you, milady? I trust your views have changed since you were down below with Kelton? Maybe when you were rescued by a certain dashing pirate captain, perhaps?" He flashed a grin.

"Well … I do believe that God still loves me … and I am terribly shamed for my unbelief."

"I understand where it came from, milady. And while it is certainly no excuse, everyone has weak moments like that because of sin; you know that, right, milady?"

She nodded, swallowing.

"Now what happened to you, sweetheart? Before you came here. What made you this shaken from what happened with Kelton? Tell me what made you so frightened of me striking you. Why did you run away from London? Tell me. Please."

She took a deep breath.

A moment passed when Caspian wondered if she would answer him or not. He hoped she had finally realized it was safe to tell him anything.

Caspian held his breath as she began to speak.

"A couple of months ago, my father announced to me I was to marry a man named Lord Clive Rutger. Mama is dead, or she probably would have put an end to it, and Adam is away. Only God knows where he is. If Adam were here, he would help Papa in his older age, and make sure we are provided for so I could marry someone I at least like. But Adam is gone. Lord Rutger ... he is a horrible man, Caspian. He only wanted me for my looks." She shivered, despite the Caribbean summer's heat in the cabin. "I-I do not understand why, but he is almost ... obsessed with me. Long before we were engaged, he tried to kiss me at a ball. He made me go with him off to an isolated room. I told him I did not want to kiss him, that I did not even like him, but he just shoved me and luckily he left with his pride hurt. I thought that would be the end of it, but it was not ...

"I did not want to tell anyone about it because they would never believe me about what had happened."

Caspian stifled a groan. He could see where this tragic tale was leading and he hated it. Hated every second of it. He almost could not bear to listen to the rest. It took everything in him not to cover his ears and ran away screaming, but he could not leave the dear, frightened girl here all alone.

"When our betrothal was announced," she swallowed back a rush of tears, "he stayed at our house because he lived far outside of London. Papa figured it would not hurt either of our reputations because he was there and so were all of our servants. Papa's room was between mine and the one Lord Rutger was staying in. That night, though, Lord Rutger came into my bedchamber. I … I guess he was very silent somehow because my father never knew it had happened."

Caspian took in a sharp breath. The poor, sweet woman.

"Lord Rutger—he had a pistol with him. He told me he would kill me if I so much as made a noise … he would kill me if I refused him like I had that night at the ball. I was so frightened, Caspian. I did not know what he would do to me and I did not doubt he would kill me. He said my body would be his in a matter of months, anyway, when we married … and then he-he …" she whispered the next words, "tried to do what Kelton tried to do to me. I was too terrified to scream for help. I was so frightened he would kill me like he promised he would if I did scream." She shook her head slightly, her eyes focusing on Caspian's chest, rather than his face.

Caspian took Eden's hand in his and squeezed it. His heart sank to see her so distraught.

"He forced me to kiss him, but when he wasn't looking, I grabbed my bed warmer and I-I hit him over the head with it. The blow disoriented him, but it did not make him unconscious. I could tell he had gotten angry with me and I knew that was my very last chance. Not only would he … ravish me, but he would probably also kill me. He was so furious, Caspian. I-I shoved him out of my bedchamber and locked the door behind him. My door was sturdy, but I heard him trying to break it down. The only reason he ended up leaving me alone that night was because he did not want to attract attention to … to what he was doing. He knew my father would break off the engagement if he discovered what had happened between the two of us. Lord Rutger had told

167

me if I revealed to anyone what had happened, he would kill Papa and he would murder my poor friends Aimee and Ivy. After that night, he tried to corner me whenever he was near. When I objected each time, he took to beating me. He enjoyed seeing me in pain. Just a few days before I left London, my father left me while he was out of town. The servants all had the day off, because we have been running out of money."

Eden pressed a hand to her forehead, her face pale. Caspian leaned forward to brush a lock of hair from her face as she continued, "Lord Rutger paid me a visit while Papa was away. When I refused to kiss him, and when I refused to go up to my bedchamber with him, he beat me in the parlor ... and he vowed to me that I would get more of it when we were married. He knows where to beat a woman, Caspian, where it will hurt her most and where no one can see it, so no one else can tell what is going on." She paused to rub her shoulder, her eyes welling up with tears.

Caspian remembered the bruise he had seen on her pale skin early in the voyage. He squeezed his eyes shut, trying to block out the image of Eden's poor body being ruthlessly battered by a man. Why, he could almost hear her screams, see her tears of anguish. It made him feel sick.

"I told him that I hated him, and that I would rather die than marry him. Finally, I escaped to my bedchamber that day, where I locked the door and pushed a trunk up against it to keep him out. After a few hours, he left, threatening me of what he would do to me the next time he saw me. Well, the next day, after my father had returned, I begged him to break off the engagement, but he refused and he got so, so upset with me. He told me he would not deal with my disobedience any longer and I would marry Lord Rutger whether I wanted to or not."

Caspian clenched his jaw. Did the man care about his daughter at all? How could he not tell the poor dear was suffering?

"So, you see I … I had no choice but to run away from home … run away from that horrible life I was doomed to. I had to leave my friends, the closest thing I had left to family. I could not live the rest of my life with that monster beating me, and doing whatever else he wanted to do to me …"

Her sobs filled the air once again like the wails of thunder in the night.

He could not bear to see her so upset like this. He took her in his arms and ran his hands through those precious, silken waves of hair. "If I ever meet that man—" he began, clenching a fist of her hair, "—or your father, for that matter, for pledging you to that man …"

"It is all right, Caspian. There is no need to upset yourself over it. What was done was done."

He squeezed her hand. "It is most certainly not all right, Eden, darling, and I assure you I *will* upset myself over it. It is never all right for a man to beat a woman like that, and what this Lord Rutger did to you was inexcusable. I promise I will never let that … *monster* come near you again. He will never touch you again, and if I can help it, no man will ever strike you again. Ever." Despite his efforts to keep it steady, his voice broke.

"Caspian … you are the sweetest man I have ever known …"

"And you are the sweetest woman I've ever met, darling." Should he tell her he loved her now? Surely not yet. He did not want to scare the dear girl.

He smoothed a stray strand of that coffee-colored hair away

from her pretty, round face. His gaze dropped to those pink, moist lips. The memory of what it had felt like to kiss those sweet little lips crept into his mind, unbidden.

Caspian lowered his mouth to hers and drank in the sweet taste of her. If he had any say in the matter, she would never be alone again. He could never let her leave and be in harm's way of another abusive man. Egad, how he wanted to declare his love for her and beg her to stay!

He pulled away and cupped her face in his hand. His thumb brushed against her cheek. It was almost hard to believe how incredibly soft her skin was.

"Has anyone told you just how beautiful you are, Eden darling?"

Her blush made her all the prettier. The girl rubbed her shoulder and glanced away shyly. He gasped when he saw the nasty bruise on her fair skin. *Another bruise.* This one, while she was under Caspian's care. His thumb brushed around the wounded area.

She flinched at his touch and he prayed it was not because she feared him striking her. He found himself cursing under his breath.

"That ... *dog* hurt you, love? He hit you just like that ... *Lord* Rutger did to you?"

She nodded, chewing on her plump bottom lip.

"Sweetheart, I am so sorry," he breathed into her hair and drank in her coconut and vanilla scent.

His elbow accidentally bumped into her stomach as he leaned forward.

She let out a sharp hiss of pain.

Caspian froze for a second. Was she hurt worse than he thought? What if there was a cracked rib or something of that sort? He could get the surgeon, but he did not want any of his sailors seeing Eden's exposed belly, surgeon or not. Caspian had to see if she was seriously injured for himself.

"What is it, sweetheart?" He moved aside the quilt that was covering her midsection.

She jerked back from him.

"Please, 'tis most improper … my dress is in shreds and my chemise is much the same." She frowned and moved the quilt back in place.

"Since when have I cared a whit about what is proper?"

She gave him a small smile and allowed him to examine the wound.

He nudged aside the tattered remains of stained chemise and made certain to only look the wound.

Another bruise darkened the skin of her belly. He knew he should look away, but his eyes were fixated on the spot. How could a man do this to a woman? Weren't men meant to *protect* the weaker sex?

Caspian brushed his fingers over the bruise lightly. Satisfied it was only a bruise and not a more serious injury, he swept the quilt back over her.

He backed away and sighed angrily. "You get some sleep, my love. I'll go see about something to put on those bruises so they don't hurt you so badly." He rose.

"No! Please, don't go. Stay. I-I do not think I will be able to get to sleep by myself," she stammered. "I will be too frightened Kelton will return … or-or Lord Rutger will somehow find me …"

* * *

"Of course, dear," he answered gently.

Uncontrollable shivers wracked her entire body.

"Would you … could you … please h-hold me?" she asked, not quite looking right at him. She knew she should be embarrassed to ask such a thing of a man, but she was too numb to think about it.

"Yes, sweetheart, of course." Caspian turned back to her and in one swoop he scooped her up into his arms and moved her to his chair with him so she was sitting, curled up on his lap.

She threw her arms around him and snuggled close to his chest, breathing in his pleasant scent of hard-earned sweat and wood and spice. A sudden sleepiness overtook her, and she realized she had never felt this comfortable, this safe, this relaxed, before, and yet she was in a man's arms.

Caspian was the only man she trusted anymore, and she was not certain how deep her feelings for him ran. She had vowed to herself never to fall in love with a man and never to marry one … but could she be falling in love with Captain Caspian Archer? It suddenly seemed quite possible, and the thought sent a shiver of both delight and fear running through her.

* * *

Tears filled her eyes, and Caspian watched helplessly as they spilled down her round, pink cheeks yet again.

He could not bear it.

Those tears and this distress needed to stop, and soon. "Eden? Please, please, do not cry again, sweetheart! It makes me feel terrible to see you upset. When you cry, it makes me feel like I did something to make you sad."

"I am fine. Believe me, I am not upset over anything you have done. I'm just so happy to be here, to be safe with you, Caspian. These are just happy tears, I guess, because I am so relieved."

"I promise I will not let anyone hurt you from now on," he reassured her. "Goodnight, Eden." He kissed her mouth quickly and rather chastely.

"Goodnight," she replied. The next was a whisper, so quiet Caspian was not certain if he had heard her correctly. "I ... I love you."

Did she truly just say that? He hoped she had. "I love you, too, Eden."

He pressed his lips against her warm forehead and relished the feeling of her soft body pressed against him, in his arms. She was a special woman and he planned to never have to say good-bye to her. A man could easily get used to having her in his embrace.

Chapter 15

Ivy rested on a crate near the bow of Captain Emery's ship. She had begun to enjoy sailing after her seasickness had passed a few days ago. Aimee sat next to her, pushing loose strands of that pale, golden hair back into her delicate coiffure.

Ivy gazed at the ocean. Eden was somewhere in front of her, and William was somewhere behind her. Every second of the day, she prayed for the safety of both. What kind of friend was she, to have not believed Eden and to have let her run away? What kind of sister was she to abandon William without anyone she trusted to take care of him? She felt awful.

"I do hate that stifling cabin, but all of this sun and wind and salt are horrible for my complexion." Aimee put a hand to her forehead.

The whining tone in her friend's voice was beginning to grate on Ivy's nerves. She had never seen Aimee like this. How could she be concerned with something like her complexion while there were far more pressing matters? Ivy could not help but to roll her eyes at her friend's vanity. "Aimee, you need to stop worrying about your looks all of the time. You are a beautiful girl without fretting about the state of your complexion."

"If I ever wish to be married, I should have a right to be worried about my complexion. What man would want a tanned, wrinkled wife?" She crinkled her nose up in disgust at her words.

"A respectable man should not care about how you look on the outside," Ivy muttered, shaking her head at the vainness of her dear friend's statement.

"Ah, and what are we talking about, ladies?" Matthew sat next to them, rolling up the sleeves of his plain linen shirt to his elbows. The sun really was burning today.

Ivy studied Aimee in interest. Her face constricted and grew red. Finally, Aimee rolled her eyes at him and stood. "I fear I have suddenly developed a most horrible headache. I shall retire to my cabin." She scurried below, her hips swaying with her.

One of Ivy's eyebrows rose.

"What did you do to her, Captain Emery, to make her like that to you?" Her friend was obviously avoiding him.

"I am not certain what I did to her, Lady Shaw. She seems to dislike me quite a bit, does she not? Oh well, she is simply a spoiled little girl who cares only about herself and what she can do to make herself more beautiful than she already is. Lady Dawson is far more concerned with her looks than with anyone else's well-being."

"Now, you do not know her well enough to jump to an imprudent conclusion like that, Captain Emery," Ivy chastised.

"All I know about that woman is she always acts spoiled and

mighty like that when she is around me, regardless of what I do or say. I can never seem to please her."

* * *

Eden snuggled close against the warm, hard body she was sleeping beside. She did not want to open her eyes. Did not want to face reality. Wanted to sleep longer, to feel safe longer.

Caspian's hand stroked her hair sweetly. He must have woken before her, or perhaps he had never even fallen asleep like she had.

Wait … Caspian …

She had been so weak last night that she had let him hold her while she slept! Eden let out a quiet groan.

How could she have *encouraged* the dear, horrible, dear man to do such a thing? It was terribly improper. She cringed to think of what Aimee and Ivy would say.

Her eyes snapped open to discover Caspian grinning down at her, an adoring expression on his charming face.

"Good morning, Eden. I pray you are feeling better today? I know that last night was terribly trying for you. No woman should have to go through something like that."

"Get away from me, Captain. I … please forgive me for allowing you to hold me while I slept, I beg of you." She shivered. But Caspian had proven his true character by her misstep. With any lesser man, her trust may have been violated. Caspian was a gentleman in the truest sense of the word, even though he was not properly bred and born in the estates of England. No, he was a true gentleman who would never do anything to hurt her. Eden was sure of it.

176

Still, it was improper to have slept in his arms. She rose and clambered to the bulkhead. When she realized all she wore besides her tattered chemise was the quilt he had placed on her last night and it was slowly sliding off of her, she wrapped it tightly about herself in a flash.

She stretched her neck, which had formed a terrible crick from spending a night in an armchair.

He smirked but sobered quickly. "I must apologize, milady. You asked me to hold you last night. Really, I had every intention of placing you back on the bed once you fell asleep, but I fear I, too, fell asleep. Can you ever forgive me?"

She frowned at the lightness of his tone.

"Must you always be so aloof with me, sweetheart? You seemed so close to me last night. I had thought maybe ... after last night ... what we both said ..."

"I am sorry, Caspian. I really am. You have been so kind to me; I should not act in such a manner toward you." She looked down, suddenly immensely fascinated by a plank in the deck.

"That is much better, milady." He chuckled and swooped down to kiss her on the cheek. His scent of salt and leather teased her nose. "And don't you forget, sweetheart, you told me you loved me last night."

Eden felt her face flush to what she was certain was an uncomely red. Had she told him that last night? She had barely come to recognize the fact herself. Her mind certainly had been in a fog after Kelton had attacked her.

The captain simply grinned at her reaction.

"As you have declared your love, might I have the privilege of a good-morning kiss?"

She frowned at his nerve. What gave the man the audacity

to ask such things of her? But as he leaned toward her purposefully, she could not resist him. She did not care how early in the morning it was and how improper it would be. All she cared about was how badly she wanted to kiss him.

His lips devoured hers, and she felt her insides and her knees turn to mush. She drank in his strength, winding her arms around his strong neck. She needed his strength.

When he finally released her, both of their breathing had become labored.

"Thank you ever so much, my love. I believe no matter what happens; now I shall have a good day at work." And with a quick wink, he strapped on his weapons and left.

* * *

Aimee plunked down onto the narrow cot and sighed. Captain Emery definitely was an infuriating little man. She did not care one whit if she had been rude to him above decks. Truly, she had developed a headache. Whenever Captain Emery was around, she seemed to acquire one.

She closed her eyes, trying to get him off of her mind and focus on the reason she had agreed to go on a voyage with him.

Eden.

Aimee felt something in her stomach tighten. They had been sailing for a long time and had not run across a single ship on the list Captain Emery had made. She could not help but think of the terrible things that could have happened to dear Eden.

She squeezed her hands together and wondered if they

would ever find her friend. Aimee glanced down, below the cot she was perched on, and scanned the deck below her. Luckily, she had not seen a rodent in a couple of days.

Captain Emery actually had done something she had asked him.

She groaned out loud. Why did every thought that passed through her head lead her straight back to the infuriating, ego-centric idiot who was sailing the ship?

* * *

Ivy had to chuckle at Aimee and Captain Emery. With how vehemently the two people despised each other, she knew there was some kind of affection or at least attraction growing between them, whatever it might be. Ivy found their squabbles quite entertaining on her voyage over to the colonies.

If only Eden were here to join them ...

Ivy missed their happy little trio. It caused her to shiver to think they might never be together again. She knew it was the right thing to do to go searching for her dear friend, but she could not help but worry about William back home, also.

She needed to find Eden and get back home as quickly as she could.

* * *

Caspian watched the myriad of twinkling stars in the midnight sky above him. They were truly quite beautiful, a work of God. But nothing compared to the woman resting in his cabin.

Eden had told him she loved him! Why, he was nothing short of elated. Perhaps she would agree to marry him when they reached the port. He definitely could not wait to claim her as his own wife if she would just have him.

He yawned and realized it must be well past midnight. His night watchman looked close to sleep, but Caspian was in too good of a mood to chastise the man for slacking on his job. He was tired of being the grouchy captain.

He thought of returning to his cabin, but after Eden had declared her love for him, and after she had let him hold her like she had last night, he knew it would be improper for them to sleep in the Captain's cabin together, even if Reed was there. A sleeping five-year-old did not make the best chaperone.

Instead, Caspian relocated down to the belly of his ship where there was a small, relatively tidy storage cabin. He hoped that down there, he could at least catch some form of rest.

* * *

Lord Clive Rutger stood at the bow of the ship he had rented to search for his runaway love. He could not be too far away from that blasted woman by now. How could she have done something like this to him, her own fiancé? Their wedding had been planned to take place nearly a week ago. Did she know what a disgrace she was bringing down upon him? After all he had been through, she had brought yet another embarrassment to his name. All of London had been snickering and gossiping both behind his back and in front of him ever since they heard she had run away.

Chapter 15

Clive would show her. He would teach her he would not be dismissed easily like some common servant. He had every right to own her and he would in time. She was his and he would have what he had been promised.

This would not turn out like last time, when she had run away into her bedchamber and barricaded herself there. He would not let the little flower escape him. Eden would learn to love him and she would be happy in time. And he would have his own wife. She was no one else's but his.

Before that happened, however, the girl would pay dearly for what she had done to him. She would rue the day she ran away from Lord Clive Rutger and rejected his advances.

Clive's gaze found at the ship they were nearing every minute under the cover of night. Was Eden on it? He somehow sensed she was.

As soon as they neared the vessel, the captain whose services Clive was paying for announced they approached a ship called *Dawn's Mist*.

After Rutger had interrogated some men at the docks, he had found out the *Dawn's Mist* had left London the day Eden turned up missing. He had been told it was sailing for the Caribbean.

Clive discussed the situation with the captain.

They came to the conclusion that, rather than starting an unnecessary battle, Rutger should sneak onto the ship and scout out any signs of the woman. He was ready to do so.

Eden would deny him no longer.

Chapter 16

Aimee watched as Ivy laid herself down on the narrow cot across from hers in their small cabin. "Any news of Eden's whereabouts?" She had been wondering about the progress they had made on the voyage, but she had no wish to talk to the captain of their ship.

"Nay, but we shall reach Port Royal in less than a week, according to Captain Emery. We should hopefully see her before then. Captain Emery checked with the docks before we left and according to their records, the only ship that left for Port Royal that day was called *The Dawn's Mist*. He says we will keep an eye out for a vessel with that name and the one Lord Rutger hired. From what Captain Emery can tell, with how the winds and the currents are acting, there is a chance we could outrun Lord Rutger and find Eden first. If not, we will have to intercept him or save Eden if he already has her."

Aimee inhaled a deep breath. Everything would be much easier if they could only find Eden first. "I certainly hope we find her before he does because I fear for her safety if that monster finds her first."

* * *

Eden lay down on the bed and leaned against the pillow, inhaling its rich smell of salt and leather. Caspian's scent. She had not seen him all day. How she missed his strong, comforting presence! Then, she began to wonder, should she be craving a man's company like that? Perhaps not. Maybe she truly was a woman of loose morals as Lord Rutger had always accused her of being.

The cabin door was propped slightly open because Eden had wanted to allow a slight breeze to enter the cabin. Heat out at sea could get quite stifling. Eden frowned when she heard a sudden scuffling noise outside the door. Was Caspian finally back? It was already later by far than when he normally came back after his duties as captain. Generally he would spend a majority of the day up on the decks with her cooped up in the cabin and in Reed's company and come back inside to her for their evening meal at about what she thought, according to what Caspian had explained to her about the ship's bells, was six o'clock. After that, he would go back up on deck and sometimes take her for a walk in the evening's cooler breeze, and he would return to his cabin about the same time as when she was preparing to go to sleep. They had formed a comfortable little routine between the two of them.

But today he had not even stopped by to eat his evening meal with her. Eden had already tucked little Reed into bed. Maybe there was trouble brewing within the crew, and Caspian was simply settling it and he would return in no time. Surely that was the case and nothing had gone terribly awry. She was afraid to go up on the main deck to find out.

Eden glanced over at Reed, who was sleeping on the bed, looking like a tiny angel. His long eyelashes were lowered, casting a shadow onto his flushed cheeks. She stepped closer to the dear boy and brushed some of those reckless blond curls out of his face, and then pressed a soft kiss onto his forehead. Not only had she grown quite fond of Caspian, but she had also come to love his little son, also. She loved him as if he were her own child.

Which she almost wished he was. Quickly, she bid the thought from her head. No matter how great of a man he was, she could never even think of marrying a man. She had vowed to herself she would never marry and she planned to stick to that promise. Even though her heart warned her against it …

Eden shook her head to clear it of those troubling thoughts and stepped up from her position in Caspian's armchair to look through the porthole at the vast night sky. The ocean was almost as black as the night, and the sky was dotted with bright white stars. She sighed. Nights at sea were truly beautiful. That was one thing besides two others she would miss if she stayed in Port Royal.

The sea seemed endless during the night, but sadly, she knew that was not so. Just a couple of days ago, Reed had mentioned seeing palm trees on the horizon during the battle. Soon they would reach land and she would have to bid Reed and Caspian farewell.

The sharp creak of a wooden plank jerked her from her thoughts.

She laughed silently at her own foolishness. The ship made

noises like that all the time. Yet why had this one frightened her? Glancing at Reed who still slept peacefully, she leaned back against the bulkhead behind her.

The door opened.

* * *

Eden could not move from her position. Her throat constricted in terror. This had to be a dream. Just a nightmare. That was all. This just *could not* be happening. It could not be real.

Lord Clive Rutger took a step toward her. She shriveled against the bulkhead. All of those old fears of being hurt by a man were reignited again in a full, petrifying blaze.

All of those fears that had finally been put to rest by Caspian's love.

Where was Caspian? Why was he not here, protecting her, saving her from this wretched man like he had promised her he would do?

Lord Rutger sneered at her and when he saw Reed lying on the bed he grabbed her by the top of her arm. Rutger dragged her out of the cabin. Eden struggled to take one last look at Reed. She knew she should scream, but the sound would wake Reed and she did not want the poor, sweet boy involved in her issues. He would not be hurt by this evil man if she had any say in the matter.

"What were you doing inside the Captain's cabin, you blasted little trollop? Are you his new mistress? Is this how you are paying for your voyage? I know your father told me none of his money was missing when you left so you had to have paid for your voyage in some other way."

Clive sneered at her, and she wished she could slap him in the face. But the last time she had done that, it had only triggered a rather harsh beating from the monster. How could she stop him from saying such horrible things about her character? She had done nothing to deserve these atrocious, degrading words.

"Why you ... how dare you?" Her voice cracked, it was so terribly dry.

She could not scream. Her throat failed her. This was a nightmare and there was nothing she could do to stop it from happening. She was forced to go through this horrible experience yet again.

Lord Rutger seized her by the waist and threw her over his shoulder like he would a sack of potatoes—a battered sack of potatoes.

Eden kicked and clawed, trying frantically to obtain her freedom. Her nails dug into his skin, drawing blood, but he did not budge. Even though she used all of her energy, she was no match for a man's strength. She had learned that fact months ago when this exact same man had overpowered her and abused her. The only hope she had of survival was to outsmart Lord Rutger, but she saw no present opportunity and right now her mind felt so weak ... so weak with terror.

Even if she had it in her to scream, she could not. If she did, Reed would wake up and try to save her and she knew Lord Rutger would hurt him without a second thought. She could not let that happen. Reed's life was much more important than hers, so she watched helplessly as she was dragged to the top deck of her Caspian's ship.

Clive positioned her differently in his arms and a ship

moving directly next to Caspian's was brought into her line of vision. The deck bowed underneath them, causing Clive to stagger. Rutger caught his balance and threw her to the deck of the other ship. She realized she was too far away from the cabin to wake Reed, but she could still cry for help and maybe one of Caspian's sailors would come to her aid.

Her weak scream was strangled.

She hit the floor with a thud. Pain knifed through her shoulder and the breath was knocked out of her lungs.

Clive jumped beside her. Eden struggled to rise. The second she filled her lungs with air, she screamed with all of her might. It was a pathetic little noise, but at least it was something. She could only pray Caspian had heard her.

She knew he had not.

Rutger slapped a hand over her mouth and dragged her away to what she assumed was his cabin. She tried to grab at the bulkheads along the way but her hands kept slipping.

He opened a door and threw her onto a bed.

She screamed.

He gave her a violent backhand that sent her sprawling from the bed onto the floor. She cowered as the ship lurched. They were speeding away. Away from hope. Away from life. Away from Caspian.

* * *

Gage was not sure why, but he had trouble falling asleep that night. He rose from his hammock and patrolled the companionways of the ship.

His stomach was queasy. Was that a cry he heard echoing

around the ship? He rushed above decks only to notice the reflective white sails of a ship was speeding off into the night. The scream had probably come from the other vessel. Maybe an amputation was occurring over there. It was odd that another ship was sailing so near to them, but under the cover of night, he supposed it was easy to accidentally drift next to another ship.

Gage headed back below decks. There was no sign of a struggle there. The noises were most likely just his imagination.

However, on his way back to the crew's quarters, the heart-wrenching sounds of sobbing emanated from the Captain's cabin. He paused at the door. Was it Lady Trenton? Had Caspian somehow upset the poor girl? Should he interfere? Maybe not.

Gage knocked on the door anyway. Caspian might be angry with him for interfering, but if the man was treating Lady Trenton poorly for some odd reason, it would be best for Gage to put a stop to it, whatever it may be.

"Lady Trenton? I trust all is well, milady?" He called, resting his forehead on the rough wood of the door.

The sobbing continued.

Gage opened the door a crack and when no one objected, he moved it an inch further.

Reed was face down on the bed, weeping into a pillow.

Gage shoved the door aside and sat down beside the distraught child. The boy spun around to face him. His blond curls were soaked with tears. His blue eyes sparkled and his little cheeks were stained red.

"Whatever is wrong, little man?" Gage brushed the hair away from the boy's eyes. Reed threw his skinny little arms around Gage's neck.

"I ... I had a bad dream, Mister Gage," he murmured shyly.

"What happened in it?" Gage urged gently. He loved children and was glad to interact with one whenever he could. If only he could find a suitable, respectable woman to marry he would have a little family by now. But, unfortunately, that was not the case, at least not yet.

"In my dream, Miss Eden was ... she was taken away by someone bad. A very bad man. He was hurting her and when I woke up, she was gone. Papa isn't here, either. No one was here."

Gage awkwardly hugged the boy. "It's all right, Reed. Lady Trenton is safe: I am sure of it. She is off somewhere with your papa, I think. I have not seen either of them in a while, but I am certain both of them are safe."

The boy studied him for a moment, and then let out a sigh. "Mr. Gage?"

"Yes?"

"Do you think Papa and Miss Eden like each other, Mr. Gage?"

Gage squeezed his eyes shut for a moment. "Yes, I believe so, Reed. I pray both of them will only realize that." He patted Reed on the back. "Now go back to sleep. I will stay here by you until you do. The captain and Lady Trenton will be back here soon I am sure. You just relax."

* * *

Lord Rutger sauntered toward her.

Eden backed away, screeching, "Get away from me. Please,

let me go!" She did not know why she begged him so. No amount of pleading with the man ever seemed to work. He actually seemed to derive pleasure from hearing her terrified pleas.

He loosened his cravat and removed his coat. "Well, my intended, are you excited for tomorrow? I know how utterly anxious you have been to become my bride." He sneered down his thin nose at her.

Eden shivered. She could not become this horrible man's wife.

She had vowed never to marry a man, but she … she discovered she would marry Caspian the second he asked her if only he cared enough to ask her. But of course he did not. He probably roved from one woman to another with how often he left on all of his voyages. Why, he probably did not want to commit to a woman any more after what had happened with his poor wife.

"I believe I have made it clearer than crystal that I will never consent to marry you as long as I live." Eden sent a cold glare his way.

"And why would you care if you marry me or not? You have no right to object. In all reality, you should be glad I will have you, soiled goods that I know you are."

Tears stung her eyes at his dig to her character, but she chose fury in place of self-pity. "How dare you speak like that? Nothing about me is soiled and you know that for a fact, sir!"

"Says the captain's whore." He sat down on the edge of the bed.

Eden felt herself blush; knowing she had kissed Caspian and let him hold her … and told him she loved him. She still found that last part rather shocking to believe.

Yet she had done nothing wrong! There was absolutely nothing immoral with innocently kissing a man as she had done. Besides, there was no way Lord Rutger had of knowing what had happened between her and Caspian. He was assuming far too much.

Eden raised her hand to slap him, but he rose and grabbed her arm, twisting it behind her violently. She bit back a cry of pain at the sharp shock that riveted through her.

"Now, listen to me, my *intended.* We shall marry tomorrow and you will obey me and be mine for the rest of your life." He sank his iron-like hands onto her waist so tightly it felt like he was crushing her insides and her bones. "Ah, you are not used to obeying a man, are you, my little flower?"

"I would not marry you even if you were the very last man on this wretched earth!" she spat at him, seething with anger.

Eden tried to wrench her arm free from his grasp but he struck her yet again. She sucked in a deep breath to keep the tears from spilling out of her eyes. Long ago she had learned that her tears only gave the man's twisted mind pleasure, although maybe if she just gave into the tears, the beating would finally come to an end.

"You have no right to choose whom you marry and you have no right to speak to me like that, *my little flower!* You will marry me or your little captain from that ship will die. That little boy who was sleeping in your cabin, also. I will make sure the boy's death is especially slow and long." He chortled. "You know that you and your father need my money. You know no other wealthy lord will propose to you when they hear what you have been doing, whoring yourself to this … this … *pirate.*" His nasally voice shook in anger.

Eden found herself backing away.

That tone of voice meant she would be struck yet again. She wanted to go cower in a corner, let him hit her again and again just so it would be over finally. But no. There was no way she would back down and be some weak little thing he could bully anymore. All that had ever led to was her running away from life … from everything, and she would not have it anymore. Eden had done enough running, whether it be from an argument with a friend or a life and death situation with Lord Clive Rutger. No. She would cower in the shadows no longer.

"I will die first and there is no way you could ever overpower Caspian, I can promise you that!"

"Ah, the blasted man's name is Caspian, then. How *sweet* of you to use his Christian name. And you just proved to me you do hold some affection for him! Well, I assure you I will make him regret ever taking you aboard his ship if you refuse to marry me. You just mark my words, little flower!" He roared, shaking her by the shoulders until she felt dizzy.

"I—I …" Eden found it impossible to say anything more. How could she have given Caspian away? Why, she had virtually just forced herself into marrying this … this fiend by revealing that she cared even a little about Caspian. She knew if she refused Rutger's proposal he would stop at nothing to track down Caspian and Reed and kill them … after he beat her to near death, most likely. There was nothing to do to avoid this fate anymore. Nothing.

"Yes. That is much better, woman. I think I rather like hearing nothing from you." He leaned closer to her, a cruel smirk on his face. His emerald green eyes sparkled. "Now while you are being silent, how about you use your pretty mouth to give a nice little kiss to your dear husband, *my flower?"*

Eden recoiled in disgust. The foul man had forced her to kiss him many times before and each time she hated it even more than the last. She certainly did not want to relive the experience.

Eden decided she would never let her lips be tainted by another man's touch and she would definitely not be spoiled by Lord Rutger. She wanted to save everything she had for Caspian and Caspian alone, if he would have her.

Rutger leaned his head down toward hers, his mouth slanting downward. His hands grasped her waist and his thumbs roved around her body, taking far too many liberties. She had to stop this. Immediately.

Sucking up all of the saliva she could find in her mouth, she spat at the monster as hard as she could. The thick liquid hit him square in the face, dripping down into his eyes.

Clive sputtered for a moment, a look of pure disgust and anger on his face, before he raised his arm and struck her across the mouth, hard. He spun on his heel and stormed out of the cabin, practically growling in anger.

Although Eden felt the sting and the sharp, bitter taste of blood in her mouth where her teeth had cut her lip from his strike, she could not stop herself from giggling. He had seemed horrified that she had even thought of spitting on him.

And the man most certainly had deserved it.

Chapter 17

L ord Clive Rutger stood at the bow of his ship, fuming. That fool of a woman was not to be tolerated. How dare she be so disrespectful of him? No woman spat upon him and got away with it. No woman ran away from him and got away with it. The last time someone had acted like that, it had been his own father. And Clive deeply regretted that he had been too small then to make the man pay for his thoughtless actions.

He sometimes wished that Lady Trenton did not force him to beat her, but if he did not do it, she would be more than out of control.

The reckless woman's father should have disciplined her more when she was a child. Really, she had to learn that she needed to obey the men in her life because they were only put there to help her. If only she had just done her father's bidding, Clive himself would not have been forced to hurt her. She just needed to learn how to obey and they would have a long, happy marriage.

If it worked out differently than his parent's marriage.

But it would, because he loved Eden.

Since Clive could remember, his father had beaten both him and his mother. He told him it was just to teach them a lesson and that once they learned it, the beatings would stop. But they did not. Whatever lesson it was, they seemed to fail in learning it. The beatings had just gotten worse as he got older and his father picked up a drinking habit.

One night, when Clive was eight years old, his father had come home, reeking of whiskey. Clive had mistakenly not done his chores that day and his sire was not happy with that fact. He thrashed young Clive until he was sobbing and bleeding and his mother woke. His mother came into the room and begged her husband to stop … but instead, he turned to the woman and in a fit of rage for defying him, pulled out a knife, and stabbed her to death. Right in front of Clive's young eyes, he murdered the child's own mother and taught him how to be a man.

Clive ran away from his father that night and spent two years begging on the streets of London before, in a twist of events, he was taken in by an earl and his wife who longed for children but had never had any little ones of their own. When the man had died in a carriage accident, eighteen year old Clive became a wealthy earl, and every day he had regretted not giving his birth father what he deserved for shaming him so.

Even though he did not get his retribution on his father, Lady Eden Trenton would get what she deserved for shaming him. He would tame the little flower's wild nature no matter what the cost.

* * *

Caspian could not sleep. Despite the discomfort of the crates he had been resting on, he knew he would still have the same problem. He had spent his fair share of days sleeping in obscure places. No, it was not the discomfort at all. It was the woman.

He could not stop thinking of her.

He could not stop thinking about how soft, how utterly perfect and *right* she had felt in his arms.

He should not have left her up there, alone, without telling her where he was spending the night. The poor, dear woman was probably out of her mind with worry. If she even cared about him. Maybe she had not even noticed that he was missing. She certainly always seemed happy to be in Reed's company and not his.

But she had said that she loved him, however disoriented she had been that night. He had to see her. In all reality, he should not leave her alone like that. Caspian climbed up the stairs and marched across the companionway to his cabin. The sun was rising, casting a soft pink hue over the ship.

Caspian hoped she was not asleep ... which was selfish, in all reality, because the poor woman needed her rest. But he wanted to talk to her. He found he had begun to crave her companionship. He could only hope she was thinking the same of him.

His hand hovered over the thick oak slab as he thought. Did he truly want to wake her? She was probably sleeping, and from what had happened in the past, the woman did not enjoy being woken from her sleep. Caspian chuckled at how upset she had been with him and how she had slapped his hands away. The woman was all the prettier when she got all riled up with him. He loved how her cheeks turned pink and those pretty brown doe eyes flashed in fury.

Just before he could knock to give her some warning of his arrival, the door burst open. Gage stepped out of the cabin. A grin sped across his face like it did whenever he saw his captain and best friend. The man never seemed to be without a smile.

"Hello, Captain! I haven't seen you in a while," he greeted cheerfully.

"Blast it, man, you startled me." Caspian frowned. What had the man been doing in his captain's cabin? In the middle of the night, while the beautiful Lady Trenton was sleeping in there?

"I am sorry, Captain. I just … I did not mean to alarm you. Umm … Lady Trenton is …" The man's eyes searched around the companionway, a worried look tightening his features.

What was going on here? Caspian had to get to the bottom of this immediately.

"Hang it, Gage, what were you doing in my cabin? You know I do not permit anyone to go in there without my bidding, not even you," Caspian stated.

He did not believe Gage, his best friend, would hurt Eden, but he could never take any chances with the woman he loved. Surely it was all some innocent mistake. Caspian peeked through the door. Reed was sleeping alone on the bed, curled onto his side. Caspian's gaze swept over the cabin but the beautiful woman was nowhere in sight. That was certainly a change.

And most likely a problem. Why would Eden be out of the

cabin at this time of night? Something was wrong. Utterly wrong.

Panic began to run through Caspian's body in thick, sharp waves. It had to be Kelton. Where had the blasted man dragged her off to now? Kelton had been locked up into the hold …

But why had Caspian not heard her screams? The only reason could be that Kelton had hurt her too much for her screams to be heard …

Caspian's heart accelerated to a rapid pace. Gage remained silent, looking down. His expression was hidden by a shadow.

"Why were you in my cabin, Mr. Thompson? What have you done with Eden? Where is she? Where's Lady Trenton?" Caspian's voice shook with emotion but he did not care if he appeared weak in front of a member of his crew, even if he was his first mate. He loved Eden and he had to discover why she was gone and where she was. There was nothing weak about being in love with a woman.

"I-I, but, I had thought-" Gage stammered.

"Quit your stuttering already, man. Where is Eden—Lady Trenton?"

"I heard a scream coming from your cabin and the door was unlocked so I entered, afraid someone was hurt. Your son had just had a nightmare, though, but he was sobbing, so I consoled him. He was terrified something was wrong because he had woken up and neither you nor Lady Trenton was there with him." Gage's words sped out of his mouth rapidly, like minnows darting into a reef.

"And Eden? What of her? Why was she not there? Where is she?"

"I had … assumed that … that she was safe with you somewhere …"

"Well, you assumed wrongly, Mr. Thompson! We must find her! Send a few trustworthy men to search with us. I'll ask Reed if he knows anything and then help search. It must have been that blasted Kelton! I thought I told you to put him in the hold and post a guard …"

Gage left, his head down, and Caspian barreled into the cabin to shake his little son awake. He hated waking the child so early in the morning, especially after he knew he had been awake with a nightmare, but he needed to get to the bottom of what was happening. Caspian had to find Eden and save her from whoever had stolen her.

"Good morning, Papa." The boy beamed at him, stretching. He yawned. "What time is it, Papa? It feels almost as if I just fell asleep." Reed peered around the room with cute, sleepy eyes.

"Where is Eden, Reed? Lady Trenton? Where has she gone?" Caspian brushed a lock of tawny hair out of his son's face.

"You mean Miss Eden, Papa?" He rubbed his eyes.

"Aye."

"I saw her before I went to sleep. She tucked me in and kissed me good-night like always. Then I had a really bad dream that some horrible man was hurting Miss Eden and when I woke up, she was gone. Master Thompson came in and he told me she was with you so I wasn't worried. She is with you, right, Papa? Miss Eden is all right, right?"

Dread clenched its bony fingers around Caspian's heart.

She was gone.

Kelton had stolen her.

She was probably lying somewhere, naked, on his own ship, sobbing, sullied. Broken.

Whatever was happening, he was certainly too late to save

her.

But not too late to punish Kelton.

He was not certain he would be able to stop himself from killing Kelton if he found out the man had done something to harm her …

"Stay right here, Reed, and do not leave unless I tell you to. I will go find Miss Eden." He could only hope she would be safe and sound when he found her, but he feared she already was not.

* * *

Gage stepped onto the main deck. He had assigned three men—the ones he trusted most to not hurt Eden, should she be found—to search for her below decks. Gage wandered above, searching in every nook and cranny he could think of for Lady Trenton, but to no avail. Where could the woman have run off to? She had all but vanished into thin air.

Gage scanned the deck. He spotted Hawthorne, the night watchmen, dozing on the main deck.

"Hawthorne!" He barked. The man leapt up, a startled expression written across his face.

"Aye, Master Gage?" The stout man rubbed a lump that was protruding from the top of his head.

Had there been a fight below decks that Gage and Caspian had not been aware of? That was odd. Hawthorne was not normally one to get into disagreements with other men.

"What happened to you?" Gage inquired, leaning forward to examine the wound.

"I-I'm not certain of that, Master Gage. I'd been a'sleepin' peacefully, when I woke to a noise. After lookin' around I saw there was a ship pulled next to us. Just as I ran to tell the Cap'n, I got knocked in me head! That's 'bout all I remember."

"Thank you, Mr. Hawthorne. That will be all. I will let the Captain deal with your laziness later."

Hawthorne gulped but stomped away.

Gage leapt down from the forecastle deck and hurried toward the Captain's cabin.

Someone must have stolen Lady Trenton. Otherwise why would there have been a ship next to theirs and why would someone have knocked Hawthorne unconscious?

The poor girl. Who would have taken her?

In his rush to the captain's cabin, Gage ran straight into Caspian. The poor man's eyes were red-rimmed and moist with tears. Gage had never seen his captain this upset, not even when his wife had died. Sure, he had been clearly upset that day, but he had not been reduced to tears in the presence of any members of his crew. It showed he truly did care something about Lady Trenton. A lot.

"Any news of her, my friend?" Caspian asked, rubbing the moisture from his eyes. His voice shook with emotion. Gage felt sorry for his captain and best friend.

"Aye, Caspian. Hawthorne saw a ship right next to ours. He was knocked unconscious went he came to alert you. I am guessing Lady Trenton was stolen."

Chapter 18

Ivy scurried up onto deck that night, deep in thought. She stepped up to the railing and glanced at the full moon that illuminated the black seas and washed the deck with a pale blue light.

She liked the calming rush of the water against the hull and she would do anything to be relaxed. It had been quite a few nights since she had last slept peacefully. Ever since they had left for Port Royal, she had been beside herself with worry. Of course Ivy was still worried about her brother's safety, but the gnawing fear inside of her belly had been not only for little William as of late. No, she had a sinking feeling something terrible was happening to Eden. It seemed like they should have found her days ago.

Her thoughts were interrupted and she started when the sound of scuffling boots came from behind her.

* * *

Matthew's footsteps seemed loud in the silence of the night as he paced about the deck. He had adopted the restless habit of pacing ever since a certain beautiful blond woman had stepped aboard his merchantman. His steps halted when he passed by Lady Shaw. Her hands were folded together and her face was tightly drawn.

"You couldn't sleep either, Lady Shaw?" he inquired, stepping up next to her.

"Nay, not with Eden in such grave danger."

"I understand." To his shame, Matthew's sleeping troubles were caused by something entirely different than worrying about Lady Trenton, however. There was just something about that blond beauty that was sleeping below on his ship that made his heart beat faster.

What was the matter with him? She was nothing but a spoiled, useless little girl like most women were. Something must be wrong with him. Maybe she had put some type of a spell on him, like a little witch.

"I am so worried about her, Captain Emery. What if Lord Rutger finds her before we do? Surely he will murder her and cover it up as a drowning or something because of the disgrace she has caused him. And, she stowed away passage on a ship—only the Good Lord knows what kind. Perhaps she was found and the crew attacked her. Mayhap she has faced her death already!" Ivy ranted, holding a hand to her hair, which was wound tightly into a proper bun.

"Milady, I know how easy it is to worry, and, may God forgive me, I am certainly worried about her also, but we must place our complete and whole trust in God. We have not found her yet. All we can do to help Lady Trenton for now is pray."

* * *

Eden sat on the bed, realizing she was far too terrified to sleep, yet her body was utterly exhausted. Rutger would return sometime soon for sure, and she wanted to be awake should he decide to attack her. She would not be left defenseless when he did.

She hugged herself against the constant chill she had felt ever since Lord Rutger had found her.

Was this what the rest of her life on this earth would be like? Lying in bed, terrified that her own husband would come home and attack her? If life went on like this, there was a large chance she would die of exhaustion and starvation before she was beaten to death by the man, if that was what it would come to be. She knew she would have no appetite any time soon with how much anxiety she was experiencing. It looked as if death was quite possible in her near future, and she had never even been given the chance to say so much as a farewell to Caspian.

Caspian.

She could only imagine how worried Caspian would be at the moment. If he truly cared about her. He had told her he loved her, but Lord Rutger had also. Those were just words. But she was certain some part of him did care … oh, what would she do, bound to a man other than Caspian all of her life? Eden would never know what it would be like to be his wife, to be the wife of a man who actually cared about her. *Oh, Caspian …*

Before Eden even knew it, her heavy eyelids drooped shut and she fell into a nightmare-ridden sleep.

* * *

Caspian swore under his breath.

He had spotted Hawthorne sleeping on duty but had not scolded him because he was as giddy as a blasted schoolboy who had just kissed his sweetheart for the first time. If Caspian had woken the man, Eden would still be safe in his cabin, under his protection.

He had failed Eden. Just like he had failed Isabelle. He clenched his fists, realizing he was shaking with anger. If he could not even manage to protect the dear women in his life, then how on earth was he supposed to care for a five year old boy, even if the boy was his own son?

"Who do you suspect took her, Captain?" Gage shuffled his feet.

"I don't know, Gage. I have no idea." Who would have something so against Eden they would steal her off of his ship in such an underhanded manner?

He vowed he would make whoever it was pay dearly for harming his love.

* * *

Caspian averted his gaze, but not before Gage saw the sheen of moisture pool in his eyes. The Captain was a strong man, but he was not beyond tearing up for this woman a second time in one night. Gage's already high opinion of her grew even larger.

"She certainly is a beautiful woman, Caspian. I don't blame

you for missing her," Gage offered.

"It is not just that, Gage. Well, from the beginning, I was attracted to her. What man wouldn't be? As you admitted, she is quite beautiful. But I do love her; I am certain of it. I cannot lose her. Not like this. Not now. Not when …"

Caspian whirled around suddenly and leapt up to the main deck, interrupting his own sentence. Gage followed right behind, concerned at how distressed his captain seemed.

Hawthorne was sitting on the main deck when they arrived there.

"Hawthorne!" Caspian bellowed, his face already an angry shade of red before even getting a response from the unfortunate night watchman.

"Aye, Cap'n!" The poor man leapt up onto his feet in a flash, startled, and backed away.

Gage knew Hawthorne could tell Caspian's despair had turned into fury in the blink of an eye. Any shrewd crew member knew the telltale signs: clenched fists and jaw, and a reddened face. Sadly, the crew saw them far too often for Gage's liking. But this wasn't just anger. Concern was mixed in, as well.

"Quit your cowering, man, and step forward already. I thought I recruited *men* to work in my crew, not a bunch of milksops," barked Caspian.

"Aye, Cap'n. My apologies." Hawthorne gulped and stepped forward ever so slightly, lowering his head.

"Did you see in which direction the ship you failed to warn me about sailed?"

"It looked t' be goin' back east some points, Cap'n."

"Thank you, sir. You will receive your punishment for sleeping while on your shift later."

Chapter 18

* * *

Aimee sat perched on the ledge by the porthole, watching the sun set. It cast hues of crimson, coral, and canary yellow across the sea. A knock sounded on the door.

"Who is it?" She called pleasantly.

"'Tis Captain Emery, milady."

Letting out a long, exasperated breath, she rose and opened the thick oak slab. "What is it you want, sir?" She could not help how harsh her voice came out. Besides, she did not care.

A hard sheen covered his eyes—those eyes that would be such a beautiful shade of midnight blue if they had belonged to anyone but this conceited little man. "I came to escort you to dinner, princess. Unless, of course, you want to go without your meals from now on. I, for one, must say that I wouldn't care if you chose to do so."

She gave him a venomous glare. How dare the man call her a princess? Captain Emery had no idea of anything about her. He had come to horrible conclusions that had nothing to do with her real self. But what could she do to stop him? There was nothing she could think of. "Where, pray tell, is Ivy? I have not seen her lately." Aimee peered over his shoulder, wondering if her friend was there.

"I met Lady Shaw on the deck. She is already in my cabin. Now, if you would just allow me to escort you to dinner …" He held out his bent elbow, obviously intending for her to put her hand inside of it.

She did not.

"Nay." She threw a hand to her forehead only somewhat melodramatically. "I fear I have developed a sudden headache,

Captain Emery. I will dine alone in here, if you please. One of your men can bring me my meal, if he would be so kind."

"You always manage to obtain a headache when you are in my presence. Forgive me for being such a nuisance to your health. As I have learned, everything revolves around you and I would hate to disrupt that for you. Ivy has informed me you are in absolute perfect health whenever I am not around," he replied dryly.

Without a single word of farewell, the grumpy man spun on his heel and hustled out of the room, slamming the heavy door behind him in a rather childish manner.

* * *

"All hands on deck! Immediately!" Caspian cried, stomping across the forecastle deck. He listened as Gage parroted his order to the crew.

Caspian moved to the helmsman. "Smithson, turn her hard to larboard. Now!"

"Aye, Cap'n. Hard to larboard."

Caspian moved away from the helm to see that his crew had appeared on the main deck, grumbling, but there. He supposed it would be better than nothing. They had a precious lady to rescue.

"Unfurl all top-gallants, men! Get to work! I want every inch of canvas spread! We haven't a minute to spare!" Both anger and urgency surged through Caspian's veins at once. He had a feeling that he knew exactly who had stolen his priceless Eden. Once he found this Lord Rutger, he vowed to kill the knave. What kind of man would attack a woman like he did—

a young, sweet, loving, gentle, innocent girl—and then have the audacity to track her down and kidnap her after she had risked her life to escape him? Why could the man not just leave her be and let her start a new life in the colonies? The dear woman never seemed to ask much of anybody. Why could she not be granted her one simple request?

He tried with all his might to pray for Eden's safety, but he was not sure he knew how to appeal to the Almighty. Would the Lord even listen to his battered attempt at a prayer? Caspian had never been good with words.

It had been a long while since Caspian had even thought about talking to his heavenly Father, but he knew he had to start somewhere in order to find Eden, for he finally realized he never had any hope of doing it on his own.

Chapter 19

E den realized she must have finally fallen asleep that night for she woke when sunlight began sprinkling in through a porthole, just as Rutger came staggering into the cabin.

"Ah, there's my pretty young bride. I have been searching for you all around the *sh-ship*. Are you ready for our wedding-ceremony?" His voice was slurred drunkenly.

A stab of guilt shot through her heart. She had obviously angered Lord Rutger into overindulging in drink. No matter how horrible a man he was to begin with, she did not like to think she could do something like that to a man.

"Here is your dress for our wedding; I brought it along for you. It used to belong to my second mother, Countess Althea Rutger. Change into it and then prepare to say your vows." He pulled an elegant dress out of a cedar chest in the far end of the cabin, stumbling as the ship rocked over a wave. The gown was a rich lavender taffeta embellished with white lace and beads and held out with layers of petticoats. It would have been a pretty dress on any other occasion, but a wave of nausea struck her at the sight of it.

She could not make herself put the dress on.

She could not physically do it.

Eden ran her hand over the smooth fabric and then took a deep breath. "No, I cannot wear that dress. Please, no-"

Her voice was cut off by Rutger's fist slamming into her jaw. She could not stifle her raw cry of pain. Ever since he had found her, Rutger had taken to beating her in more obvious places. He probably thought it did not matter if he made marks on her face anymore, since she had no way of escaping him now.

"You can and you *will* wear this dress, even if I have to strip you and dress you in it myself. If you don't hurry about it, I will be doing it for you quite soon, my little flower."

"What have I ever done to make you treat me so? Do you truly want to spend the rest of your life with a woman who hates you? Please, Clive, I do not want to do this. I cannot do this," she sobbed at him, trying to plead to some inner decency that she knew could no longer exist inside the man.

"You were *promissed* to me and I will finally have you, woman. Do not think that your weak, pathetic *liess* will help you in any way. You will not leave me like you did before. No, you will become my wife, and we will be together until our last days. *Trusst* me, my little flower. You will grow to love me in time like I love you. You *jusst* have to learn to love me. Besides, I will never *ss-strike* you again if you will only obey me like I ask of you. A wife must learn to be obedient. But no matter. When you *off-officially* pledge your life to mine, you will be vowing to obey your husband. You won't have to worry about me *s-striking* you if only you will be the wife you ought to be.

"Now, my flower, you will change your dress and join me on the main deck for your wedding." He stumbled toward her. "Come now, Eden. Do not fight me, and you will find I will make you quite the happy woman."

He paused, studying her. She knew he could tell she recoiled in disgust from him. Maybe he was right, though. If she was a little more agreeable toward him, maybe he would be kinder and her life would not be filled with endless beatings. But she could never love him. There was no way she could ever love a man who beat her and constantly insulted her character. No, she could never even think about loving a man other than Caspian.

"Ah, but you like your captain, don't you? Is that what you were thinking about? I knew there was something going on between you and that man. Well, if you do not marry me, I shall have to report your captain to the authorities. He shall be tried and found guilty of piracy. Ah, yes, it would be quite satisfying to see his carcass hanging. Besides, I am sure you will see soon enough that I am much better of a man than he could ever be." Clive leaned forward, tugging a strand of hair out of her eyes. His breath reeked of wine.

She remained still. "You would not. Besides, they would never believe you. There is no reason to! I am so sorry to foil your wicked plot, but Captain Archer is a privateer, not a pirate." She raised her chin and stood up to her full, intimidating stature of five foot three. It did not seem to have the intended effect.

"They will believe a nobleman's word before a privateer's any day, my flower. Who would have the insanity to believe a glorified pirate? Marry me unless you wish to see your precious captain hanging." His hands gripped her waist so

212

tightly she had no hope of breaking the bond.

"Maybe they would believe a nobleman over a privateer, you are correct—that is, a nobleman by birth, not a peasant by birth like you." Eden felt horrible speaking like a spoiled, wealthy girl, but she would not let the man stand by and say such things about Caspian.

"Why you lying, conniving little witch! How dare you speak of such things?" He struck her across the chest with his arm so hard she was sent flying and all the air was forced out of her lungs. She hit the floor with a dull *thud*.

* * *

"A sail, Cap'n, a sail!" Sults climbed down from his position in the crow's nest with all of the skill of a monkey.

"Where away, Sults?" Caspian inquired, squinting off at the horizon.

"Three points off our starboard bow, Captain."

"Johnson, steer her three points to starboard!"

"Aye, Cap'n. Three points to starboard," the stout man parroted, wiping his forehead with a bandana that was tied about his wrist.

They were approaching the ship. Gaining on it.

A fresh sense of anxiety swept through Caspian. He would not fail this time. He would save the woman he loved.

He gazed at the ship through his telescope. What was that flicker of white on the faraway deck? A high-pitched voice was muffled by the still great distance. There was no doubt it was a female voice. Eden? Could it be?

"Man the swivel guns!" he shouted.

Caspian strained his eyes for a glimpse of his Eden. She had to be aboard that ship. He somehow knew it, deep inside.

"She is nearly within our range, now, Captain," Gage reported.

"Perfect. Tell Mitchell to aim for her gun deck. I do not want any flesh wounds. My intention is only to disarm them at the moment. Be watchful, however, because I may change my mind after a while."

"Aye, Captain." Gage relayed the orders to Mitchell, Caspian's master gunner.

The ship shook as the cannons fired. He anxiously waited for the thick smoke that he had become accustomed to smelling to clear so he could see the damage that had been done.

* * *

Thirty minutes later, after recovering from the tumble she had taken on account of her fiancé, Eden stood on the main deck of the ship Lord Rutger had hired to find her. Her body ached all over from the beating Lord Rutger had doled out last night. It was a familiar ache, one she had come to know too well in the past few months.

Please, God. Please save me from this somehow.

Rubbing her bruised ribs gingerly, Eden glanced up at the sky. Pink and orange tinted clouds soared high above her. Dawn was breaking. A smile spread across her face when she remembered a blissful day only a week or so ago. Caspian had roused her early and persuaded her to watch the sun rise with him. She had come to truly enjoy the mornings at sea. Except for this one, of course.

She snorted when she remembered the first time Caspian had woken her early in the morning. In all reality, she had been quite rude to him. Her mind shifted back to the morning they had spent watching the sun rise together. He had wrapped his strong arms around her, and held her tight and she had felt so safe and protected it was almost unbelievable. It was most improper, really, to feel completely and utterly safe in the arms of a rogue. Then again, nothing at all was proper about her Caspian ... how he dressed, how he kissed her, the way he stared at her all the time, how she felt about him deep inside ...

For goodness's sake, he was a *pirate*! How on earth *could* he be proper? Yet, she realized that was one reason why she had grown to love him. She hated society's idea of proper gentlemen. The lot of them were far too shallow. Lord Clive Rutger in particular.

Thunder shook her back into reality. Lightning knifed across the sky that was darkening by the moment. She felt the flash as if it had sliced straight through her heart. Lord Rutger grabbed her hand, gripping it tightly, and the man in front of them began the ceremony. He still smelled of wine, but he had seemed to gather himself in the last hour. His words were no longer slurred and he stood more steadily.

Was it wrong of her to pray for lightning to strike a man?

Eden squeezed her eyes shut against the onslaught of tears that threatened to shatter the brave façade she had stubbornly built. She had done all that was within her power to escape this beast. And now she would be his wife. A shiver creaked through her body. What a great way to end things.

But she must do it for Caspian. She would not be able to

live with herself as a free woman, knowing that Caspian or poor, sweet, darling Reed had died or suffered from her own selfish actions.

God, please get me out of this situation. If not for me, then for Reed. The child needs a mother and I would be so glad to provide one for him. Please.

"A sail, Captain! A sail!" The shout drifted from the shrouds above.

"Be silent already, man! I will not tolerate any interruptions on my wedding day! I thought I told all the men that already!" Lord Rutger swung around, his face turning red. His grip on her hand could have crunched her bones into powder.

Rutger twisted to face the captain standing in front of them. "On with the ceremony!"

The captain before them was tall and thin, with curling blond hair and blue eyes. He appeared to be quite bored with the situation and far more interested in the sails on the horizon than with the wedding vows he was reading.

Eden fidgeted with the borrowed lavender dress and chewed on her bottom lip. Sweat trickled down her back and a lock of long hair blew across her face in the gusty wind, tickling her nose. She grabbed the strands and twirled them about her finger. A glance over Lord Rutger's shoulder revealed a ship approaching them at a fast rate. It almost looked like … like they were being pursued.

She held her breath and dared not to let her hopes up by thinking that perhaps Caspian had come to save her. If she did, it would only make the pain that much more palpable when the ship passed by without a second glance.

Rutger removed his hand from hers and placed it on her waist as the captain in front of them opened a book and began to read out loud. A light, steady rain began to fall from the sky, darkening Eden's mood all the more.

Why should she think Caspian would waste his time to come rescue her? She was not anything special. Rutger proved that every time he hit her. Why would Caspian go out of his way in order to save her? He had business to tend to in Port Royal. Surely he was too concerned about exacting revenge for his wife's tragic death. Why, he would not be interested in saving some useless girl—a stowaway—from her own fiancé.

Besides, how could he know where she had gone to? He had no apparent way of knowing. It was most likely that he just assumed she had fallen overboard and drowned. Who would ever think she had actually been snatched straight out of Caspian's own cabin?

Her thoughts drifted back to reality again when Lord Rutger snatched her hands, pulling them away from where they had unconsciously become entangled in her hair. The man had forced her to wear her hair down and loose, like a normal bride, as if this were a typical wedding in a church. He clucked his tongue and leaned forward to whisper into her ear, "We don't want you pulling out those beautiful locks, my little flower."

Eden refused to look into his eyes and instead turned her head aside. She did not wish to see the lust and greed in the emerald depths.

Eden glanced at the horizon out of the corner of her eye. The ship was near, so near. 'Twas obvious she was approaching them; why did Lord Rutger do nothing? Her eyes moved to the hull of the ship. She squinted to make out the name: *Dawn's Mist.*

Caspian.

Thank you, God. Thank you, thank you, thank you.

He had come for her.

He had come to rescue her from Lord Rutger!

A loud blast rent the air. The racket was shortly followed by the deck shaking riotously beneath her feet.

Clive whirled around. A string of foul curses spewed from his mouth and then he backhanded Eden, but she was too busy grinning like a fool to feel the sharp sting.

Caspian had come for her. Why, he truly did love her! He had not abandoned her! She would not have to marry this horrible man any longer. Maybe … maybe Caspian would even consider marrying her in Clive's stead.

Lord Rutger turned to the captain, who had shut his book and appeared about ready for battle. "Do something, man! I will not have my *wedding* interrupted by a foolish little battle. Who is this, anyway?"

The captain ran a finger over his blond moustache. "Well, sir, whoever it is does not appear friendly. I don't know if this is avoidable. I can't just sit here performing your wedding ceremony while me ship is attacked, now can I?"

Clive fumed. "Do what you must, but be quick about it. I will not have this wedding delayed any longer!" He tugged Eden closer to himself, running his hand up and down her waist.

She shivered. *Please, God. Please let Caspian save me. Please, please, please.*

"Man all the guns. Check for the damage. Fire at will!" The Captain screamed at his crew.

Most of the men disappeared below in a flash, bloodthirsty cries on their lips.

When the smoke cleared from the hit they had taken, she

noted Caspian on the forecastle deck of his handsome ship, fists planted firmly on his hips. She couldn't resist a smile at him, the picture of confidence.

She moved closer to the rail for a better view.

The ship shook as the captain called his men to fire upon Caspian. Eden covered her ears and coughed as the smoke entered her lungs.

She prayed that the shots had not hit Caspian's ship. If anyone was harmed, or … or died on her account, she would not know how to forgive herself.

Chapter 20

Anger shot through Caspian in waves as he saw the man who he assumed to be Lord Clive Rutger shove Eden down onto the deck. He had no right to hurt the sweet lady.

Eden rose and her eyes snapped to his. Caspian could not help but feel manly pride creep into his heart. He was the first person she had turned to. She could have looked to Gage, but no, she looked straight at him. That sent his heart soaring.

Caspian gave the dear woman a comforting smile and a wink, hoping she was not too frightened. He prayed that the wretched man had not hurt her badly. But this Lord Rutger would regret ever harming Lady Eden Trenton. Caspian would make sure he saw to that.

Gage turned to Caspian. "She raises her white flag, Captain."

Caspian had guessed that the coward would. The enemies were under-gunned, and Caspian had the element of surprise. He was glad Lord Rutger did not have a warship or something of that kind. At least rescuing Eden would not be as hard as it could have been.

"Good. Grapnels ready. Prepare to board her, armed, but do not attack until you have my command. I want to see if he will talk civilly first before we need to shed any blood."

"Very well." Gage relayed the orders to the crew.

* * *

Lord Clive Rutger appeared to be seething with anger about the interruption of his wedding.

Eden slipped away from his grasp and hugged the main mast in an attempt to be out of the way of his wrath. Caspian had told her the main mast tended to be one of the safer places on the main deck of a ship during a battle because it was at the center of the deck. It was likely a cannon ball would hit the edges of the ship before the center. She had chosen the main mast because she feared there would be some type of battle this day.

Eden watched intently as Caspian boarded the ship. He grabbed onto a rope and swung over in one quick swoop, the thick muscles in his arms bulging. Eden felt her knees weaken. He certainly was quite the handsome man. Disregarding Lord Rutger completely, Caspian sauntered straight toward her.

Everything will be over in no time, Eden reassured herself. She was safe with Caspian here. He would protect her and he would take her back to his ship where she would be safe. A cold tear of relief slid down her cheek. *Thank you, God.*

Caspian strode toward her, ignoring everyone else.

"You came for me." She could not stop the tears from pouring down her face as she gazed up at him gratefully.

Caspian enveloped her in his warm, strong embrace. He wiped her tears away with a single finger. "Of course I came for you, my love. Why would I not? I love you, sweetheart. Don't you ever forget that."

Rain began to pound down on them like a thousand tiny pebbles. Eden had completely forgotten about the storm when she had seen Caspian.

"Captain," Master Thompson's voice came out rather timidly.

Letting out a groan, Caspian faced him, releasing her.

Eden already missed the strength and warmth of his arms wrapped around her.

"What is it, Gage?"

"The crew wishes to know when we can search this ship for treasure. They await your directions, Captain."

The sea rioted, sending murky waves lapping all the way up onto the deck. It appeared that the dark sea was equally rebellious as Caspian's money-hungry crew.

"Not now," Caspian ground out, turning to face Lord Rutger with a clenched jaw and fists held tightly together. Eden had only just realized the man was approaching them. They would have to deal with him before Caspian would be able to take her back to his ship. She did not want to think about the other possibility. "And you, sir; I shall have to challenge you to a duel."

Lord Rutger snorted. "You wish to fight me for this ... this pirate's whore? I daresay she is not worth it," he sneered.

"Believe me, the *lady* is worth it. I will fight you to the death if I must because of what you did to Eden. You kidnapped her and obviously have beaten her since last night. She did not have that bruise on her cheek the last time I saw her and her lip was not cut yesterday. By fire and thunder, I saw you strike her just moments ago!"

"It was an accident. The clumsy woman simply tripped and hit her head on the deck. She has always been uncoordinated. But very well. We shall see who will die in a fight to the death. But better be warned, I have been trained extensively in sword play," Lord Rutger cautioned, a cocky smirk painted across his face.

"No, Caspian! Do not do this! Please, I can't let you die. Not when it is my fault. Please do not fight him, I beg you, Caspian." Eden gripped Caspian's arm, fighting back tears.

But Caspian looked extremely calm for a person in his situation. Almost too calm. Should she be worried or was that a good sign?

"You have naught to fear, Eden. I am the most feared pirate in the Caribbean; you know that, sweetheart. I can take care of one little English lord. I am sure of it." He winked at her.

Lord Rutger glared at Eden. "Very well."

Both men drew their swords and Rutger moved his first, swinging at Caspian's blade.

The sailors around them, Lord Rutger's hired crew and Caspian's crew, all took a step backward, forming a small circle around the two men. They shouted and cheered, some placing bets on who would win the fight.

Eden closed her eyes, fear taking over the urge to watch. She could not, would not, see Caspian come to his death before her very own eyes.

* * *

Caspian easily parried all the blows Lord Rutger sent his way. Soon the earl was panting from exertion when Caspian had barely even broken a sweat.

As Caspian fought, all he could think of was the bruise on Eden's cheek. There was no way something like that had come from a fall onto the deck. No, the monster had been beating her while Caspian wasn't there to protect her. That propelled his rage enough that he was certain he would be able to fight for hours if he was needed to.

A loud scream sounded from Caspian's and Lord Rutger's left. A feminine scream.

Both men stopped in their fight immediately.

The sailors around them all spun around, their shouts fading.

Caspian swiveled to discover Kelton bolstering a knife to Eden's throat.

Blast it, he had forgotten about the whelp! He had no doubt escaped while there was no guard over him. Why had Caspian called all hands on deck? This was *entirely* his own fault.

"Forgot about me, didn't you, *Captain?*" Kelton sneered, drawing the blade tight against Eden's delicate throat.

Her face was white with terror. Those pretty brown eyes pleaded with his.

"Don't you worry, *Captain.* Everyone seems to forget about me. Even the guard you stationed to watch me forgot. Well, from now on you will not. You see, I will be taking your ship. And your little stowaway here. She shall serve nicely as my mistress, don't you think?" He leaned his head into Eden's hair, which was down, loose like a bride's.

A tear cut its path down Eden's pale cheek, mingling with the rain that was pouring down.

Caspian's gut clenched with disgust and anger. "No, I'm afraid you will not be taking my ship, boy. You would have to have the support of my crew, and from what I have seen, you have none of the sort." Caspian clenched his jaw shut tight. He needed to think of something he could do to rescue Eden. Quickly. He would not let this jackanapes take her and his ship. He *would not* leave her in his hands to be tortured.

The blade sliced deeper into her throat, drawing a trickle of cherry-red blood.

"Ah, but I will. For if you object, I will just have to kill your precious little Lady Trenton."

Eden's brown doe eyes widened and pleaded with Caspian. So trusting. So innocent. *Sweetheart, I'm not sure I have a way out of this one*, he answered with his eyes. She had such faith in him that he almost wanted to cry. He could not fail her like he had failed Isabelle. The Lord had put Eden on his ship to protect her, and he would do just that. Somehow.

Caspian wiped a sleeve across his forehead to remove a bead of sweat that had formed there, even though chills of dread spread down his spine.

"Please, Caspian. Just let him kill me. I will not have this … this *ninny* commanding your ship and I defiantly *will not* be his mistress. I would gladly die first." Fire shot from Eden's eyes as she turned her head to glare up at Kelton. That sweet voice of hers was cut off with a gargle as the blade pressed tight against her throat.

* * *

Gage crept up behind Kelton on silent feet, pistol securely in hand. If he could strike the man unconscious with one blow to the head, he could save Eden. He would just have to make certain that the blow was hard enough so he only needed to strike him once. Otherwise, the man might turn on him with the knife or dig the blade deeper into Lady Trenton's throat, no doubt killing her.

Gage knew Caspian would be proud of him if he managed to succeed in his plan.

One more step brought him almost directly behind Kelton. He retrieved the pistol from his belt and raised it above his head, but the man shifted his weight just as he was about to strike. Gage only succeeded knocking into Kelton's upper arm.

Kelton whipped his head around, roaring in rage.

Lady Trenton let out a cry of pain as she was shoved to the side by Kelton, his blade cutting into her shoulder.

The woman fell into a heap on the deck. Caspian rushed to her side.

Gage gripped Kelton's arm that was holding the knife in his hand, twisting it in order to force him to release the weapon.

He resisted, and Gage dropped his pistol in the struggle. Kelton's blade dug through the front of Gage's arm, and he stifled a cry.

Gage kicked at Kelton, preparing to punch him square in the jaw before he was cut again. He could barely hear the sounds of Lady Trenton sobbing and the Captain trying to soothe her.

After several punches, Gage dislodged the knife from Kelton's hand just as the Captain approached, fully armed.

Caspian grabbed the man by the shoulders and knocked him in the head with the hilt of his cutlass.

Gage let out a heavy breath as Kelton crumbled to the floor, unconscious at last.

* * *

Eden remained on the crate Caspian had moved her to while Master Thompson fought Kelton. Rain poured down, drenching her. She pressed her handkerchief against the cut that continued to bleed on her shoulder.

She rose but swayed under a wave of dizziness. Gage moved next to her immediately and steadied her until Caspian came and took her in his arms.

"Are you all right, sweetheart?" He inquired, studying the slice on her neck, and then moving his gaze to the deeper wound on her shoulder.

She nodded, realizing that despite the little scratch in her neck and the cut on her shoulder, she was safe now. Kelton was not going to hurt her anymore. "Thanks to Master Thompson."

Gage offered her a charming wink. He really was a sweet man.

Eden leaned forward into Caspian's chest but then glanced back over his shoulder.

Lord Rutger was approaching.

With Kelton's attack, she had almost completely forgotten about Lord Rutger. The man had sunk back like the coward he was during the tussle.

"Caspian!" She warned, gripping him around the shoulders.

Her Captain whirled around, unsheathing his cutlass and swinging it at Lord Rutger in defense.

He sliced the man's upper arm. Rutger winced and reflexively lowered his sword. It appeared he would leave them alone finally.

Caspian turned and wrapped her in his strong, warm embrace again. "Thank God you are safe," he whispered, planting a tender kiss on the center of her forehead. Caspian glanced at Gage and Eden smiled gratefully up at the grinning man.

"Thank you kindly, my friend. You saved her life. I am in debt to you, Gage." Caspian shook his first mate's hand and clapped him on the back.

Cold arms gripped Eden's waist and dragged her toward the railing. When she screamed, a vicious elbow jabbed at her stomach.

She writhed in the man's grasp, gasping out in pain. She would do anything to escape his malicious grip. Lord Rutger only chortled at her cries, drawing her closer yet and inhaling a deep breath of her hair.

Adrenaline rushed through her veins. Everything around her began to twirl in a devilish dance. She squeezed her eyes shut, trying to stop the stubborn bright lights from flashing in front of them.

"Unhand her at once!" She recognized Caspian's voice and heard him charging at them.

"Na-ah-ah, Captain. One step closer and I promise I will throw Lady Trenton to the sharks." Rutger's voice rang in her ears, hardly discernible.

Slowly, everything around her became a dark, swirling blur. The edges of her vision darkened until she could see no more.

"No!" Caspian howled, lunging at her and Lord Rutger. Eden's dizziness overtook her and she crumpled down, knocking her head on the hard wooden deck. Everything faded to a

Chapter 20

dull black.

Chapter 21

Caspian saw Eden hit the deck, but he knew she would be safer on the ground than with Lord Rutger holding her. Rain poured from the sky, soaking her unmoving body.

Caspian drew his pistol as quickly as he could, but it became stuck inside its encasement.

Lord Rutger grabbed Eden by the shoulders and lifted her lifeless form up onto the railing, leaning towards the sea.

It dawned on Caspian then. The man had every intention of throwing her overboard.

Primal anger swept through Caspian's entire body as if charged by the lightning that was cutting across the black sky. He knew it was wrong, but he found he hated this man for all he had done to Eden. She was an innocent. She deserved none of this.

God, I would appreciate some help here …

Caspian charged at the man, grasping Eden by the waist lest she fall back over the rail.

Rutger reared backward, trying to yank Eden back into his own grip.

Lord Rutger teetered back and forth in the violent wind of the storm. Caspian tried to reach out to grab the man, but as Rutger stumbled backward over the ship's rail, Caspian realized he was tugging Eden down with him.

He had to save Eden. There was nothing to do but hold on to her limp body tightly and let Lord Rutger regain his own balance or fall into the abyss.

With a final grunt, Caspian pulled Eden down from the rail onto the deck then watched as Rutger slid over the edge with a cry just as loud as the thunder that was echoing across the sea.

The man's arms swung about madly. He was trying to catch hold of something, anything, before he plummeted to his death.

Unsuccessfully.

After a moment, Rutger hit the water with a splash that was drowned out by the sounds of the storm.

He sank below immediately, disappearing in the riotous waves.

Caspian trained his eyes on the spot where the man had vanished for minutes, but to no avail. His head never popped back above the surface.

Finally, Caspian tore his gaze from the tragic site.

* * *

The rain ceased just as Caspian scooped Eden up in his arms

and carried her across the bulwarks and back to their cabin, where it was blissfully dry.

The moment they entered, Reed rushed up to them from where he had been sitting in one of the leather armchairs. "Papa, what happened? Is-is Miss Eden all right?" He spoke the words tentatively, as if he was afraid that just by saying them he would make his beloved "Miss Eden" not all right.

"She-she fainted, is all, Reed." Caspian suppressed a sigh. He did not need the young child underfoot at a time like this. "Umm, Reed, why don't you go up on the main deck? You can ask one of my men to take you over to see if Master Thompson needs any help. I am certain he would be pleased to have it."

Reed simply stared at Eden, his bluish-purple eyes wide as saucers. The child was no doubt every bit as worried about the woman as he was. Well, Caspian could understand that. Lady Trenton was a special woman and she had suddenly become close to both him and his son. Caspian decided he needed to comfort the child in at least some small way.

He stooped toward his son. "Reed, I assure you I will notify you if she recovers or for some reason something worsens. She will be fine, son. You have no need to worry about her. Go."

Reed studied his father's face for a moment, looking back and forth between him and Eden. Finally, he nodded slowly. "You promise to tell me if anything happens, Papa?"

Caspian's throat constricted when he realized his son cared for this precious woman just as much as he did. They would become a pleasant little family, if only the lady agreed to be the wife and mother. He hoped she would. He fingered the chain around his neck that held his mother's old ruby and gold wedding band. She had given it to him, her sole child, before she died, and told him when he had a wife of his own it could be hers. That day had been far off since he was only five years old at the time, but he had kept it around his neck every day since then. Isabelle had objected to taking the ring, claiming it was frivolous and they should just sell it. Caspian had bought her a simple metal band instead and kept this one close to his heart as a reminder of the mother he could barely remember. He had a feeling Eden would appreciate this ring and cherish it as he did. That was if she would accept the promise that accompanied it.

Caspian gently deposited Eden on the bed, and then took a step back to examine her. Her long black eyelashes were lowered onto her creamy cheeks. Those brown curls of hers were tangled about her head and that normally bright face had grown pale and ashen. A tick of worry floated through him. Maybe he should have sent Reed for the ship's surgeon.

He ran his fingertips across her scalp, searching for bumps or cuts and lingering as he went. Caspian thanked the Lord when he realized she had no fatal head wounds; she had just been knocked unconscious. Maybe she had even fainted rather than suffering a blow to that pretty little head of hers.

At his touch, her eyelids fluttered open.

"Caspian." She blinked rapidly.

Relief swept away his anxiety like a cool breeze on a hot Caribbean afternoon.

"Yes, 'tis me, milady." He nearly laughed in relief, and then gently slid the back of his hand across her forehead and moved to caress her cheek.

"Where is ... where is Lord Rutger?" That familiar tiny line appeared between her dark, delicate eyebrows.

"You know, milady, I should like it if I were the first thing you thought of when you woke, not that wretched dandy named Lord Rutger," he teased, kissing her hair and feigning a wounded look.

She whacked his arm playfully. Well, it was a good thing she felt up to joking around with him. That had to mean she was not in too bad of shape.

Soon, however, her expression slid back to all seriousness. "What happened? I ... I guess that I must have fainted again. But what happened between then and now? I know we are back on your ship now, but is Lord Rutger still bent on taking me? And ..." She gulped. "Killing me? What happened, Caspian?"

"Lord Rutger fell into the sea trying to do just that to you. I caught you by the waist just before he lost his balance or you would have fallen over with him." Caspian shook his head, trying to clear its image of Eden falling over the rail, her arms flailing, her hair flying. He cringed at the *splash* his mind conjured up.

"You mean Clive—Lord Rutger is ... dead?" She brought her hand over her chest.

"Aye, my dear lady. He drowned just moments ago. The storm was so violent we could do nothing to save him. His head sunk under right away and never resurfaced.

"I disliked the man greatly, but I did not want to see him die like that. I would have much preferred to see him to spend the rest of his life in a prison or be executed by the law for what he did to you, sweetheart." His voice shook with emotion.

She looked down at his comment, but not before Caspian noticed the sheen of tears in her eyes and the pinkish hue that rose on her cheeks. "What ... what happened to his ship?"

"I made Master Thompson the captain of Rutger's ship. We

captured the previous captain who had been sailing Rutger around. He's in the hold. That man had to have known Rutger's plan all along, and a man like that should not be free to roam as he pleases. Besides, it's not like I could use that ship. Gage deserves to be a captain after how he saved your life when I could not. He is sailing beside us to Port Royal," Caspian explained.

"Master Thompson is a good man." She smiled sleepily.

"Aye, that he is, milady. And a wonderful friend at that," he added. "How are you feeling? You've taken quite a few hits to that sweet head of yours ever since you met me, sweetheart." He gazed at her face, glad to see much of her pretty coloring had returned there.

"I have a headache and I am tired, but other than that I think I'm fine," she answered.

Caspian gazed down at her tenderly and noted how heavy her eyelids appeared. The poor dear had been through a lot lately and even a strong man would be sleepy by now. He glanced down at her dripping wet clothes. Maybe he should not have set her on the bed after the pouring rain they had been through.

"You just change out of those wet clothes and then get some sleep, love. I will stay out of here and make sure Reed remains with me so you can sleep peacefully. Right now, you need some rest and I think after that you will feel worlds better."

* * *

As soon as Caspian left the cabin, Eden removed her dress and undergarments which had been soaked through and tossed them into a corner. She was far too tired to fold them or lay them out to dry. Besides, she did not want to see that lavender wedding gown ever again.

Eden selected a white nightdress from the trunk lying next to Caspian's sturdy desk and draped its warmth over her arms. Although she probably should wash the muck off her face from the past few days and brush her hair, she was lucky to even lift her arms due to fatigue. She had endured a lot today.

Instead, Eden crawled into the bed and fell asleep almost immediately when her head hit the pillow.

* * *

Eden awoke hours later to see Caspian leaning over her, grinning. Reed stood behind him, a similar smile on his adorable little face.

She yawned and stretched slowly.

"Good morning, milady. How do you fare?" The handsome captain leaned forward and planted a light kiss on her forehead. He brushed some hair out of her eyes.

"I-I feel much better, thank you, Captain. What time is it?"

"It is almost five o'clock in the morning, milady. You slept straight through the evening meal and all the way 'til dawn. You went through a terrible ordeal yesterday. I can't say I know many women who have had a knife at their throats who were nearly as brave as you proved to be." Caspian took her hand and helped her up from the bed.

She glanced down, grabbing a quilt from the bed and wrapping it around her shoulders. "I was not very brave, Captain. I do believe I fainted."

236

"That you did, milady, but who could blame you?" He gently chucked her under the chin. "Now, I want you to change out of that nightgown and put on a pretty dress. I have a surprise for you when you can come up on the deck."

"A-a surprise? For me?"

With a simple wink and a nod, Caspian exited the room, silently closing the door shut behind him.

Eden quickly removed her nightgown and donned a turquoise, silk gown, her favorite of all that were on this ship, all the time wondering at the thought of a surprise from the man.

Reed remained by her side, politely looking away as she stepped behind a screen Caspian had found a couple of days ago for her to dress behind.

"Reed, darling, do you know what surprise your papa has planned for me? I am certainly eager to learn what it is."

"Not at all, Miss Eden. He did not tell me of a surprise."

She poked her head around the screen at the boy. He looked terribly confused about the whole situation and slightly disappointed.

"Well, I promise I shall tell you what my surprise was as soon as your father lets me come back down here. Now you be a good boy while I'm gone, and I will return as soon as I can." She tapped her finger on his nose lightly.

Eden approached the main deck as fast as she could, eager to find Caspian and to discover what her surprise was. Why, she had no idea what it could be. What would Caspian have or know to give her or tell her as a surprise? Maybe he had some good news for her. Maybe they had discovered where Adam was or something like that. She sighed and cancelled that thought out. That was just dreaming.

Eden discovered the Captain standing at the rail, overlooking the sunrise that cast a golden-pink hue on the horizon. His hands were planted firmly on his hips, like he owned the entire sea and not just this ship.

"Whatever is my surprise, Caspian? I have to admit, I have been most eager to find out." Eden placed her hands on her hips.

He slowly drew something out of his pocket and kept it cupped in his large, strong hands, a mischievous grin illuminating his handsome face.

"Close your eyes, sweetheart, and I will show it to you. Close them tight."

She immediately clamped her eyes shut, her heart fluttering like a nervous butterfly. Eden felt like a little child, unable to wait to take a peek at her gift.

Caspian slipped something cold and hard around her left finger. She opened her eyes a crack to see an exquisite ruby and gold ring. The ring Caspian had always worn on a silver chain around his strong neck.

"I didn't tell you that you could open your eyes yet, milady," Caspian teased, winking at her. "You are nearly as impatient as little Reed." Amusement sweetened his deep, masculine voice.

Eden giggled in response and found herself looking into those crystal blue eyes, unsure if she understood the meaning behind the gift he presented. What did he mean by that ring? Was it just a trinket for her to remember him by when they reached Port Royal and she had to say good-bye or … or … did he want it to mean something … more? Because he always wore it around his neck, she assumed it held some significance to him. The man did not seem to be one to collect feminine trinkets.

"What …"

He wrapped her in his arms, kissing her as in reply. That was all the answer she needed.

Eden threw her arms around his neck and responded to the kiss, happier than she could imagine at what the ring surely meant. She would quite enjoy being his wife. She was certain of it. After a long few moments he pulled away from her, panting for air.

She was doing much the same, feeling almost lightheaded, either from the excitement of the kiss or the lack of oxygen.

"I would be honored if you would agree to be my wife, Lady Eden Trenton. Would you, sweetheart?" He bowed low and brought her fingers to his lips.

"Yes, of course, Caspian, but …" she gave him a saucy grin and a coquettish fluttering of her eyelashes, "perhaps I just need a little more convincing."

"I know exactly what you mean, milady," he laughed heartily, his voice coming out husky. And with that, she slowly drew his face down to herself and kissed him, not caring if the entire crew saw.

Chapter 22

❧

Only a matter of days later, Caspian sat at his desk early in the morning, watching his beautiful wife as she ate her breakfast of porridge in one of their armchairs. She giggled with Reed, who sat across from her. His little body was dwarfed by the large armchair. The boy had been overjoyed when Caspian told him Eden would be his mother.

Caspian studied Eden. Her cheeks were flushed a light pink from laughter. The sweet woman's doe-like eyes flashed with excitement, and her umber curls fell in wild disarray about her shoulders, untamed and not yet combed. He decided he liked her like this. She had left her nightgown on and simply wrapped a blanket about her shoulders because she had decided it was much cozier than getting into her normal dress so early in the morning. Reed had joined them in their cabin even earlier after spending the night with Gage. Reed had been eager to see his "Mama" as he now called Eden.

Caspian could not help but grin at how charming his little

family was.

Just a day after Caspian had proposed to Eden, they had arrived in Port Royal. They were married days later in a small chapel in the city—a chapel that was completely out of place with the corruption of most of Port Royal. Caspian knew he should leave his wife and Reed safe on land while he went in search of Moore, but he could not bear to leave them behind, especially Eden, when they had only been a complete family for all of a day. He had decided they would be just as safe with him, rather than him leaving them unprotected in Port Royal.

Glancing at his son, Caspian realized he would have to either get a new ship or do some remodeling. Although he loved this one dearly, he would need a cabin for Reed to stay in rather than allowing the boy to tag along with him and Eden all of the time. A man and his wife needed some time alone, and that would never be accomplished with a child in the room.

Caspian would like some of that alone time right now. He rose from his desk where he had been attempting to map their route in search of Moore and moved over to his wife and his son.

"Why don't you go up on the main deck, Reed, and watch the sun rise over the ocean?"

Reed glanced back and forth between his father and Eden before answering. "By myself? Or will you and Mama come with me?"

Eden glanced at Caspian. He gave her a reassuring wink.

"We won't be joining you just yet, Reed. I want to talk to 'Mama' first, but maybe we will join you later. You just go on up for now," Caspian explained, feeling a little bad that he was wishing his son's absence. But wasn't it normal for a man to want to spend some more time alone with his new wife?

"As long as you and Mama come soon." The boy left the cabin, humming a tune Caspian had caught his wife singing to Reed as she had tucked him into bed one night.

As soon as the door shut behind his son—their son, Caspian moved to take his little wife in his arms. He loved the soft feel of her body against his. Caspian pressed his lips to her forehead and began trailing kisses down her neck, stopping at her collarbone. Then he buried his face in her neck, inhaling her sweet vanilla scent.

Eden giggled. "Stop that, Caspian, it tickles me!" She playfully pushed against his arms. After a moment she gave up her struggle and leaned her head against his chest. He tilted her face up to his with his hand and pressed his lips to hers, softly at first. Warmth flooded through him at his wife's response. Snagging his fingers in her mass of brunette curls, he gently cradled her head with his hands. She let out a soft moan of pleasure.

A knock sounded on the door, ending their intimate moment.

Groaning, Caspian pulled away from Eden just barely and called out, "Who is it?"

"'Tis Wilson, Cap'n. I wouldn't have interrupted, but I saw your son leave. We spotted a ship, sir. She's headin' straight for us and she doesn't appear to be friendly."

Caspian left the warmth of his wife's embrace with a moan. Who could be after them so soon after their wedding? He had freed them of Lord Rutger, but now they obviously had a new enemy. Could it be Moore? He grimaced at the thought that the monster could have found them before Caspian had hardly even begun his search. The man had run away from a fight last time, but maybe he was better prepared now.

Whoever's ship this was, Caspian vowed he would protect Eden and Reed with his life.

* * *

Eden sped about the cabin like a madwoman, searching to find a dress to wear for the day. Her husband winked at her as he grabbed his plumed captain's hat and perched it atop his black curls.

She beamed back at him, selecting a coral-colored gown from the armoire. Deciding to just put it on over her nightgown and stays, rather than getting out her petticoats, she set it on the bed and tried to tighten her stays, but her fingers betrayed her and kept slipping. At home, she had a servant who helped her with it, but normally, on the ship, she just spent a couple of moments before successfully tightening them. Now, however, there was no way to be dressed in time if she had no help.

Eden moved toward her husband, who had a deep frown on his face. When he saw her looking at him, a grin spread across his face. "Caspian, would you please … help tighten my s-stays? I can't seem to tie them quickly enough this morning." She felt herself blushing furiously, speaking of her undergarments to someone, a man, no less.

Her husband.

Her anxiety lessened as she smiled at the thought.

Caspian gave her a roguish grin, his glacial blue eyes twinkling. "But I so thoroughly enjoyed helping you out of them last night, darling," he proclaimed innocently.

Eden's face flooded with heat yet again at his reference to

243

their wedding-night. The skin on her back tingled pleasantly as his large hands fumbled with the laces of her stays. His warm breath feathered on her neck and sent a shiver of delight running all the way down her body.

He stopped to press a kiss to the top of her head and then continued his attempt at untangling her laces. He swore lightly under his breath and leaned toward Eden. "How about you don't wear your stays today? I do not understand how you women can stand being confined in those blasted things anyway. You, my dear, look just as perfect without them as you do with them."

"But, Caspian—a proper lady never goes without her stays. My mother taught me that long ago," Eden objected, although she already knew she would do anything Caspian asked of her when he gave her that charming grin of his.

"My dear lady, no one will notice your missing undergarment, I assure you. For heaven's sake, you are on a pirate ship! What do a bunch of uneducated, grimy men know about women's fashion? Besides, I know you don't care about what is perfect and proper anymore. If you did, you would never have married me. And need I remind you that when I first saw you, you were dressed in men's trousers? Surely that was most improper, as well," he chuckled.

Eden smiled, and quickly tossed her dress on over her nightgown. She did enjoy the feel of wearing no stays. Almost as much as she had enjoyed wearing Adam's trousers.

* * *

Caspian felt dread clench around his heart after he had peered at the other ship through his telescope and saw her name. *Neptune's Poison.* Moore. And the man must have been prepared for battle this time, or he would not be approaching them.

Caspian had tried to tease his wife, to not let her notice his fear, but that did not stop the dread from numbing every nerve in his body right now.

He did not even feel Eden's warm hands on his arm. He ignored his son's cheerful greeting as the boy skipped up to them. All he felt was horror at what situation he had just brought his newly married wife and his son to face.

"Caspian, darling, what is wrong? Who is it?" Eden wrapped her arms around his waist from behind. His mind clouded pleasantly like it always did when around his wife.

That was not good at all. No. He could not have the beautiful woman distracting him at a time like this.

"Eden, I need you and Reed to go to our cabin and lock the door behind you right now. Push my desk up against the door and do not come out until I personally tell you to. Do not leave that cabin for anyone other than me, you understand, sweetheart?" He did not need her distracting him or getting harmed. Or worse.

He spun around, wrapping her in his arms in a whirl and drawing his son close at the same time.

"Why, Caspian? Why are you not telling me who that ship is, darling? Why must we go below?" Eden asked, pulling away from Caspian and drawing Reed's little body next to hers. The boy was studying him with those wide, blue, violet-tinged eyes that made Caspian conjure up an image of the child's biological mother. He would not fail his family yet again. He would keep them safe and sound in his cabin this time, even if

245

he had to drag them both kicking and screaming. He would lock and barricade the door before he let anything happen to them.

"Just obey me, Eden, please, for once. I will not have either of you hurt. You go into our cabin and do as I asked. Please, sweetheart." He ran a hand from her shoulder down her arm and held her hand in his.

Caspian's words may have been harsh but he tried to make them kinder by his expression and the begging in his voice. He did not have time to explain they had run into Moore, and he did not want her unnecessarily worried about him. "Eden, go below. I will come for you when it is safe. Please, I will not have you dying in some battle like Isabelle a mere day after we have been married. Go to our cabin immediately."

She sighed and tears sprouted in her pretty brown doe-eyes. "But, Caspian, don't you realize that I feel the same about you? What if *I* lose *you*?" Her voice cracked with a sob.

"Please, darling. It is Moore, the man who killed Isabelle. I will be all right. Gage is sailing next to us with his new crew. Most of his men agreed to become privateers rather than being kept in the hold. He will join us. Don't worry about me, sweetheart, and go below and take care of our son."

The sobs he knew she was trying to control caused him to swallow back some tears of his own. He could not stand seeing his little wife like this. Finally, after what seemed like ages, she nodded and grabbed Reed's hand. "I will go below, Caspian."

Before she turned, he grabbed her by the waist and gave her one last quick kiss and squeezed his son in his arms.

"I love you, Caspian. Remember that. I need you to come back to me. I don't know what I would do without you," she whispered.

"I love you, too, Eden. Reed as well. You two stay safe for me, all right?" His voice broke with emotion.

Eden nodded at him and led his son—their son—down the companionway. As Moore's ship approached close to their firing range, he prayed with everything in him he had not just kissed his brand new wife good-bye.

Chapter 23

After Eden had locked the door to the cabin and shoved her husband's sturdy oak desk against the entrance with the help of her son, she sat on the bed with her legs drawn up below her and motioned for Reed to join her. The poor child's eyes were filled with tears. He jumped up onto the bed and rested his little head on her lap, curling his legs up behind him. Eden forced the wetness from her eyes. Reed was frightened, and she knew her crying would only make things worse.

"Mama, what is happening? Why was Papa so worried about us?"

Her heart felt the tiniest bit lighter when the dear boy called her his "Mama." She had always longed for a child of her own, but until she and Caspian had a baby, Reed would do just fine. As long as she lived, she knew she would think of this precious youngster as her own son.

She stroked his tawny curls away from his forehead. This situation was far too stressful for a five-year-old. "Well, Reed, some very bad men want to attack our ship. Have you been in a battle at sea before?" Surely he had. Where else would he be when his father attacked enemy ships?

The child nodded. "Yep. They are loud and Papa makes me come down here by myself so I don't get hurt like he said my mother did."

"That's right, sweetheart. And he made us come down here so we are safe and sound. You see, those bad men on that other ship are the same ones who hurt your mother when you were just a baby. Your papa is just worried, and he doesn't want anything to happen to us because he loves us both so much." Eden rubbed his back in small circles.

Reed wrapped his arms around her neck and hid his face against her shoulder. "I hope they won't hurt you like they hurt my other mama, Mama," he declared sweetly.

"No, they won't, darling. We will be safe in here and your papa will be all right, too. Don't worry, Reed."

Boom! The ship shook violently. Eden had sailed on the ship long enough to recognize that disruption as a cannon being fired.

A similar sound echoed in the distance, ending with a splash. The battle had begun.

Eden leaned down and hugged Reed close against her chest, humming a hymn to him she had always loved to sing in church. She hoped the words she recited along with it in her head gave her strength and stilled the stubborn fears that churned inside her belly. Suddenly, she remembered a passage from Isaiah, "Fear thou not; for I am with thee: be not dismayed; for I am thy God: I will strengthen thee; yea, I will help thee; yea, I will uphold thee with the right hand of my righteousness."

She did not need to be afraid. God was with her.

Even though she had been frightened into running away from every trouble she faced in her life, she now realized God was really the One who controlled everything. He would stay with her always and protect her.

The shouting that sounded above was followed by another boom and a crash. The crunching of wood filled her ears. A crash that was near where she and Reed were sitting. Their ship must have been hit. Eden had to force herself to keep her arms around Reed to keep from running up there to find her husband and check if he was safe. Deep screams of terror rent the air. She squeezed her eyes shut against images of Caspian's strong body limp, bloody … lifeless.

Reed moaned, burying his little face in Eden's chest, sobbing. She stroked his hair, keeping her tears at bay. If she allowed herself to cry, she would never stop. It would only succeed in worrying the dear boy.

"Reed, it's all right. It's all right, darling. Shush, sweetheart," she murmured over and over into his hair, all the while pleading with God to keep her husband safe.

She cupped her hands over her son's ears, attempting to block the vicious sounds of the on-going battle. Reed stared up at her, his pink cheeks stained wet from crying. He reached out and covered her ears with his own little hands.

"Thank you," she mouthed to him, pressing a kiss on his forehead.

She closed her eyes and they waited … and waited … and waited. The muffled sounds of a fight never ceased. That was good, though, right? If there was no battle, then that would mean someone had won … if no one had yet become a victor, then that meant Caspian was alive, right?

Chapter 23

A pounding sounded from the companionway leading to the cabin. Caspian? Had he come to let her and Reed out of here? She gently removed Reed's hands from her ears, hoisted him up onto her hip, and stood so she could hear more clearly. But none of the gruff voices she heard belonged to her husband. Two voices grew closer to her door, before stopping. The doorknob clicked like it was being moved. Luckily, she had locked it behind herself. But what would happen if they made it past the lock? What if her makeshift barricade failed to work? Why had everything grown more silent?

Shouting came from the other side of the door and she heard a thump. "This is the Captain's cabin! Surely he has some of his prized possessions in here."

His most prized possessions.

They could not know that she and Reed were in here. Nonetheless, Eden sped about the cabin, searching for something she could use to defend herself. She spotted one of Caspian's cutlasses, but she knew it would be entirely too heavy for her to lift and might just have the opposite effect of what she wanted.

She glanced at little Reed, who had laid his head against her shoulder and was squeezing his eyes shut. The men outside pounded on the door. Eden spotted a pistol in the bottom of the trunk in which she had found most of the clothes she had worn throughout this voyage.

She knew how to shoot a gun. Eden laughed silently when she remembered how terrified of her own husband she had been when they had first met.

So terrified that she had shot him in the arm. And little Reed had slept right through it. She pushed the memory aside when the heard the men beginning to bang into the door. Could they break through that thick oak? Were they that strong? She doubted even Caspian could make his way through the heavy wood. There was no way these men could be more muscular than her husband.

But she heard at least two voices out there. Surely multiple men would be able to break it down. She could take no chances. Not when she had to worry about both her own life and her son's.

Eden stooped down to grab the pistol and ran to hide between the leather armchairs and the bulkhead. She grabbed a quilt from the bed along the way.

As she squatted down behind the furniture, she set young Reed in her lap, draped the quilt over the both of them, and squeezed him close. The child slipped his arms around her neck and she inhaled his sweet, innocent scent. Boisterous cheering drifted over from the main deck. Eden cringed at the foul language that followed it. She certainly hoped Reed would never grow up to speak like that. At least his papa—her husband—did not. But what did the cheering mean? She had no way of knowing.

The pounding on the door grew louder and more frequent.

"What's going to happen to us, Mama? Where is Papa? He should be here with us."

Although his voice was quiet, they could not afford the risk of speaking out loud. "Shhh, Reed, darling, we must be quiet so the bad men don't find us in here," she whispered as silently as she could, "we are going to be all right, love. I am most certain your Papa would love to be here with us, but he is the captain of this ship and he needs to be up on the main deck during the battle. He belongs there, commanding his crew. He is their leader. We both need to understand that, dear. We just need to calm down, my darling, and this will be over in no time. Those men will not be able to get in here. The door is too sturdy, and your papa's desk is in front of it."

Eden heard a great crack, but could not bring herself to look at the entrance to the cabin. She knew what that sound meant. It had to have been the cracking of their door. That meant the pirates would make their way in here sometime in the near future.

She could not bring herself to think of the horrors that would befall both her and her son if they were discovered.

She did not bother to quell the tears that were burning in her eyes any longer. They spilled out onto Reed's golden hair. He peeked up at her, no doubt confused at the wetness on his head.

His eyes filled with fresh tears and she hugged him closer. "Mama, we should pray. The Bible tells us to pray when we are in trouble, and He will deliver us, right?"

"Yes, darling, you are perfectly correct about that. But let's pray in our heads so the men do not know we are in here, all right?"

Reed nodded, and she watched as he bowed his head and closed his eyes. She did the same and squeezed him even closer when she heard another thump and the crack of wood splitting. The men had made it past the door and now they were only slowed by the desk.

* * *

Caspian clenched his fists, letting out a deep breath. With his family below, barricaded in his cabin and Master—Captain

Thompson sailing next to him, there was no possibility of harm assailing his son and his wife.

He glanced across the bulwarks of his ship to see Gage commanding his crew, his shoulders thrown back in the stance of a true captain. Caspian did miss having the man as his first mate, but it would be unfair to restrain his talent from reaching its full potential.

Neptune's Poison sailed closer every second, and rows of guns peeked out from her sides.

"Prepare the guns, men. Immediately! We will take her," Caspian shouted.

He saw Gage's newly acquired crew rushing to do much the same.

Moments later, *Neptune's Poison* shot a cannon ball straight at the *Dawn's Mist*'s hull. It was too short, however, and hit the water in front of the ship with a *splash.*

There was no doubt. The battle was about to begin.

Although *Neptune's Poison* was undermanned, she was not under-gunned.

A bit of fear sliced down Caspian's spine at the thought, but he forced it down. After all, as he had only realized recently, God was on his side.

A crack sounded as Gage shot at the enemy. His shot hit with a resounding bang.

The cry of pain that accompanied told Caspian it had been a flesh wound.

"Fire, men!" Caspian shouted.

After his guns were fired, he blinked his eyes against the smoke, straining to see what they had accomplished.

The main mast of *Neptune's Poison* had been struck. Her main mast was cracked and leaning heavily to the side.

Another boom sounded.

"All hands down!" Caspian dropped to the deck with the rest of his crew.

The ship shook beneath him, and a feeling of dread sliced through Caspian. They had been hit and his first thought was for his wife and son.

Slowly, Caspian rose. "Are all men accounted for?"

"No, sir. Elliot was hit ... he's not responding, sir." A man announced.

"Davis! See to Elliot. Everyone else, prepare for battle. Fire the cannons again! We can't let them get an advantage over us."

Caspian glanced across at Gage, who was moving his ship in the opposite direction. Good. It had been their plan to surround Moore whenever they found him, even if this was not how they had planned to catch the monster.

Within minutes, after many more booming cannon shots, Gage was on the -other side of *Neptune's Poison*.

Caspian had expected Moore to raise his white flag of surrender.

But no. Instead, the man's entire crew raised their weapons and roared.

What kind of fool was this man? Did he plan to split his crew and have them perform hand-to-hand combat against two different ships?

Caspian identified Moore on the main deck of *Neptune's Poison*. He was wearing a purple waistcoat over his paunch of a stomach, a plumed hat on his head. His brown, straggling beard was streaked with gray.

A ruthless look was on its face just as it had been the day he had murdered Caspian's first wife.

While he had been thinking about Moore, *Neptune's Poison* approached the *Dawn's Mist* until Caspian's men were close enough to board her.

"Should we board her, Captain?" Smithy inquired with two pistols in his hands and a cutlass at his hip.

"Nay. Let's wait to see what they will do. I want everyone to stay armed, though, and ready for battle," Caspian replied.

Caspian's entire crew bristled up, preparing for the imminent battle.

The moment they were close enough, the crew of *Neptune's Poison* split into two groups, boarding Caspian's and Gage's ships at the same time.

Each group was rather small, but large enough to cause trouble.

Caspian grimaced. He hoped he would make it through this battle without losing any of his men's lives.

A collective cry rang out as cutlass clashed against cutlass. Pistols fired.

Caspian noticed Moore wormed his way onto Caspian's ship, brandishing a sword.

He could hear his blood rushing through his ears like the water that rushed against the hull of the *Dawn's Mist.*

Caspian knew he could retrieve his pistol and exact the long-awaited revenge for Isabelle's death, all the while helping the law by removing one more pirate from the waters. His hand twitched and moved toward the firearm almost of its own volition.

But he also knew the revenge and the hate he had felt for the man all of these years was wrong. God told everyone to love their enemies.

Caspian unsheathed his sword, charging at the vicious

Captain rather than shooting at him.

The man roared at Caspian's blow. Caspian leaped to the side. He just missed a hit from another man to his left.

Moore propelled his cutlass straight at Caspian's head with a *whoosh*, but he ducked just in time to avoid it.

Moore's gray eyes widened when he finally appeared to realize who he was fighting. "Ah, if it ain't Cap'n Archer himself. Have ye come t' finish me off finally? Ye're the fool who kept a woman on his ship, on the main deck in the midst of a battle. It's yer own fault yer wife died."

Caspian knew full well he was a fool without being told. He swung back at Moore and successfully sliced the man's arm.

The cut barely affected Moore. He kept on fighting like a man without any wounds.

"You murdered my wife, Moore, but that's not why I'm chasing you anymore." Caspian lunged forward to avoid the collapsed body of a man who belonged to the enemy's crew. "I'm a privateer now, so you are facing the law."

Moore snickered. His blade dug into Caspian's thigh.

Caspian out in pain. He staggered for a moment but then thought of Eden and Reed waiting for him in the cabin and steadied himself. Adrenaline pumped through him, helping him ignore his wound.

He would not lose to this man. He would not give him the chance to harm his family again.

Someone struck Caspian in the neck from behind. It took him several breaths to steady his vision.

He hefted up his sword, feeling every muscle in his body ache as he did so.

He had to stay strong.

He had to stay strong for Eden. For Reed.

He had to use God's strength that He had given to him.

A cry sounded from somewhere, but Caspian had to take a moment of concentration to realize it had come from directly in front of him.

Moore lay in a heap, breathing, but unconscious.

Letting out a sigh of relief, Caspian glanced around to find the battle was over. Moore appeared to have knocked himself in the head on one of the ship's flying jibs.

Caspian's crew was standing, battered, but alive, and awaiting his direction. He squinted across the sea and found much was the same for Gage and his crew.

Moore's crew was either dramatically injured or captured.

They had defeated Moore at last. Caspian may have wanted to murder the man at some point, but now, he would keep him in his hold and hand him over to the authorities.

Caspian faced his crew with instructions to burn *Neptune's Poison*, but not before a feeling of foreboding crept into his gut. His crew may have fared well, but what about Eden and Reed?

Chapter 24

Caspian returned to his cabin exhausted and eager to see Eden's and Reed's beautiful faces. He had obtained a victory over the man who had wronged him long ago. Since he knew it was wrong to seek revenge as he had for so long, he just considered it as a normal victory, ridding the sea of pirates as was his job. This one just happened to be the monster who had murdered his late wife. But maybe her death had not been so bad after all. If Isabelle had never died, Caspian would likely have never been in London. Had he not been in London, Eden would never have stowed away on his ship and he never would have met her. Fallen in love with her. Married her.

He still found it difficult to believe the woman was actually his wife. Caspian grinned at the thought and sped up his pace down the companionway, impatient to visit his family. His smile soon faded, however, when he saw three men pounding on his cabin door.

He had thought all of the enemies had been taken below or

impressed in Gage's or Caspian's crew.

Dread and hatred filled him almost equally at the sight. They were planning on hurting his wife and his child. Caspian's first instinct was to attack the men, but he knew that would be useless and foolhardy. He knew he was strong, but not strong enough to ward off three men on his own. He glanced at the men, who appeared to have cutlasses but no firearms, and ran as silently as he could in his heavy boots to go find some members of his crew to aid him.

He rounded up some men who carried pistols and took them down to the entrance to his cabin. When the intruders spotted the guns, they quickly dropped their swords and cutlasses and raised their hands in an innocent gesture.

"We—we didn't mean no harm, sir, really!"

"If you'll only just let us go, Captain, please!"

Caspian grunted in reply. There was no way he would fall for their pleas. Had these men gotten into his cabin, something terrible would be happening to his wife and his son at the moment. "Smithy, take these men to the hold with the others." He shoved the man closest to him toward Smithy. Smithy and another crewmember led the offenders down toward the brig where Caspian would make sure they stayed for a good long time before giving them a choice: a second chance as a sailor on his ship or a report to the authorities for performing piracy. Most of the men he captured preferred the first choice.

Caspian clenched his jaw, realizing just how close to losing his family he had been. He moved to open the door but realized it was still propped shut with a large piece of furniture. His desk. Eden was a smart woman to listen to his suggestion. That desk had probably saved her life.

He knocked on the door gently. "Eden, you can move this

desk now. It is just me, dear."

He heard a scuffling sound followed by a light hiccup. "Caspian? Is that you out there?" Her sweet voice came nearer to him. She was just on the other side of the desk now, and it was almost unbearable to wait to take her in his arms and hold her tight.

"Yes, sweetheart. It is really me. You can let me in. Just move this desk aside."

"Th-those wicked men are gone now?" Her voice wavered and he wondered anew if she had been harmed at all.

"Papa?" His son's voice chimed in.

"Yes, Eden, Reed. Let me in." A scraping sound was followed by a soft, feminine grunt. Caspian gave the door a shove to help move the desk. After a moment, the door opened a passage barely big enough for Caspian to get through, but did not care. He squeezed into the room and was greeted warmly as his wife ran up to him and kissed him. Reed wrapped his little arms around his father's knees. After kissing his wife, Caspian leaned down to kiss the child on his head.

"Are you all right, Caspian?" Eden chewed on her bottom lip and ran her soft hands along his arms and his chest in a distracting manner.

He decided when he glimpsed his gorgeous wife he was not quite so tired after all. But his whole body still ached from sword fighting for almost hours on end.

"Yes, darling. I am sorer than any man should ever be, but I was not hurt. No need to worry; I am simply rather exhausted," Caspian explained, slowly stretching his right shoulder.

"Well, I am certainly glad you are all right, Caspian. You have no idea how worried we were about you down here." Eden gnawed on that plump lip yet again.

"We prayed for you, though, Papa!" Reed outstretched his little arms. Caspian had recently realized that meant the child wanted to be held.

He scooped the boy up in one arm and balanced him on his hip, still holding his wife close to his other side.

"You prayed for me, Reed? Well, I thank the both of you very much for that. The battle was close for a while, but eventually we beat them."

"What about Moore?" Eden's gaze found the slice on his thigh. She immediately began fussing over it.

"Moore knocked himself out fighting with me. He's in the brig now, and I'll drop him off at the prison in Port Royal. He'll probably be hanged for piracy."

Eden was crouched down in front of them, examining his wound through the hole in the leg of his trousers.

"I am all right, woman. Quit your worrying." He gently grabbed her waist and nudged her up so she was standing straight. "It's just a scratch, sweetheart. It already stopped bleeding."

She frowned but seemed to believe him and leaned her forehead against his chest. Her sweet scent of vanilla erased all traces of the battle he had just faced.

He moved toward the other side of the cabin and plunked himself down onto the bed, drawing both Eden and Reed down with him. They giggled, and Eden moved over so the boy could lie between them.

"I believe I could just sleep here for a couple of days ..." Caspian teased, closing his eyes.

Eden laughed. "I wouldn't blame you, husband. I do not even know if I could hold one of those wretched cutlasses for more than a minute, let alone fight with it." She leaned against him, snuggling her head against his chest and closing her eyes.

"Oh, I bet you could for a little while, sweetheart. You are stronger than you might think, my little doe."

"I bet Mama could fight off anyone with a sword!" Reed offered, grinning up at them.

Eden shared an amused glance with her husband. He winked at her and crossed his arms behind his head. Slowly, he felt exhaustion tug at his eyelids and he was soon asleep.

* * *

Eden glanced over at her slumbering husband and could not suppress a grin. He had slept the whole night through and was still snoring lightly during the first light of dawn. Reed was as well. She glanced over at the two of them and grinned at the sweet sight. Caspian's arm was entwined around her waist and Reed was laying his head across Eden's lap. The three of them did make a cute family. Her husband's dark hair was lying across his face in a most endearing way. She could not stop herself from brushing the locks away from his handsome face and pressing a light kiss against his now exposed temple.

Those striking crystal blue eyes opened wide the moment her lips touched his brow. That charming, lazy grin stretched across his lips and he swooped down to steal a kiss.

"A man could grow to love waking up like this every morning, milady."

A shiver of excitement shot through Eden at her husband's deep, husky voice.

She looked down to find Reed stirring. He stretched his little arms up over his head and yawned before he gazed up at her and sent her a charming grin much like that of his father's. "Good morning, Mama and Papa."

"Good morning, dear." Eden kissed the top of his forehead.

Caspian moved his hand to ruffle the child's blond curls.

"I wish I could sleep in here with you and Mama every night, Papa." Reed cast his innocent blue-violet gaze up at his father.

Eden had to bite back a laugh. She peered up to gauge her husband's reaction.

His face reddened and his eyes sparkled with amusement. Before he could respond, however, they were interrupted by a knock on the door.

Caspian groaned before standing up. The joints in his legs cracked. "Who is it?"

"I—I'm sorry, Cap'n, to interrupt you again, but we spotted a ship and she is headin' straight for us, Cap'n," came the voice of Wilson.

Eden sighed. Could she and her husband and her newly acquired son never have a peaceful moment alone? And who was after them now? Her husband seemed to have more enemies than she had first thought.

* * *

Once they had prepared for the day as quickly as they could, Caspian took his wife by the hand and led her to the forecastle deck. Reed trailed behind them. Caspian took a spyglass from Wilson and scrutinized the ship that was bearing down on them by the minute. He squinted in order to read her name. *Cross's Victory*.

Eden laid a gentle hand on his arm. "Who is she, Caspian?

Are we going to have another battle again, so soon after the last?"

"The *Cross's Victory*," he answered, lowering his glass, "I do not know who that would be. A merchantman, perhaps? I see no need for a battle yet, but if they continue to approach us in this manner ..."

Eden frowned. "Really? The *Cross's Victory*?"

"Aye. Do you know her?" He looked to his bride, baffled. Could it be some former suitor from England, coming to rescue her? Some proper English gentleman, come to take her away from Caspian and return her to her pampered life in London? Suddenly feeling more than a tad bit overly protective and jealous, he put a hand on the small of her back, keeping her close to his side.

"Yes, Captain, I believe I do know her. 'Tis the name of Matthew Emery's ship. Mr. Emery is a dear friend of mine who attends the same church as I. But why would he be pursuing us all the way over here? He is merely a merchantman, not a pirate or privateer. I know he wouldn't ... he would not be trying to steal from us or cause us any problems. Maybe there is another ship with the same name ..."

Caspian ignored her inquiry. All he heard was that this Matthew Emery was a friend. "Just what type of friend, my dear, would be here, chasing us?" He mumbled, clenching both his jaw and his fists. Before Eden could see the anger and jealousy burning in his eyes, he spun around quickly. Even if he was one, he did not want her to think him an insecure fool. He tried taking in a deep breath to calm his temper, but it hardly seemed to have an effect.

She took a slow step closer toward Caspian and turned him

around before studying his face for a moment. He forced himself to look her in the eyes. "I do believe you might just be a bit jealous, my husband." Eden giggled and ran a hand over the stubble on his jaw.

He lightly placed a kiss atop her head. "Do you blame me, my dear?"

She gave him a rather impish little grin. "Nay, Captain; I am certain I would feel much the same if our roles were reversed. You have naught to worry about, darling, Matthew is just a good friend from church." Her appealing smile faded. "But why would Matthew be chasing us? What would he want from you?"

"He most likely sees the ship Lord Rutger was using—Gage's ship—next to ours and is coming to rescue you after he heard of your mysterious disappearance. Why, probably thinks the terrible man stole you … that is, if he knew of all this."

* * *

Eden's friends had come to her aid. Even though it had not been Aimee and Ivy, someone had come for her. Her heart warmed at the thought. Someone besides just her loyal husband seemed to care for her after all.

She glanced over at the ship sailing next to theirs. Gage stood at her bow, fists on his hips. The role of captain seemed to suit him quite nicely, almost as nicely as it suited her handsome privateer husband. Gage's imperious gaze drifted over to the *Dawn's Mist* and he winked at Eden before striding toward the rail to speak with Caspian.

"I swear your wife has become prettier since the last time I saw her, Captain Archer," Gage proclaimed, bowing slightly.

"Aye, I must agree she has."

Eden felt heat rush to her face at her husband's overly kind compliment.

"But you will do well to stay away from her as she is my wife and no one else's, Gage."

Eden glanced over at Caspian. The man was protective of her, but she did not mind. She knew he was only teasing his good friend.

"Of course, sir. I am well aware of that." Gage nodded humbly.

* * *

Aimee and Ivy cowered on the quarter deck, fearing an oncoming battle. Ivy could not understand how some men could stand seeing death around them every day in battles and wars. She could only pray Eden was on that ship and she was safe and sound. If Lord Rutger had not found Eden yet, then at least Captain Emery could intercept them first.

Aimee clutched at Ivy's arms, squealing in terror when a cannon shot from the gun deck of one of the ships that were now only a matter of yards away. She had no idea why there were two ships together, but Captain Emery had told her he was certain one of them was the ship Lord Rutger was using. He had guessed Lord Rutger had run into trouble and the other ship was helping him.

"What are we doing, Ivy? Does Captain Emery not realize those ships are together? We don't have a chance of defeating them!" Aimee lurched forward toward Captain Emery.

Ivy yanked her back and spun her around. She did not need her friend starting another fight with the poor man. "Stay here, Aimee. I'm sure Captain Emery knows what he's doing."

Please, God, have Eden be all right.

Ivy knew Eden could use all of the prayers she could get. She hoped they could stop Rutger before he discovered Eden because she knew just how cruel the earl's anger could become.

Chapter 25

"W hy on earth are you firing on them, Caspian?" Eden screeched, running up to her husband. She grasped his arms. "That ship belongs to my friend. He has not even fired upon us at all or given any sign they plan to."

"Aye, my dear, I am fully aware of it. 'Twas simply a warning shot. I am just telling them they would regret firing upon me so we do not have to worry about that."

Eden sighed at her husband's actions. The poor man was simply jealous over nothing. He did not need to fire upon poor Captain Emery who was not armed. But Caspian's plan had worked; Matthew was soon raising a white flag of truce.

"He motions for us to heave to," shouted Scruggs, her husband's new first mate.

"Heave to, gentlemen! Be ready to prepare all weapons at my command."

The *Cross's Victory* slowed down beside them.

"Prepare the ropes, men!"

Eden caught a glimpse of blond and red curls bouncing across the main deck. Ivy and Aimee? No, it could not be …

Yes!

She rushed to the rail, eager to jump over and greet her friends whom she had not seen in far too many weeks. "Aimee! Ivy!"

Their eyes widened in shock when they saw her. "Eden!"

Eden tried to climb over the rail immediately but only succeeded in getting her legs all tangled up in her skirts. She ceased struggling as her thoughtful husband grabbed her by the waist.

"Just wait a moment, sweetheart. It is too dangerous to try to board her before these vessels are even lashed together. You could be crushed." He pressed a gentle kiss to her ear and kept his arms wrapped about her protectively. She decided she loved the feel of his strong arms around her waist.

* * *

Aimee took a startled step back as the man dragged Eden back and put his arms around her waist. He was wearing an elaborately plumed captain's hat, and by his attire, she guessed he was some sort of a pirate. Her breath caught in her throat. Really, he was quite handsome.

But he was a pirate.

What kind of trouble had Eden gotten herself into? Yet Eden actually appeared quite happy. Was this the same woman who had been telling Ivy and Aimee just weeks ago she would never marry any man? What had gotten into her? The man whispered in her ear and she giggled up at him. After a moment he hefted her in his arms and used a dangling rope to swing them both over the bulwarks.

As soon as the man released her from his embrace, Eden ran over and hugged Aimee and Ivy. Tears streamed down her face. "I missed both of you so much!"

"Thank God you are safe, Eden! You have no idea how worried about you we have been this entire time," Ivy whispered. Aimee laid her head on her friend's shoulder.

"We searched for you for so long. For goodness' sake, we had thought perhaps Lord Rutger had found you."

Eden shook her head, her brown eyes growing wide. "Lord Rutger is dead."

"Dead?" Aimee echoed in disbelief, frowning at her friend.

"Aye. Rutger fell off of his ship and drowned while he was trying to kill me. He wanted to throw me overboard because I would not agree to marry him, but he slipped over the edge himself."

"We are safe from him then?" Ivy inquired.

"Yes. He will never hurt me again. We are safe."

Aimee hugged her friend. "Oh, thank God!"

* * *

Caspian could not help but grin at his little wife's happiness. But who were these young women? Her sisters, perhaps? Nay, they looked nothing like her, and she had never mentioned sisters. A brother, yes, but no sisters. These women were most likely just her friends.

Caspian cleared his throat. Eden turned around, a sheepish grin on her pretty face. "Forgive me for not introducing you to them, darling."

"That is perfectly all right, milady," he smiled, bowing slightly.

She moved back to the women. "Caspian, this is Lady Ivy Shaw and this is Lady Aimee Dawson. They are my good friends from back in London. I have known them practically since we were babies. Our mothers were good friends," explained Eden.

Caspian bowed deeply. "Nice to meet you, ladies." The girls seemed to be younger than Eden by a year or so. They smiled back at him, nodding politely in reply. The blond, Lady Dawson, batted her eyelashes rather coquettishly.

He averted his eyes.

"And Ivy and Aimee, this is Captain Caspian Archer, my husband."

Her friends gasped. "Your husband? Since when are you a married woman?" The girls both objected in unison.

"Aye, Caspian is my husband. We married only a matter of days ago."

Caspian's heart rose at the giddy excitement in his wife's voice when she mentioned their marriage.

Caspian leaned toward Eden. "I will go speak with this Matthew Emery while you catch up with these ladies." She nodded and he squeezed her hand before turning to Emery.

* * *

"You are happy, Eden? Married to that man?" Ivy inquired with a concerned look on her face.

Eden giggled at her friend's concern that was entirely

misplaced. "Yes, of course I am happy, Ivy! I love Caspian with all of my heart." She felt a blush rise on her cheeks from talking about her husband in front of them. Would they think her foolish?

"You told us just months ago you never wished to marry and that you would just become an old spinster," supplied Aimee.

"Well, I simply changed my mind when I met Caspian, is all." And with that she told them the tale of how she had come to be a wife, all the way from stowing away on Caspian's ship to his proposal. The girls oohed and aahed at every turn of her story.

"I hope I find a man like that someday," Ivy sighed.

"Me, too," Aimee agreed, glancing over at Captain Emery with an odd expression on her face.

* * *

Caspian and Matthew's discussion was drowned out to a dull buzz in Gage's ears. He did not see Eden or the blond woman who was standing beside her.

Nay, all he could notice was the beautiful redhead next to the both of them. She wore her golden-orange curls pinned atop her head in the tightest bun he had ever seen, although a few red wisps had escaped their confinement. Her nose and cheeks were splattered with dark freckles and her eyes were a stormy shade of gray-blue. Those brilliant eyes snapped to his and her cheeks flushed to a vibrant purple-pink when she caught him staring.

He supposed he should be embarrassed, as well, but he found he was not. All he could do was continue to stare at this pretty young lady.

* * *

Ivy felt herself flush as she caught a rather handsome pirate on the deck of the ship Eden had come from staring at her.

He flashed a grin and winked at her.

She shook her head in order to clear it and then closed her eyes tight.

Eden grabbed both her and Aimee's hands in her own. Ivy forced herself to draw her attention away from the handsome rogue and transfer it to her friend.

"I am afraid I will be staying here in the Caribbean, my friends. Caspian is going to build us a nice house somewhere in Jamaica, I think, so Reed and I don't have to be on the ship all the time if we don't want to. We might even go looking for Adam sometime. I am afraid I will not see the two of you much at all anymore." Eden chewed on her lip as she spoke.

* * *

Eden swallowed back a sob and tried to hold back the tears that were burning in her eyes.

Aimee did not even attempt to halt the water pouring down her own cheeks. "I guess this is good-bye, then. For good."

"I suppose so. But we simply must write letters back and forth, as often as we can. I'll have to hear of all your new beaus and your new families and your children … I am sure Caspian will take me to visit London every once in a while, since he sometimes has business there. Maybe you two could even come here and stay with Caspian and me for a couple of weeks."

"Maybe." Ivy pulled Eden into an embrace.

Aimee lunged forward and wrapped her arms around the both of them. "We will miss you so much."

* * *

Caspian gathered his crying wife into his arms and swung her back over the bulwarks to his ship. She waved to her friends until their ship was just a tiny speck on the far horizon.

He kissed the tears off of her pretty, creamy cheeks. "It is all right, Eden. Everything is going to be all right. You'll see. You will be able to see your friends again someday. Besides, you can write letters to them." He drew her against his chest and breathed in the vanilla scent of her. His wife.

* * *

Eden leaned against Caspian's chest and closed her eyes as he wrapped his arms tightly about her waist. He kissed the top of her head until her tears slowed down and finally ceased.

"I know, Caspian. It is just that I will miss them so much." Eden pressed the palm of her hand against her forehead.

"But you do not regret marrying me, sweetheart, do you?" He spun her around to face him.

"Of course not, Caspian; I would never even think such a horrid thought. I love you and I know I will never regret our marriage."

He gave her that charming grin of his that she loved to see and hugged her, and then began to nuzzle her neck. "We shall visit them. Don't worry. I have business in London at least every year, sweetheart."

"But not too soon, I hope." There was a mischievous lilt in her voice.

"And why would that be? I thought you said you would miss your friends."

"Why, I have only just arrived in the Caribbean, and I could count on one hand the times I have spent alone with my own, brand new husband ..."

He laughed, a hearty sound she had grown to adore. "I believe I like your way of thinking, milady."

Reed skipped up to them and latched himself onto Eden.

Giggling, she fell into Caspian's arms.

Aye, she had everything she needed right here. With this man. She had this ship, her freedom, a son, and her handsome pirate captain.

The End

About the Author

Bestselling author Heather Manning is a young lady who loves to read—and write. Her first trilogy, Ladies of the Caribbean, quickly became bestsellers. After graduating from Stephens College with a degree in Theatre Arts, she moved to Orlando, Florida where she works in the hospitality industry. In her spare time, she enjoys kayaking, hiking, and biking through all of Florida's beautiful State Parks.

You can connect with me on:
🌐 https://www.heathermanningofficial.com
📘 https://www.facebook.com/heathermauthor
📷 https://www.instagram.com/heatherm_author

Subscribe to my newsletter:
✉ https://mailchi.mp/e5e9e7498f8e/join-my-newsletter

Also by Heather Manning

Dancing through history with a dash of romance and a hint of adventure.

Carried Home, Book Two, Ladies of the Caribbean

The Caribbean is no place for a society lady of London, yet after a daring quest to save a friend, Lady Ivy Shaw finds herself trapped far from home. Now, driven with worry for her young brother, she is determined to return to England in all haste. So, when a new acquaintance offers to sail her to her brother's side, she jumps at the offer, scarcely caring that the man is a privateer.

Captain Gage Thompson is just learning how to be a captain. He sailed for years under the command of his longtime friend, Caspian Archer, but serving a captain and being a captain are, as he soon discovers, two very different roles. While struggling to gain the respect of his newfound crew, he now faces the distraction of beautiful Lady Shaw. He finds himself entranced by her and promises to give her passage home.

After a brief stop in Port Royal, Ivy and Gage discover an abandoned child. They both decide to bring her with them on their voyage to England. But problems soon arise in the form of hurricanes and enemy pirates, and Ivy and Gage find themselves scrambling to not only care for a lonely child, but also gain command of a motley crew.

Will love bud between Ivy and Gage as they journey home?

Tossed Together, Book Three, Ladies of the Caribbean

Lady Aimee Dawson is the perfect picture of an English society lady—except when she is around Captain Emery, who simply makes her want to scream. Much to her dismay, she finds herself stranded in Port Royal with the man. As if her week could not get any worse, she is stolen by a group of pirates who want to sell her at an auction.

Captain Matthew Emery is a merchant man, but all he really wants to do is become a missionary. His plans take a turn, however, when he finds a group of pirates attempting to auction off Aimee. The only way Matthew can think to save her is to claim she is his betrothed—something he had never thought would come out of his mouth.

Much to Matthew and Aimee's chagrin, the pirates agree to let Aimee go free, on one she must marry Matthew right then and there to prove they were truly betrothed. Left with no other options, the two sworn enemies exit the tavern as man and wife. They reluctantly set sail for home, but trouble brews in the form of a handsome but mysterious translator and more than a few detours.

What will become of Aimee and Matthew after they are tossed together?

Stuck in Time (Coming Soon!)

Ember Appleton thought she was in for a lousy afternoon when she got stood up on a blind date—little did she know she would end up in the wrong century! Focused on her love of art, Ember pays little attention to the world around her, until a freak accident sends her whirling back into Kansas City, in the year 1933. There she witnesses one of the city's most gruesome catastrophes in history right before her eyes. However, her day gets a little brighter when she is rescued by a handsome, concerned reporter who cannot take his eyes off of her...

Daire Kelley has worked his whole life for this moment—an opportunity to capture history the moment it occurs and cement his name as a world-class reporter. That is until a bewildering woman materializes in front of him, stopping him in his tracks and catapulting him into a quandary he never expected: capture the crime of the decade on camera or rescue the intriguing woman who is standing in the crosshairs of the biggest mobster shootout in Kansas City history.

Danger lurks in every corner of 1933 Kansas City, a city run by the powerful mafia machine. Can Ember survive the unexpected dangers of this complicated era? And will Daire be forced to set aside his lifelong dreams in order to keep them both alive? These two may be stuck in time, but could they have found each other for a reason?